Prologue

2000

Freddie Henriksen sat at his desk revising for his upcoming University exams, trying to force his brain to remember how to solve the Laplacian equation using the separation of variables method. He got up and stared at the large whiteboard he had installed in his room a few years previously and tried to recreate what he had just written down in pen and paper at his desk. After a couple of minutes of staring blankly at the white space, he finally started applying the method and found that he did, in fact, know nothing at all. He sighed, exasperated. This wasn't even meant to be one of his hardest modules, how the hell was he going to learn all the material for the other five he had to sit in just over three weeks' time? A bout of anger welled up inside him and he cried out in frustration, going over to his bed and bashing his pillow until he was breathing heavily and had worked out all of the negative energy he was feeling towards being a student.

"For God sake," he cursed at himself. "Pull yourself together. Come on, you've done this before and no doubt you'll be doing it again. You know what you have to do; work, work, work. Practice makes perfect and eventually you'll get it right. Just be patient, come on man you always do well in the -"

Freddie snapped back into the real world as the intrusive bell of the house phone began screeching outside his room. The previous owners had put the bell in. An old couple that were hard of hearing and had needed the bell at a level so high that it could have been used as the warning signal during the Blitz.

The phone continued to scream at Freddie, who considered ignoring it as he knew it would inevitably be an Indian chap from a call centre called 'Dave'. No doubt this 'Dave' would try to sell his dad an extension to their TV package, not that there was anything more they could add to their existing deal. They had all of the channels for the sole reason that you had to have all of them to actually get the three or four that were actually any good.

"Answer the bloody phone!" Freddie imagined a neighbour shouting at the wall that adjoined their houses together.

Freddie gave up trying to wait out the cries of the phone and twisted the knob on his door, which had been installed upside down. The door had been like that when the Henriksen's moved in 9 years ago, and as the door still functioned in that it was able to be opened and closed, the family had left it that way. In fact, come to think of it, Freddie wasn't entirely sure his parents even knew the door was upside down. It was a detail he had noticed long ago but thought nothing of as it hadn't particularly affected his life in any way.

The phone sat on the landing just outside his bedroom. Freddie didn't bother to leave the comfort of his chair to pick it up, instead bending and stretching his body around the frame of the door until the phone was in his hand.

"Yello?" Freddie tried to say cheerfully.

There was a pause at the other end, followed by some static and a click that Freddie immediately knew meant he'd picked up from a call centre. But, due to the fact he was struggling with revision and at this point would take whatever opportunity he could to procrastinate, he didn't immediately hang up and instead waited for 'Dave' the Indian bloke to try and sell him something.

"Hello is this a Mr Henriksen?" A female voice with a thick Asian accent asked.

"Yes, this is *a* Mr Henriksen, though I imagine not the one you are actually after." Freddie smirked at his own wit, probably the funniest thing he had said since he'd come home from University and that was saying something.

"Ah! Hello! Mr Henriksen can I have a minute of your time?" The Asian girl chirped.

"You can, but I would like to say you are talking to Mr Henriksen's son, and not the man himself."

"You are the householder yes?"

"No, I am the homeowner's son."

"The householder is in?"

"No, I am in, the homeowner is not, it is just me, there are no pets in, no fish, there's not even that much food if I'm totally honest. Just me, the homeowner's son. How can I help you?"

"Oh. Do you speak on behalf of householder?"

"That depends entirely on what you want."

"Okay well Mr Henriksen my name is Claire…", Freddie stifled a laugh, "and I would like to ask you a few questions if that is okay? Okay can I proceed?"

Freddie was about to reply, but Claire ploughed on anyway.

"Okay, first question for you Mr Henriksen is do you mind that this call is to be recorded for training purposes?"

"No, that's perfectly fine."

"Good, good, good, that is good. Thank you. Okay, next question Mr Henriksen is are you happy with your current TV package?"

"Yes, I'm perfectly happy with it."

"NO, MR HENRIKSEN!" She shouted excitedly down the phone, and Freddie wondered if it was her first day on the job. Anyone with this much enthusiasm surely could not have been hung up on from 95% of the people they called everyday for a prolonged period of time. Then again, maybe she was so enthusiastic because he was the *first* person who hadn't hung up on her straight away in a long time.

"No?" Freddie asked, somewhat sceptically.

"NO!" She continued her shouting barrage. "Your package is much out of date! I see you don't have the haydee package! You need the haydee package!"

"Excuse me, what is the haydee package?"

"The haydee package is the package for you, Mr Henriksen! You need the haydee package. Hundreds of new channels all in haydee! You will view them never the same again! I have this package, Mr Henriksen; I know haydee is the best! You need it!"

"Oh! You mean Hey-ch Dee. Well it does sound rather interesting, why don't you tell me a bit more about what it is and what is involves."

Freddie put the phone on speaker on his desk and went back to his whiteboard as Claire started furiously jabbering down the phone about all the pros that upgrading to a HD package would bring. As great as some of the reasons she gave sounded, he very much doubted the HD package's ability to prevent his eyesight worsening over his lifetime, and indeed followed up this thought by cleaning his glasses on his t-shirt. The damage was already done with his eyes; his father's genetics had seen to that long ago.

After a couple of minutes of reattempting the Laplacian problem on the whiteboard whilst trying to drown out the sound of Claire ranting on, Freddie decided enough was enough.

"Look Claire, this sounds really interesting and great and all those other positive describing words you have used in your description of this package, but at the end of the day we are talking about a box that sits in a room in your house. Well, in my dad's house actually. I have seen things in HD before and quite frankly, they look very, very similar to things I have seen in normal definition. Most programmes I watch were filmed in normal definition anyway, and quite frankly some of the faces I watch on TV I would rather not see in any more detail. I have to put up with enough ugly faces in real life. If normal definition TV makes them look better than they actually look in real life because we can't see the craters from acne on their faces or the crumb on the top of their lip from the sandwich they had for lunch, then it's all the better for me. In fact, had you rung up today and offered a package with even more standard definition than the one we currently have, I may have been more inclined to listen to you and not put the phone down as you jabbered on in an accent I can barely even understand. Now I am sorry for being so bloody rude but you have been bloody boring. I am sure you are a lovely person, but come on; you're trying to sell TV packages to a teenage boy over the phone. Is this your dream job? Is this really what you want to be doing with your life?!"

Freddie probably would have said all of those things if he was a braver man, but he was not. Instead, Freddie picked up the phone, pressed the big red button, and put it back in its charger slot just outside his room and prayed that it would be the last call he received that day.

Freddie swizzled back on his chair and faced his whiteboard again. He had gotten literally nowhere in over 20 minutes of struggling. The exam was only two hours long and a question like the one he was currently attempting would be worth about 5% of the paper. He didn't have anywhere near the amount of time he was currently spending on it to spend on it in an exam situation.

Brilliant, Freddie thought and buried his face in his hands, rubbing his forehead with his fingers. *Just brilliant.*

He checked the time and saw it was fast approaching 12pm. He did a quick calculation in his head and realised if he went down to make lunch now, it would be ready at exactly 12 on the dot. Perfect timing as far as he was concerned, and the perfect excuse not to do anymore work until after lunch. It looked like Claire had her uses after all in getting him close to the holy time of day that Freddie liked to call 'whatever time he was eating next'. Despite this love of eating, Freddie wasn't particularly fat; in fact he would argue that his arms were skinny. He had a bit of a potbelly, a dad-bod from drinking too much cider at University, and he did really enjoy his food. Freddie, still sat on his big, black leather, swizzle capable chair, drifted off in his head thinking about what he could cook up. He was so wrapped up in chicken chasseur and steak with onion puree and a red wine jus that he almost didn't hear the phone go off again. If indeed the phone had been one that rang at a normal human level, he probably would not have heard it at all.

As it was, the piercing scream of the phone penetrated through his food defences and broke his happy thought process. Frowning, and pissed off, at yet another intrusion into his procrastination, Freddie picked up the phone faster this time.

"Yes?" Freddie said sharply.

Again there was no immediate reply. Freddie let out a groan and hung up, not bothering to wait for the call centre click.

He picked himself up out of his chair and drooped out of his room. It was amazing how quickly a couple of call centre calls could dampen a mood. He looked at himself in the mirror that separated his bedroom door from the bathroom door at the top of the stairs and raised an eyebrow.

"Jesus, I need a haircut." Freddie muttered as he leaned closer to the mirror to get a better look at himself. Other than needing a haircut he didn't think he looked too bad considering he had done pretty much nothing but revise alone in his room for two weeks. His skin was clear for the most part and surprisingly tanned for this time of year. He'd always been blessed with olive skin, but coming out of winter it was usually a much lighter shade than it currently was. His eyes looked a little bloodshot, but he had rubbed them whilst listening to Claire going on and on, so he wasn't too surprised at that. Plus the stress of not being able to solve a simple Laplacian equation with boundary conditions would take its toll on anyone's eyes.

He continued on past the bathroom and down the stairs, which had been newly carpeted. They were stripy, with the landing taking on a light shade of fawn from one of the stripes. As he moved from the base of the stairs into the kitchen, the phone went off again. Freddie decided to answer it one more time, figuring that the chances of it being another call centre were slim. His aunt was ill after all and it was best to be on the safe side in case of an emergency.

"Hello, Freddie speaking."

There was a shuffle on the other end of the line, and Freddie thought it was his Aunt Erin. At the very least, it wasn't the usual noise you get from a call centre that is trying to connect you to one of their team.

"Hello, is that you Erin?"

There was another shuffle on the other end of the line.

"It's me, Freddie. You just called me. Are you okay? Do you need me to come over?"

A loud screech built up on the line, quietly at first but then it became a great, deafening, piercing noise that was so brutal on the ear that Freddie instinctively jerked his hand away from his face, letting go of the phone as he did so. It clattered a couple of metres away from him onto the hard kitchen floor.

"Christ!" Freddie cried as he rubbed his ear and scrambled to pick up the phone again.

"Erin, what the hell was that? Are you all right? Have you fallen on something?"

Freddie heard the screech building up again and instantly hung up; he didn't think his poor young heart could take that noise a second time. It was like the noise you would expect a piece of chalk on the chalkboard from hell to make as the devil wrote on it.

"What is going on today?" Freddie frowned, before remembering the time and putting the noise to the back of his head as he realised it was time to put food on.

*

That evening, Freddie watched the latest episode in a TV series called Born Again. It was a show about the descendants of Dracula in Transylvania, some of which wanted to go back to the glory days of feasting on human flesh and invoking fear and carnage on humanity, whilst a second group wanted to integrate with the humans as they had done since Draculas demise and live off animal blood. The difference in opinion, Freddie suspected, was building toward a grand finale where there would be a full-scale outbreak of war. So far, the glory day hunters had murdered four humans in Transylvania and there were whispered rumours about the return of the dark lord himself to the haunted lands.

The episode ended with the arrival of a character called Helsinga. Hard of face, and yet fiercely beautiful, she arrived wielding a stake and claiming that a great war to come had been foretold. She had been born in a village 40 miles away where the children were trained from a young age to be able to track, identify, and kill vampires.

As the credits began to roll, Freddie let out a huge yawn. He went to the bathroom to brush his teeth and get ready for bed. Freddie lent toward the washbasin as he brushed his teeth, and then spat into it, running the tap as he did so. As he pulled his head back up, he did a double take, his heart catching in his chest. He saw movement behind him in the pattern of the window. He turned sharply, moving his hands up to protect his face and splattering toothpaste everywhere. He looked at the pattern in the window closely, and saw nothing. Freddie laughed sheepishly before looking at the mess the toothpaste had made all over the door and floor. He sighed for about the 20th time that day and used the towel hanging on the radiator to clear it up. It was impossible for there to be any real movement at the window, the bathroom was on the second floor. It must have just been a bird flying past the window, he just happened to look at the wrong time and scare himself

Freddie went back over to the washbasin, removed his glasses and put them down next to the tap, before washing his face in cold water. He used the towel he'd just used to clean the bathroom to dry his face, and then put it back onto the radiator. As he was about to unlock the door to leave, he glanced in the mirror and looked at the patterned window behind him, expecting the worst, but Freddie saw nothing. He shrugged and made a note to himself not to watch the vampire programme directly before bed again, he had always had a very weak constitution for anything slightly frightening or gory.

*

Consciousness found Freddie suddenly. He was sweating hard despite the room being cold. It was pitch black. He sniffed his nose, which was running, and wiped his brow before heaving himself up to a sitting position. Freddie shuffled down to the end of the bed and reached for his phone on the bedside table, which due to the shape of the room couldn't fit by the side of his bed and had to live at the bottom of it instead.

He pulled it off the charger and checked the time, 02.37am. He licked his lips with a tongue that was dry with thirst. Freddie was also desperate for a piss. He wiped his nose again as he got out of bed and fumbled his way toward the door. As he stepped into the landing he trod on something sharp and cursed, throwing his hands out on either side of him and pulling his foot away from the offending object. His right hand hit the wall. He felt something touch it ever so lightly, followed by a sharp pain in the tips of his index and middle finger. Freddie cried out and swung his head around, expecting to see a burglar or worse, but there was no one there. Freddie shook his head; his mind was playing tricks on him again. He used to have night terrors as a child and when he woke up from the dark dreams, often he would find that he was still living in them and it could take up to five minutes for them to subside. Once he had even punched his own mum in the face because she had the appearance of one of the monsters from a nightmare she had woken him up from.

He pulled his hand back toward his body and regained his balance, looking down at the spot he'd trodden on but failing to see anything untoward in the dark. He passed the mirror between his bedroom and the bathroom, this time not bothering to glance in it, and went straight for the toilet without stopping to pull the hanging light switch. He lifted the lid and relieved himself, wiping his nose with the back of his free hand as he did so. Before he flushed, Freddie grabbed some loo roll and blew long and hard into it, trying to clear the snot. Then he washed his hands and moved back out onto the landing. He shuffled along, being careful not to step on the creaky area so that he wouldn't wake his parents up and slid back into his room, closing the door behind him. Freddie then rolled the chair back in front of the door, as he always did, and got back into bed. He drifted back to sleep almost immediately.

*

Freddie woke again, and was surprised that it still wasn't light, but then felt the thirst present in his mouth He checked his phone for a second time that night, 02.59am. He hadn't even been back asleep 20 minutes. The realisation struck him that he had forgotten to have a drink the first time he had gone to the bathroom. Freddie let out a long breath that was deep with frustration, and pulled himself out of bed. He moved the chair, went back onto the landing, and wiped his nose, which was still running, on his sleeve. This time he forgot to avoid the creaking patch and whispered "shit" under his breath as he stood on it, hoping it wouldn't wake up his parents in the room opposite his, and continued into the bathroom. Again, he didn't bother with the light, turned the tap on and stuck his head under it, lapping up the water with his tongue like a dog would. Once satisfied, he grabbed another tissue and blew his nose again, before flushing it down the toilet and returning to bed.

*

Freddie woke up coughing sharply, and felt something at the back of his throat. He tried to clear it, failed, and coughed harder. It felt as if his throat was swollen. Still spluttering, he reached for his phone, but couldn't find it. He reached for the floor and put his hand on his charger, and traced it to the end of the cord, but his phone wasn't attached. He coughed again, and remembered he must have moved it the last time he picked it up when he went to the bathroom.

Eyes now streaming slightly from the coughing, he wiped his nose on his arm and got up to go back to the bathroom to get more water, this time to try and clear his throat. He suspected he was coming down with something, rotten timing considering how much revision he still had to do and how far behind schedule he was.

He thought about Claire again and instantly regretted ever answering the phone. "Those five minutes I spent listening to your shit might have been the five minutes where I was destined to remember how to solve the Laplacian equation," he mumbled to himself as he unconsciously moved the chair for the third time that night and stepped into the landing.

He coughed again, and grimaced as his throat felt like it was now on fire. There was a dull pain in his foot and also in his fingers, but he couldn't be bothered to check them out now and would wait until the morning.

This time he did pull the cord in the bathroom, shutting the door as he did so and went over to the toilet to pee again. He must have drunk too much water on his last bathroom trip. As he went to pull his pyjama bottoms down, he noticed a red smudge on his arm. *Weird*, Freddie thought as he relieved himself.

His nose had continued to run, and as Freddie shook out the last few drops of pee, he glanced down and saw as a drop of blood fell down into the toilet to join his pee. Hitting the surface and dissipating out. His eyes widened with curiosity, and he moved his free hand up to his nose and wiped across his nostrils. As he pulled his hand away, his fingers were covered in blood. Looking back at his other arm, he realised that was what the smudge must have been.

Freddie flushed the loo and then washed the blood and germs off his hands before unwinding the loo roll and making two plugs for his nose. He pushed them in and went back to bed, deciding he would sort it all out in the morning. The distraction of the blood had made him forget all about the itch in his throat and the dull pains in his foot and hand, which had now stopped bothering him.

*

Freddie's eyes burst open as he gasped for air, his hands instinctively reaching up toward his throat. Panting, he tried to get his breath back. He looked toward his door and saw a man standing dead still watching over him. His heart pounded in his chest and he recoiled back towards the wall, scrambling for a pillow that he brought around to put between himself and the man as a defensive barrier. The man didn't move towards Freddie, who blinked a couple of times and cleared his vision. There was no man stood watching over him, it had just been his dressing gown hung up on the back of his door.

"Jesus," Freddie whispered, "what a night this is." He reached for his phone, before realising he hadn't found it the last time he had gotten up and gave up, making a mental note to find it in the morning. He glanced back at his door just to make sure that it was only his dressing gown there, and was relieved to see that it was. His heartbeat slowly returned to a more normal level.

Freddie tried to clear his throat from some phlegm that had built up, but in doing so managed to irritate it again and he began coughing uncontrollably, each one a fresh fire in his throat. After about 20 seconds, he stopped coughing, but no longer felt tired. Freddie decided he would get up see if his nose had stopped bleeding. This time he did glance in the mirror as he went past it and was shocked to see big dark smears all over his face of what he presumed was blood from his nose. He went into the bathroom and turned the light on again. Looking in the mirror he confirmed that the big smears were the dark reddish-brown colour of dried blood and looked disgustedly at them. He bent down toward the tap and turned it on, splashing his face with the cool water. He opened his eyes and saw the light red-brown colour the blood was turning the water as it swirled around the drain. Remembering he still had the nose plugs in, he pulled them out expecting the blood to have clotted in his nose. Instead, as soon as he pulled them out, the blood that should have been clotted started streaming down his face and into his open mouth as if he had just turned the tap to his nose on. Freddie's eyes widened with panic and he gagged and spluttered, trying to get the taste of warm iron out of his system as quickly as he could. He scrambled for the loo roll from next to the toilet, but succeeded only in knocking it onto the floor. His right hand caught his eye, blood was pouring out of his index and middle finger. Freddie was too shocked to scream. Feeling slightly light headed and ill from the sight of all the blood, he reached out again for the loo roll that was now on the floor, and bent toward it.

As he did, the blood stopped pouring down his face and into his mouth, and instead started free falling onto the floor, making a sound similar to that of the shower after you just turn it off and the last few drops of water escape the showerhead. Freddie picked up the roll whole and lifted it under his nose. At the same time, he pushed his bleeding fingers into it as hard as he could to try and stem the blood flow. With his left hand, he scrambled for the door handle, no longer worrying how much noise he was making. He stumbled into the hall and finally found his voice as the initial shock began to subside. He screamed out for help, desperate for his mum or dad, as they would know what to do. They must have been in a deep sleep because no one came out of their room, so Freddie banged on the door using his left hand as his right still held the whole roll to his nose, and then burst into the room shouting that he was bleeding and needed help.

He'd opened the door into an empty room. Freddie stared dumbfounded at the neatly made bed that hadn't been disturbed that night, before cursing again. His parents weren't in. They weren't even in the country. They'd gone away for the weekend to Paris as a late birthday present to his mum, a fact he'd forgotten entirely about during all of his late night issues.

"Fuck, fuck, fuck, FUCK!" Freddie cried out as his nose continued to pour into the roll, he was now feeling extremely dizzy and realised if he lost much more blood he would definitely pass out. That's the last thing his parents would want to find when they got back tomorrow. He turned around to grab the phone and call an ambulance, giving up with the now soaking loo roll and tossing it aside. He dialled 999 and waited for the connection.

"Hello, emergency services how can I help?"

"I'M BLEEDING, MY NOSE AND FINGERS, HELP!" Freddie screamed. He wavered on his feet and thrust out his bloody right hand to grab onto the bannister. The blood made it impossible to grip and he slipped down onto the floor.

"Where are you my dear?"

"At home. Andover! The Avenue!" The panic was overwhelming; the dizziness was beginning to take hold. "Please find me." Freddie's voice was weakening and he threw up.

"Please tell me your house number." The voice on the other end of the line was calm but quick in delivery.

"Hello? Please tell me your house number." The voice asked, even quicker this time.

But it was too late; Freddie had lost the ability to speak. He stared down into the dark, deep red pool that had just come out of his mouth, then slowly turned his head to the right, where he saw a pair of bright green eyes attached to a creature standing motionless, head cocked slightly to the left, staring right back at him.

Part One

2016

Chapter One

Fete

Marvin ran up to his mum and pleaded with her to give him some money so that he could have a go on the shoot'em'up game. He had just watched his friend Harry win a huge teddy bear by managing to get three shots in the smaller of three rings that were on a piece of white plasterboard about 10 metres from the shooting position. The fete worker had jumped triumphantly when Harry hit his third shot and had excitedly exclaimed that he was the first person to win one of the big prizes that afternoon. Marvin had jealously watched him first get the three shots on target and then had even more jealously watched as Harry was presented with the biggest teddy he had ever seen in his life. Confident that he could do the same, he had bounded over to his mum, weaving past children and parents and grandparents, all of whom were enjoying this year's edition of the fete, and begged her for a pound coin so that he could win one of the massive bears too.

Anne eyed him up suspiciously. "Now Marvin, shooting is the last thing I want you to try, let alone find out you're good at! I don't want you getting any ideas about joining the army, you know my heart couldn't take it!"

"Please mum!" Marvin huffed at her, "If Harry is allowed to why can't I? I promise I won't ever join the army, I just really want to win that big teddy else I'm never going to hear the end of it from Harry, and every time I go to his house he is going to go on and on about that time he won the big teddy and I wasn't even allowed to shoot. Please mum I don't even like the army I double pinkie promise, cross my heart hope to die, that I won't join the army! Just let me win the bear please!" Marvin dropped to his knees theatrically as he begged his final plea and looked up at his mum with puppy dog eyes, "Please mum, you'd become my favourite parent ever in the history of everything ever if you do!"

"Oh alright! Get up off the floor I don't want the knees of your trousers getting dirty. I only washed them the other day and they need to be clean for when we go camping on Friday."

"YES!" Marvin shouted gleefully. "Thanks mum you're the best!"

Anne dipped into her purse and fished around for a pound. She didn't have one and so made it up with spare change that she then dropped into Marvin's outstretched hand.

"Now make sure you don't shoot yourself! And if you don't win with that pound I'm not giving you any more money do you understand?"

"Yes, yes, whatever mum I'm going to win with this, don't worry! If Harry can do it then I definitely can too!"

Marvin swivelled on his feet and ran back towards Harry and the shoot'em'up game.

Anne turned back to the bookstore she was standing at and continued her search for the

Charlotte Brontë book 'Jane Eyre' that had so far proved fruitless. Unfortunately, the books weren't arranged in any sort of order. They had all been piled up into boxes straight from donations that people had given to the fete. Anne spotted a couple of books that she herself had donated, all grouped together, and realised that each person who had donated books probably had their own little section in the stall. She wondered where the Baker's family section might be, as they were the sorts of people that might donate a number of Charlotte Brontë novels, and she continued searching through the boxes hoping to strike gold.

As she finished sifting through the second to last box, there was a tap on her right shoulder. She looked over it to see who wanted her attention, but saw no one there.

Anne frowned and looked off to the right, expecting to see Marvin or her other son James running off, laughing at their hilarious prank, but spotted neither. She turned back to begin her search through the final box, when there was another tap at her shoulder. Anne whipped her head round to catch the culprit. But again there was no one behind her. She brought her head back round to the –

"BOO!"

Anne jumped back startled as her friend Cath roared with laughter.

"Gotcha!" Cath grinned triumphantly.

"Jesus, Cath!" Anne laughed back. "You do know how to age a woman prematurely!"

"Oh get off it, I'm just trying to catch you up to the rest of us mums. There is no way you are 40! I simply don't believe it. You still look like you're in your late 20s! What is your secret?" She whispered the last question as if it were a great secret that Anne held and was hiding from the world. It was whispered in such a way that Anne knew if she did have a secret to divulge, she could tell Cath there and then and it would never be uttered to another soul for as long as Cath lived.

"Well," Anne whispered back suspiciously, looking around to make sure that no one else was listening in. Cath's eyes lit up and she leaned in closer to hear what Anne was about to say.

"My great secret is my anti-aging Anne drink." A look of disbelief spread across Cath's face as she began to suspect that Anne was winding her up. However, a second glance at Anne's face led her to believe that what Anne was about to tell her was the truth. Cath looked around, also making sure no one could overhear the secret that Anne was about to reveal.

"The ingredients are as follows; you might want a pen," Anne continued in a hushed tone. Cath quickly produced a small pen and pad from her bag.

"200ml of semi skimmed milk, 10 grams of almonds, 5 grams of pecan nuts, 3 medium sized strawberries, one-third of a banana, seven pomegranate seeds..." Cath wrote all this down hurriedly, anguish not to miss a single detail out. "...The juice of a quarter of a lemon, and finally my secret ingredient which absolutely no one can know about, do you hear me?" Anne stared directly into Cath's eyes trying to see whether or not Cath would be able to keep her great secret. Cath nodded vigorously. "The smallest pinch of a rare spice called abifatly." Cath continued to write fast. "Sorry," she whispered back at Anne, "I didn't quite catch it."

"I said, a small dash of abifatly."

"I've never heard of that; how do you spell it? Can you only get it online or something?"

"It's spelt a-b-i-g-f-a-t-l-i-e."

Cath scribbled down the letters as Anne spoke them and then looked at the word as a whole once Anne had finished dictating. Her body slouched as she realised that Anne had gotten her back, and so easily at that.

"That's what you get for scaring me!" Anne laughed at Cath, who looked genuinely put out. "Skin like this is one in a million, I'm a lucky, lucky gal!" Anne continued to tease as Cath gave her a rueful look.

"How are you anyway?" Anne asked changing the subject, "How are your boys?"

"Yeah really good, I'm fine thanks, just gearing up for our big holiday in Egypt this year. I told Rod to pick up the currency the other day. The one thing that he was in charge of and of course he completely forgot about it and hadn't even ordered them which put me in a frightful panic…" Cath cut herself off as she spotted one of her sons jumping off the top of the slide in the children's playground just off the village green where the school fete was being held.

"Sorry Anne, I've got to go and do some pest control! I'll catch up with you later!" She shouted back over her shoulder as she had already begun scurrying off to have a go at her son. Anne watched her go fondly; Cath had been the first friend she had made when she had moved with Pete and her boys to the new town a few years back. She was a peculiar woman and acted like a child a lot of the time, but she was good fun and an especially good and kind friend.

Anne smiled absentmindedly and turned back to the final box of books, hoping beyond hope that she could find Jane Eyre. She was about three quarters of the way through the last box, and had given up any real hope, when she stumbled across what she believed to be the Baker's family section of books, or, as she liked to call it, the mother-load.

The first couple were books that she had read a long time ago. The third one, however, was what she had searched through hundreds of books to find. Jane Eyre. Anne was pleased; she had wanted to start reading some of Charlotte Brontë's novels, feeling she was an author everyone should have read something by before they died, and what better place to start than Jane Eyre? She planned to start reading it on the camping trip. Anne picked it up out of the box and began reading the first page as she went over to Helen, Harry's mum, who was running the bookstall.

"Hi Helen, how much is this one?" Anne asked brightly.

"Hey Anne, how are you doing? That one is £1.50 please."

"I'm doing really great thanks!" Anne replied cheerfully as she fished around in her purse for the correct change, before realising she had given Marvin most of her remaining coins. She looked at Helen ruefully, "I'm afraid I've only got a twenty."

Helen smiled and said that would be fine, before accepting the note and collecting the change to give back.

"You're going on your camping trip this weekend aren't you?"

"Yes! This weekend. Friday night actually, after the boy's finish school for the term. Pete will drive us all down there. It should be good we're all really looking forward to it!"

"Yes, I am sure! How exciting!" Helen beamed as she passed Anne the change. "Are you all set for it?"

"Yes, yes, everything is ready! Just need to make sure the boys remember to pack everything."

Helen laughed, "No doubt you'll get halfway there and James will pipe up that he forgot to put any underwear in!"

"It's not James I'm worried about; Pete is the worst one!"

"I bet!" Helen glanced at Anne, her eyes immediately changing the tone of the conservation as they flicked from left to right to check that no one was listening in. "Hey look, I'm sorry I couldn't make the meeting the other day. My babysitter wasn't well and I couldn't find anyone else at such short notice. David was having some problems with the machine up north too. Was there any new information?"

"No not really, it was the same old, same old. Nothing that hasn't been said before. Just a final confirmation of everything. You know how they all like to go on and on and be completely thorough in every single last detail. They all think they're so important, I find it all rather dull really. Let's just get on with it shall we? Why do we need to go over everything for the thousandth time? I'm pretty sure I could have written out the entire meeting word for word without even attending and would have gotten it 99% right." Helen looked relieved, and then Anne looked at her a little more seriously.

"Are you prepared for this weekend?"

Helen gave her a knowing look before glancing around again to make sure that no one was eavesdropping. People loved to find something to gossip about and a school fete was generally the perfect place to find something juicy. "Yes, everything is set. David is getting back around 6 on Friday night and so everything should be sorted out soon after that I would imagine."

"Good, that's excellent." Anne said nodding, before looking around and passing Helen a small, folded white piece of paper. Helen carefully pulled the paper apart; it was no bigger than three or four square inches, with one rugged side where it had been torn from a larger piece of paper. Helen glanced at what it said, then looked up at Anne and smiled before mouthing a 'thank you' and slipping it into her pocket. Anne nodded a 'you're welcome' back.

"Right, well I better get on then and see if Marvin has managed to win that gigantic teddy on the shooting stall that Jackie is running."

"Oh yes, I did see that. Bit odd to have a shooting game at a school fete don't you think?"

"Yes, I thought it a little odd, but Jackie does it at the carnival and they have kids younger than ours using the guns. Apparently it's odds on to make the most money this year, in which case it'll be about next year too!"

"Yes, no doubt!"

They smiled at each other again and Anne gave Helen a little wave as she turned to go and find her sons to take them home before they spent anymore of her money.

Chapter Two

Runner's

"Have you packed your underwear, boys?" Anne shouted from the kitchen up to her two sons. She checked her watch; Anthony would be home any minute and would want to be on the move straight after dinner.

"If I come up there and find that you haven't packed your underwear, I will take that blasted games console off you both and you'll never play another game so long as you live! Do you hear me?"

At the mention of losing their prized games console, both boys looked at each other, dropped their controllers, and rushed towards their respective chests of drawers. Marvin pushed his younger brother James to the floor and James let out a little yelp as he scrambled to try and get to his feet. Meanwhile, Marvin had reached his chest of drawers, grabbed a handful of socks, and another handful of pants, span and ran towards his suitcase which was in the middle of his and James' shared bedroom floor.

Marvin, after chucking the underwear on and around the suitcase, which was zipped shut, stood up victoriously and shouted down to his mum, "I'VE DONE IT AGES AGO BUT JAMES HASN'T SO HE SHOULDN'T COME ON HOLIDAY!"

James, now scared that his mum would see sense in Marvin's words, threw his own underwear in the general direction of his suitcase and in turn shouted down the stairs at his mum. "MINE IS DONE! HE'S A BIG FAT LIAR, MUM! I DID IT AGES AGO PLEASE LET US KEEP PLAYING!"

Anne, sensing the fear in her sons that she might take the console away from them, decided to have some fun. "If I reach the top of these stairs and find that your clothes are near your suitcases and not neatly packed in them, I am going to be extremely angry. And when I am extremely angry you know that means that you will not be allowed to play your games for at least a week. I'm going to start coming up the stairs now. You have 10 seconds to make sure everything is neatly packed away… 10… 9…"

As Anne climbed the stairs and continued her count down, she heard the scuffle as her boys tried desperately to squeeze all the clothes they wanted to take into their suitcases and smiled to herself.

"6… 5…"

She heard Marvin call his brother in a strained voice to come and sit on his suitcase so that he could close it, followed by the patter of James' feet as he crossed the room.

"3… 2…"

"HELP ME WITH MINE!" James couldn't keep the volume down; he was scared witless about the possibility of not being able to play on the console anymore. This time Anne heard two sets of feet running across the room to James' suitcase, followed by a dull thud as Marvin planted himself on top of the suitcase and the sound of a zip being hastily fastened.

"1… ZEROOOOO!"

As Anne shouted the word zero, she burst into the boys' room and was met with a scene of total chaos. In the middle of the discarded clothes that had been deemed unfit to travel, and the hundreds of toys and dress up clothes and plastic swords that littered their room, the two boys stood bolt upright. Their heads thrust back so far they were almost facing the ceiling. Their right hands pressed into their foreheads in a salute to their mum.

"See, we told you so! We packed ages ago!" Marvin piped up.

"Is that right?"

"Yessum." James replied, unconvincingly.

"You have packed everything that you need yourselves?"

"Yep," Marvin nodded.

"Well that's very good of you both, I guess I will let you continue to play your games until we leave then…"

"YAY!" Marvin and James both shouted as one and turned to pick up their controllers.

"…If you can pass the following series of questions." Anne finished with a smirk.

The boys' had frozen, both bending towards their controllers. Their faces dropped as they looked sheepishly back towards their mother.

"Do we have a deal?" Anne asked them both.

"Okay..." Marvin replied, "Just please don't let them be super difficult!"

Anne began pacing slowly, taking care not to step on loose blocks of Lego or PlayMobil soldiers. The boys watched her nervously as she moved.

Anne stopped dramatically, and then swivelled to face them. "WHAT... is the capital of England?"

Marvin's hand shot up, quickly followed by James'.

"Yes Marvin?"

"London."

Anne stared him down incredulously, and Marvin's eyes widened as he worried that he had gotten it wrong before he was put out of his misery, "Correct." Anne began her pacing again.

"WHO... is our current Prime Minister?"

Both of the boys looked at each other apprehensively, praying the other would know the answer. James was struck by a moment of inspiration.

"Mr Harson?"

"Is that a question or your answer?" Anne looked at James, feigning sternness.

"Mr Harson!" James said back confidently.

Anne let a smile slip across her lips, before regaining control and looking at James with a hard expression again, "Correct."

"And finally..." the boys gave each other a relieved look as the interrogation was coming to an end, "Which one of you has forgotten to pack your toothbrush?"

The boys, who had for the most part continued to remain standing bolt upright this whole time, slouched simultaneously. Who had forgotten the one thing mum had always banged on about remembering? There were, after all, no convenience stores in the middle of the forest where you could buy a new toothbrush. But who hadn't put their toothbrush in? James couldn't remember if he had or not, and neither could Marvin. In their rush to quickly throw everything they possibly could into their bags, who knew what had really made the cut and what hadn't?

The boys glanced at one another, trying to see in each other's eyes if the other had packed their toothbrush or not. Marvin decided to step up to the plate, he was sure he hadn't packed his toothbrush, which meant that James must have done.

"It was me, mum." Marvin said as quietly as he could.

"Pardon?"

Marvin raised his eyes from the floor and brought them up to look at his mum. "It was me, I have forgotten."

Anne studied him carefully. "And what about James? How do you know that he packed his?"

"Because only one of us packed it and I know I didn't, so he must have."

"But I didn't pack mine." James said, frowning. "Maybe you packed yours without knowing?"

34

"No, I know I didn't pack mine." Marvin replied. Then both boys looked at each other in realisation of what their mum had done.

"You tricked us!" Marvin exclaimed.

"You're so sneaky!" James said shaking his head at his mum.

Anne was laughing, "Well, I guess this means you're not allowed to play your games for a whole week!"

"Noooo!" Both the boys shouted, utterly distraught. But then Marvin realised something.

"Wait a minute, we're going camping so we wouldn't be able to play them anyway!"

Anne continued to laugh and nodded her head, "Well I'll say, aren't you a clever little chicken! I guess you are right; you boys are lucky to get away with it this time! Now come on, get your things together, your dad will be home from work any minute and he'll want to head off straight after tea. If you aren't fully packed by then it'll be tough luck. I'll force you to use a twig to brush your teeth for the whole trip!"

Marvin and James threw disgusted looking faces at one another, before running past Anne, towards the bathroom, to fetch their toothbrushes. Anne turned around to go back downstairs and was just about to leave the boys bedroom when she spotted a mask the boys must have been using during dress up. Next to it on the floor was something she couldn't remember having seen before. "What has your father gotten you boys now?" She spoke absentmindedly to herself as she bent and picked it up. She turned the object over in her hands. It was almost a cube, but one of the faces was slightly curved, and there were weird markings all over it in red, dug into the faces. Anne thought it was a funny Rubik's cube type thing at first, but then it didn't seem to have moving parts to it. It really was a peculiar object. Pete must have found it in a charity shop and thought the boys could use it as some sort of Pandora's box for their PlayMobil soldiers.

Anne put it back down on the oatmeal coloured carpet, which in the boys' room was darker than the landing and her and Pete's room from mud and general dirt worn into it. Boys their age, and she'd had this confirmed by the other mums, who picked their sons up from school, were outrageously filthy. Even if they had just had a bath, the likelihood would be that they would find a way to get covered in mud not 10 minutes later.

As she was making her way down the stairs, the front door opened and Pete called out, "Honey, I'm home!"

Anne quickened her pace down to the bottom of the stairs and then embraced her husband. "Hello darling," she said cheerfully before kissing him, "How was your day?"

They released each other and Pete started climbing the stairs, telling Anne about John, the office prick, who thought he was better than everyone else. This was despite having been disciplined by Pete, who was John's boss, less than a week before for a truly abysmal report that he had submitted to clients who had complained and asked to be given an entirely new person to look after their account. Pete himself had to grovel with them and said he would take over their account when he got back from his camping holiday in a week, but in the meantime he would get his second in command, David, to go through all the nitty-gritty details and produce something that the clients would be happy with. A big old fu…dging mess was how Pete decided to describe it in front of his boys, who had just finished packing and stuck their heads around their door at the worst possible moment.

"Hello boys! Are you all packed up and ready to rock and roll?"

"Yes, we are!" They both beamed up at him.

"Excellent, excellent! Well look, let's have some dinner shall we? Then we'll hit the road! We don't want to have to try and put our tent up in the dark do we? Remember the last time we had to do that? It took us half the night, didn't it? In fact, I seem to recall you boys left me to suffer on my own and went and sat in the car with your mum!"

The boys laughed, "But dad it took sooo long!"

He chuckled as he went into his room, before checking himself in the mirror and popping his head back out the door, "Go and be good boys and lay the table for your mum, she's been working hard, packing and cooking, all day."

"No dad, we packed our own stuff!"

"Is that right? Well in that case, go and lay the table whilst your mum has to repack for you!"

Pete continued to laugh and shut the bedroom door so that he could get changed in some privacy.

He was in an exceptionally good mood; he'd been waiting for this day for a very long time.

Pete wandered downstairs in a pair of bootcut jeans and a red and white plaid shirt, open at the chest, revealing a large volume of dark, curly brown hair.

"You look like a lumberjack!" Anne laughed as Pete sauntered into the kitchen with a pleased look on his face.

"Big, strong and handsome? Why thank you darling!" Pete winked at her.

"No; smelly, fat, and with a horrible taste in clothes!" Anne winked back. Pete laughed and rolled his eyes.

"Something smells good, what are we having?"

"On the menu tonight is baked sea bass with a romesco sauce." Anne announced proudly.

"Well that does sound wonderful!" Pete exclaimed as the children pulled funny faces. The boys hated fish in general, but they doubly hated fish with peppers and almonds.

"And for the boys, sausage and pasta bake!"

The boys stopped pulling their faces and looked much happier with what their mum had made for them. For a minute they had been worried they would have to eat fish, something they both hated with a passion after the time they had gone over to Billy and Joel's house and had to endure the sloppiest, slimiest fish pie anyone had ever created.

Anne dished up the two different mains and set them in front of her family, before sitting down with them to enjoy the meal.

"Right boys," Pete announced as he finished off the potato on his plate, "You've got 20 minutes whilst your mum and I have a coffee and then we're heading off. Can you please be strong, young men and bring your suitcases down and put them by the front door ready to go?"

The boys shot off upstairs to grab their things, and made a racket as they dragged their suitcases down the stairs, banging on every step on their way down despite the fact the bags could be worn on their backs using the straps.

"Hey, cut that out and carry them properly won't you?" Anne shouted.

Her and Pete finished their coffees, then quickly washed everything up. Pete heaved all their bags into the boot of their Toyota as the boys strapped themselves in to the back of the car. Anne did a final bathroom check to make sure everyone did indeed have their toothbrushes. Once satisfied, she joined the boys in the car, ready to set off for their holiday.

Chapter Three

Drive

It was a long drive from the Runner's house in Leicester to the spot they had chosen to camp at in the New Forest, on the Beaulieu river, roughly halfway between Beaulieu and Bucklers Hard. There was a small clearing between the forest and the river where the Runner's had decided to make camp, and Pete believed he could get the car relatively close to the camping area. Though they would have to walk the last 300 metres or so. This meant carrying the tents and all of the equipment and clothing that they had packed, as well as the fishing rods and food and other general supplies that they needed for the week. Not forgetting a blanket that Pete's mum had thrust upon him a couple of weeks after he had said that they were taking the boys camping in the New Forest. His mother had warned him not to let them get too cold, as hypothermia is all too real, she'd read about it in a feature in her knitting magazine. Pete had laughed her off but accepted the blanket anyway. He'd been grateful for it as he probably would have forgotten to pack one otherwise and then been told off by Anne as the boys shivered their way through the week. His mum only had their best interests at heart after all.

Slow evening traffic meant that it took them a couple of hours to reach Oxford, and by that time both Marvin and James had complained that they needed the toilet. Pete pulled into a service station and told them to be quick, whilst he wondered in to find a newspaper and also some sweets to make the journey a bit more bearable.

"Two-fifty for a few fruit pastels?" Pete muttered to himself shaking his head, before deciding to buy them anyway. He picked up a paper and went over to the cashier, searching in his pockets for some change.

As he put the paper on the counter, a headline caught his eye:

COPY-CAT MURDERER SENTENCED AGAIN

Pete couldn't find the right money, so handed the cashier a fiver and glanced at the text accompanying the article as he waited for his change:

Jacob Wicombs sentenced to second life imprisonment for the murder of Freddie Henriksen after fierce court battle. Mr Wicombs, already in prison for the murder of Price Hatchet, was sentenced at London Crown Court at 4pm this afternoon...

The cashier handed Pete his change. He thanked him, picked up the paper and sweets, and went out to wait near the toilets.

Pete remembered the first time that Jacob Wicombs had been arrested and then convicted for one of the most gruesome murders of the time. There had been rumours he had used a pneumatic drill that he had designed and developed himself to cut holes into the fingers of his poor victim Jane Hatchet whilst she was still alive. Her body was found with deep gashes slashed into it. There had been murders like it before, and it turned out that Jacob had been part of a secret cult who had fetishes about killing in this way. It was almost a religion in how they worshipped the type of kill. There had been a national sigh of relief when he had been caught, and now he had been convicted of this other murder that had gone unsolved for years.

Pete leaned against the wall opposite the entrance to the toilets and finished reading the article, which turned out to not be very long. Apparently, Jacob had admitted to one of his fellow prison inmates that he had killed this boy in the exact same way as the one he had already been convicted for. The inmate who he confided in had sensed his opportunity to get off more lightly and reduce his prison sentence and had told the police everything Jacob had told him.

Pete was surprised he hadn't heard more about the case in the news, but it didn't sound like it had been a particularly long affair. Signed, sealed and delivered once the testimony from the inmate was given. A jury was unlikely to have much sympathy for an already convicted murderer after all. He never stood a chance.

Pete continued to daydream about Jacob Wicombs when Marvin pulled at his top.

"Dad? Come on, we're ready to go. What are you doing?" Pete snapped out of his daydreaming, he had completely missed James, Marvin and Anne coming out of the loos.

"Sorry Marvin, I was off with the fairies! Where's your mother?"

"She's gone back to the car with James, we were stood for a whole minute in front of you waving! Mum even got a video, it's so funny! We thought you were going to start drooling!"

Pete chuckled, "Well, maybe I *am* going to start drooling!" Pete said as he lifted his son up and gave him a slobbery kiss on the cheek.

"Ew dad! Get off me!" Marvin exclaimed horrified, "That's disgusting!"

Pete dropped him to the floor and Marvin ran off back to the car with Pete following behind.

Once everyone was strapped in, they began the second half of their journey, which thankfully was quicker than the first as the traffic had improved significantly. What made it even better was the fact that Marvin and James had both fallen asleep and so the usual chants of "Why are we waiting?", and "Are we there yet?" which Pete normally suffered on longer journeys weren't to be heard.

They had to park the car quite a way from where they were making camp. They drove right up to the river edge through the forest, but where they were making base was actually a few hundred metres through the forest to the left of where they were able to pull up. Pete thought it would be a good way of having to explore their immediate surroundings anyway before they properly looked around tomorrow.

"Right boys, wake up we're here!" He called out to his sons, who groggily opened their eyes. They looked around the car and could only see water ahead and forest behind and to the sides.

"Oh, I mean almost here." Pete said looking at the boys, "It's just a short walk but we're going to have to carry our stuff." Pete looked around and noticed that the sun was beginning to set.

"I think tonight we'll just take the tents over and set them up then go to bed. We can get the rest of the stuff tomorrow morning before we have breakfast."

Pete opened up the boot and pulled out the two tents. Anne came round to help him get them out. They decided the best way to carry them with their suitcase was to hold one end of each tent and to balance their suitcase in the middle. James and Marvin's luggage had straps so that they could carry them on their backs. Pete decided that he wanted to take his guitar that night too so they could all have a sing song once the tents were up before bed, and he strapped it over his back.

"Right-oh, come on then let's find a good place to set up camp before the night catches up with us!" Pete said cheerfully, "Ready Anne? Three… two… one… lift!" Anne picked up her ends of the tents and Pete did his, and then they were off.

They had to walk a little way through forested area, tracing the river as a guide. It was tough going, particularly for Marvin and James who struggled to pull their cases across the terrain that was made difficult by surfaced roots and fallen leaves.

"Keep up boys! It'll be a nightmare if we lose you guys in this forest!" Pete shouted back towards his sons, who hurried up and caught their parents. After a couple of minutes they broke through the edge of the trees and found themselves in a clearing.

"Ah-hah!" Pete exclaimed and stopped, putting the tent down with Anne to give them a minute to rest before continuing to find the best place to pitch them.

"See, that wasn't too bad was it? And look at this!" Pete said, blown away. He extended his right arm out and panned it across the river. The sun was low in the sky and was glinting off the surface of the water, resulting in a red glow on the faces of the Runner family. On the other side of the river were more trees, and opposite the Runner's, slightly to the left of where they were standing, a deer was dipping its head into the water to quench its thirst. Behind it, a smaller deer was moving tentatively towards the edge of the river. It brushed into its parent, who looked back at it and encouraged it to get closer to the river, showing it what to do by leaning its head down to the water and licking the surface. The doe inched closer to the lake, leaning its head in from far back. It spread out its legs slightly to try and get a better grip on the surface and make sure it wouldn't fall in. Eventually, the doe put its head near the water and stuck its tongue out. When it realised the water wasn't poisonous and in fact tasted nice, it drank more deeply. The large deer withdrew its head, and then looked up and stared right at James, before nudging its doe, who also looked up. They stared for the briefest of seconds before bolting back into the forest behind them.

"Well, wasn't that something!" Anne said warmly.

"He looked right at me, that younger one, I bet he wanted to play." James said excitedly.

"See! This will be fantastic!" Pete said brightly, "Now come on, there'll be plenty of time in the week to come to admire the animals of the forest, let's get these tents put up and then get a good night's sleep so that we can finish our camp and make it homely tomorrow."

Pete began unloading the boy's tent. He had recently purchased a new one that only took about 20 minutes to put up, so he thought he'd get that out of the way first before tackling his and Anne's, which he had bought much less recently and hoped that the instructions were still with.

"Anne, why don't you and the boys nip into the forest and get some dry wood so that we can get a fire going and I'll get the boys tent set up. It's only really a one-man job anyway. Don't go too far though, I don't want you three getting lost! That would be a terrible start to the holiday!"

Anne laughed, "I'm sure we'll be fine, don't worry. We'll be back in 10 minutes."

"Okay darling. Boys you heard your mother, go and help her gather wood for a fire so we can stay nice and toasty."

As the boys and Anne went off in search of wood, Pete began to construct the boy's tent. He'd got them a three man one so there would be plenty of room, enough he had hoped at the time of purchase to prevent them from banging into each other in the night, though not quite large enough for them to be able to have a full scale war in there should they cross paths during the night. It took him even less time that he thought it would to assemble, and he was finished with it before Anne and the boys were back from the forest with the wood. Pete had been a scout in his younger days and was very used to putting up tents that were difficult to make. These new ones practically put themselves up and were certainly no match for his talents. He decided not to wait for Anne to return to get started on their tent and cracked on with it. As it turned out, the instructions were in with it.

After 10 minutes of sorting through the pieces, Anne and the boys returned carrying arms full of firewood.

"Sorry we were slightly longer than expected, the wood nearer the edge was damp so we went further in. How are you getting on?" Anne asked Pete who was crouching over a pile of poles.

"Yeah good, the boys tent is done and I've just begun sorting through ours. You'll be pleased to know that I remembered to pack the instructions!"

"Good! I'll help you in a minute once we get this fire lit. Come on boys help me get it going and then I'll teach you how to look after it and be masters of fire!"

The boys gave each other excited looks as they rushed to help their mum, and Pete looked up as the three of them started constructing the base for the fire. The shadows they were casting were long, the sun was setting faster than he would have hoped, and he sped up his work to get the tent done.

Anne returned a few minutes later and working together they were able to erect the tent quickly and it was ready for use just after 10pm.

Anne said that she had spotted some slightly larger logs that they could use to sit on at the edge of the woods and so Pete went with her to get them so they could sit around the fire and enjoy the evening together.

Chapter Four

Fire

The campfire threw smoke up into the cool night air as the Runner family sat in a circle around it on the logs that Pete and Anne had collected from the edge of the forest. The sun was close to fully setting, resulting in a dark red-orange canvas painting the sky. The few clouds that did drift across the sky were dark grey in colour, not because they were heavy with rain, but due to the shadows that spread across the earth below.

"Tell us a story dad, you know like the ones you used to." Marvin asked his dad expectantly, and James sat up straighter as if to confirm his interest in story time.

"You know as well as I do that the reason I don't tell you stories like those anymore is because you and your brother cannot sleep after hearing them, which means your mother and I are not allowed to sleep either!" Pete teased, though with a somewhat serious note to his voice.

"Please dad!" James piped up, "I promise we'll sleep just fine and if we do wake up we promise that we won't disturb you or mum!"

Pete looked towards Anne who shook her head with her eyebrows raised as if to say 'if you scare them witless, you will have to suffer the consequences. I'm not staying up all night to look after them.'

"Please dad, pleeeeeease!" Both of his sons now said in unison.

Pete laughed and took his gaze off Anne. "Oh all right then, what's the worst one story can do?" he chuckled.

The boys excitedly adjusted how they were sat so that they could more easily hear their father across the crackle of the fire.

"Nothing too scary, Pete." Anne asked him gently.

"Don't worry dear. Right, are you both comfortable?" He looked at them both to make sure they weren't going to fall off their logs, and then picked up his guitar and softly played a chord that drifted through the smoky fire and out into the night sky.

"It was about a decade ago, on a night not all too dissimilar to this one. It was a touch colder perhaps, and there were no clouds at all in the sky. The stars were out on their own twinkling up with the moon. The Parkins family were sat underneath the stars, keeping them company–" Pete paused for a second and looked menacingly into the fire, before lowering his voice to be just louder than a whisper "-When the creature came to town." He thrust his hand down sharply on the guitar, producing a horrible, twanging noise that cut through the night. He glanced at his sons, each one in turn, and saw that they were both gripped and frightened already. He didn't look at his wife, but felt a stern expression burning on the side of his face.

"The Parkins were an ordinary family. There were four of them. The dad was an extremely intelligent man who was said to be the brightest technology expert in the whole entire world. He was able to build a computer from scratch without any instructions, and had recently created a working robot. Because he spent a lot of time handling oil when building his robots, he was always extremely dirty. In contrast, his wife, as if to make up for her husband's dirtiness was always immaculate in both her cleanliness and her fashion sense. She always wore beautiful dresses, even when she was doing housework. They were happily married with two children, both of them boys. One was called Jack and the other Tom. Jack was 12, and a year and a half older and much bigger than his younger brother. They both had light blonde hair and loved nothing more than to have a good scrap with one another, a lot like you boys. However, on this particular night, both were too tired from their adventures exploring the nearby forest and running on the beach to want to scrap and instead they were content to sit by the fire, much to the relief of their parents. The fire was spitting and crackling in the late day sun, and billowing up smoke into the air. Their dad, whose name was Anthony, was telling his boys a scary story. Except the story he was telling his sons was not a true story. Anthony was making his scary story about Dracula up on the spot. The story I am telling you about the Parkins family is also a scary story, though unlike Anthony's story the one I am telling you is true. It happened not far from where we are now, just down towards the coast from here. In fact, I would say it is in walking distance of this very spot."

Pete paused again and looked at his two sons, who were staring at him wide eyed, listening intently, hooked on his every word.

"On that cool evening in August, as Anthony told his tale about the great Count Dracula and all the blood that he loved to suck from his victims, the air became chillier and in response to this, the fire crackled louder in defiance to the cold. One of Anthony's sons shivered and he realised he had left the blankets in the car, so picked up a torch and went to fetch them. When Anthony returned to the fire to continue his story, he found that his wife and two sons were no longer there. He sat back down anyway and picked up his guitar, figuring that one of the boys had needed the loo and Jane, his wife, certainly wouldn't have left one of them alone near the fire. He waited for them to return and started strumming his guitar in the meantime, playing nothing in particular, just chords like this one." Pete strummed his guitar again.

"After about 10 minutes his family still hadn't returned and Anthony began to get worried, even if the boys had needed a number two..." Pete's sons giggled at the mention of others having to go to the toilet, resulting in a sharp look from Anne, which quickly stopped their giggling.

"...As I was saying, even if the boys had needed a number two..." Pete winked at his sons, "They never normally took this long. Worried that his family had gotten lost in the dark, Anthony put his guitar down and stood up, looking around to see if he could spot them coming back from the woods that were about a minutes walk from where their tent was pitched. When he was satisfied he couldn't see them coming, he tried to ring Jane. It went straight through to voicemail. He shouted in the general direction of the trees, calling their names *'Jane? Jack?, Tom? Are you all right?'*

"There was no reply, Anthony assumed because they had wondered in slightly too far and the trees were blocking out the sound of his voice. He jogged back to the tent to fetch a torch, switched it on, and made his way toward the trees, being careful not to fall over any branches. Anthony continued to call out his wife and sons names, but there was no answer. He walked on a little further, shining his torch left and right, hoping that they would see it or hear him and come out. After another 15 minutes, Anthony began to really worry, but then thought that they may not have come into the woods at all. Heck, Jane wouldn't bring them out here in the dark without a torch; she was far too smart to do that. They'd probably gone slightly further in another direction to pee and that was why they couldn't hear him shouting, he'd gone wrong all along. Anthony decided to stop and turn around. But just as he brought the torch in an arc around his body, he spotted something move just out of the light. "Jack? Tom? Is that you?" He asked the darkness. There was no reply, so he assumed it must have just been the shadow of a tree and went to head back.

"That is when he realised he didn't know how far he had turned around. Had he turned 180 degrees and was now facing the way he had come, or had he turned less than that? Had he even turned around at all? Panic coursed through Anthony's veins and he began running through the trees. After 5 minutes running practically blind, he stopped and panted heavily, reaching out with his hand to rest it on a tree. "OUCH!" He shouted as he cut his fingers on a sharp piece of bark. "Just what I needed, great." Anthony's phone then started ringing. Thinking it was Jane at last he picked it up. However, on the other end of the phone, there was a long, loud screeching noise. Anthony threw the phone away, crying out in shock. He looked all around him and shook his head. He started walking again in a direction that he thought was best, though really he had no idea where he was going, he just wanted to get out of the forest and hopefully back to his family. After what seemed like an eternity of walking, Anthony breathed a sigh of relief as he came back to the edge of the forest where he had entered and made his way back to the camp. He could see a child sat by the fire on his own with his back to him and felt even more relief, it looked like Jane and the boys had made it back safe. As he got closer to the fire, however, he noticed that the colour of his son's hair was darker than normal. "Tom, what have you been rolling around in?"

"Anthony stopped dead in his tracks. The boy sat with his back to him was a good half a foot shorter than Tom, and now that he was close enough to see the back of his head he realised that he was right that the hair was darker. It was black. Not blonde. "Hi there, are you okay? Where are your pa-?" Anthony's nose began running and there was a sharp pain in the back of his throat, which caused him to cough.

"He pulled a tissue out of his pocket and blew his nose. He looked at the tissue as he went to fold it and was surprised to see that it covered with blood. His hand with the tissue in flinched away from his body, but not before he noticed that the ends of his fingers were also covered in blood. He thought it was very odd that he couldn't feel what should have been an obvious pain in them by the looks of the wounds.

"He continued to cough, unable to properly clear his throat. His cough was rasping and seemed to come from deep within him. His eyes were wide open and panicky now as he wiped his nose again. His situation then became worse as blood began to pour from his nose and down into his mouth, which was open from coughing and the fact he couldn't breathe through his bleeding nose. Anthony gagged the blood up and leaned over, now completely oblivious to the stranger who was still sat facing in towards the fire.

"Tears began to stream down his cheeks from the pain of the cough that was now overwhelming him as much as the blood was and he slumped down onto his knees, bending forward. Blood fell out of his nose and began to puddle on the floor beneath his face. Anthony stared down into it, gagging now instead of coughing. He threw up a dark red paste.

"Unknown to Anthony, the stranger stood up from the bench and turned to face him. With the last ounce of strength left in his body, Anthony looked up from the floor into two, big green eyes and screamed."

"PETE!" Anne shouted at him, and he blinked suddenly back in the world from his story. His two sons were huddled together under a blanket and were both ghostly white.

"Shit sorry I – *damn*! Pardon my French kids!" Neither of them laughed at something they would have usually found funny, they were both petrified.

"Come on boys, it's getting late. Come with me to the forest so you can go to the loo and then we'll do our teeth."

She ushered them up towards the tent but neither of them moved. "Come on, it wasn't that scary!" She huffed. "Your father was just trying to scare you, don't give him the satisfaction!"

"Yeah come on boys, everything will be fine don't worry!"

Reluctantly the boys got up, fetched their toothbrushes, and followed their mum into the forest.

Part Two

2005

Chapter Five

Jane

Jane crawled on all fours across the forest floor. Her elbows and arms were bleeding from scratches that she had received from the stray, sharp twigs that littered the ground. It was so dark that she couldn't see where she was going; she was so scared that she didn't care where she was going. All she knew was that somehow she had to find her boys. She still couldn't believe how she had gotten into this mess, and kept running it over and over in her head. When Anthony had gone off to get the blanket for Jack and Tom, Tom had complained that he needed the loo. She didn't feel right about leaving Jack out by the fire on his own and so had made him come too, despite him moaning that he was old enough to look after himself for 5 minutes. Jane had insisted he come anyway for her sake, to protect her because she was scared that the monsters from Anthony's story would get them. A nice twist she had thought at the time, and persuasive enough as it turned out to get Jack to come along, wielding one of the smaller sticks that was lined up to be used as firewood, claiming he would be their great protector from the dark.

    Jane guided them a few paces into the forest away from their little camp and told Tom to do his business. Jack had decided he too needed to go. As she had been waiting for the two boys to finish, Anne had heard a rustle in the leaves to the right of the trees where they had set up stool. She wandered over to see if anything was there, but it was too dark to make anything out and she assumed it must have been a small bird or maybe a rat out hunting, using the night as cover.

"Are you nearly done boys?" She asked as she went back toward where they were peeing.

Neither of them replied.

"Boys? Are you finished yet?"

She could no longer hear the sound of their pee hitting the forest floor.

"Come on boys this isn't funny, I don't want you to get lost out here or we'll never find you before light! And you know how your father will be; he doesn't even know where we are! He'll have a panic attack if we're not back soon! Now come on!"

She heard another rustle to her left and turned quickly this time hoping to spot one of the boys. Again there was nothing in sight. Jane was worried, how had she let them get away from her so easily, they were peeing 2 yards away from her not 2 minutes ago! Where in god's name were they?

She heard a child giggle, and let out a little sigh of relief. They were hiding behind a tree and were going to try and scare her. She really had to stop Anthony from putting these ideas into their heads, mainly because she couldn't cope with these consequences. Still, she believed she had them right where she wanted them. She approached the tree slowly and started talking out loud to herself.

"I can't believe I've lost my boys! Where on earth could they be? My only children, out lost in the wild, perhaps never to be found again. Oh what will their father say?" She continued, as she got closer to the tree that they were hiding behind. "Lost out here in the wild, with all the foxes and other dangerous animals out on the prowl, anything could happen to them out here!" Now inches from the tree, she prepared to jump out at them. She heard another giggle, bent her knees, and leapt out from her side to their side of the tree shouting, "GOT-CHA!"

But she didn't have them.

There was no one behind the tree.

She looked around confused. She hadn't heard the footsteps of them running away after the last giggle. What was happening? She did a loop of the tree. It had an extremely thick base, and must have been hundreds and hundreds of years old.

Her children were somewhere out in the pitch black, in a forest that they had only briefly explored earlier in the day and surely would have no recognition of in the dark of the night. She checked her phone but found that she didn't have any signal. Anthony would soon begin to worry that they had gotten lost. She couldn't believe that this was happening, and on the very first night too.

Deciding to take matters into her own hands, Jane turned the torch on her phone on and wandered further into the woods, calling out her son's names. She could hear the adrenaline pounding in her ears and the noise of it made her movements erratic. She could barely concentrate on what she was looking at and the forest was passing her in a whir as she made her way deeper and deeper into it. Jane kept twisting her head this way and that, hoping her boys would suddenly appear in front of her, popping their heads out from around a tree shouting, "We got you mum! We had you so scared you should have seen your face!" And at the beginning of her search she thought this a very real possibility. Her sons had always been cheeky little sods and were always pulling pranks on her and Anthony. But this didn't feel like one of their pranks. This wasn't a whoopee cushion under the pillow of her chair, or sugar in the saltshaker. This was a dark forest, late at night, a long way from home and a long way from help. The minutes began to drag on.

Jane continued crunching her way through the forest, stepping on twigs and crisp leaves, straining her ears to hear any sound of her children against the thumping of the adrenaline. She continued to shout, but there was less conviction in the names that she was now calling. The hope was draining rapidly out of her body; she could physically feel it seeping from her pores.

Eventually, breathing hard from her searching, she stopped and looked around her position, utterly defeated. She was hideously lost. Only now did she contemplate the foolishness of chasing her children through the forest. She was about to start crying when she suddenly realised another mistake she had made. Jane had assumed that her children would have wandered further into the forest. Could they simply have peed, tried to hide from her to scare her, realised they had done too good a job and that they'd actually lost her, and then just headed straight back towards camp instead? The idea that they had done that filled Jane up with hope, but also hit her with a slight dread. She had been so preoccupied with finding them that she hadn't paid any mind to where she was actually going. In the dead of night, especially with the overhanging trees blocking out the days remaining light, she wasn't entirely sure on how to get back to camp.

Jane knew that she had been walking in a roughly straight direction looking for her sons, so decided the best course of action would be to turn right around and head back. At the very least if she managed to hit the edge of the forest again she would spot the fire and be able to find the camp. Her mind flickered back to Anthony, and she prayed that the children were back with him. Because if they weren't and he'd also gone running into the forest... She stopped herself abruptly from following that line of thought, and instead made the decision to focus her efforts on getting back safely. She turned around, and using the light on her phone, began to move again.

Jane wasn't entirely sure how long she had been trying to track down her children, the adrenaline that had been flowing through her body had made her unconscious of time, but she imagined it couldn't have been more than 30 minutes since she had lost them. She checked her phone, which displayed 10.57pm. Later than she had thought. Factoring in the adrenaline that had gotten her this far into the forest, she assumed it would probably take her about an hour or so to get back to the camp. Anthony would have come into the forest to look for them by then, if he hadn't done so already. She knew she had to try and get in touch with him. She checked her phone again, but there was still no signal.

*

The forest had become more and more alive with the sound of creatures as the night had worn on, so much so that once or twice Jane could have sworn she heard the mutterings of her children. Though, when she looked in the direction that she thought the sounds were coming from she saw nothing but blackness and the shadows cast from the light of her phone.

Her phone buzzed, and Jane looked down hoping for a message from Anthony. Instead, she was dismayed by the message that was displayed:

10% battery remaining.

Panic shot through her body, but she took a deep breath and tried to steady herself. 10% was still enough to get her out of the forest, especially if she was just using the torch. Unfortunately, Jane knew that this probably wasn't true. Her phone was old and temperamental. 10% battery actually meant she had anywhere from 5 minutes to an hour left of power. Jane prayed that it would be the latter of the two.

She tried to recognise trees from her journey into the forest with the boys or from her brief time spent in it earlier, but knew it was a fools' game. Everything looked different in the dark, especially under the weak light from the torch on her phone. All of the trees looked identical anyway.

On she continued, desperate yet determined to find her way out. She checked the time on her phone again, 11.24pm, and thought she must be getting close by now. She was feeling tired herself. This was the latest she had been up in a long while and the most exercise she had done too, especially after the hike the family had gone on earlier in the day.

*

The torch on Jane's phone went out, and she was thrust into darkness.

"Oh," was all that she could manage. She stopped walking and crouched down on the floor, thinking hard about what to do next. She could always just lie down and try and sleep through the night, then find her way back to the camp in the morning, mark the ground with an arrow so that she knew which direction she had come from. She decided to mark an arrow pointing the way she wanted to continue going anyway, just in case whilst stopped she accidently lost her bearings. She dug the arrow into the ground deep enough so that if she did lose her bearing in the dark, she would be able to feel around on the floor and find it. Once she was satisfied that the arrow was deep enough, she returned her concentration to the current predicament. In her mind she had decided to assume that her children were now with Anthony. She hadn't heard him come after them and as she had supposedly been walking back towards the camp, if he had come looking for her shouting she would have heard him by now. There was a twang of fear in the back of her head that perhaps the reason why she hadn't heard him shouting for her or the kids was because she was heading in the wrong direction, but at this point in the night Jane couldn't afford to get caught up on those sorts of details. She had to remain positive above all else.

Jane was frightened and knew that her head would want to lead her down a great many dark paths. She had observed in her job a long time ago that humans have a habit of creating fear in their own minds often in times when it is unwarranted, leading them to do truly terrible things in order to improve their own situation. She had always believed it to be connected to a humans strong will to survive - by expecting danger at all times you were always ready for it. So she knew that she had to be headstrong above all else. Extraordinarily so. Her heart could ache for her children and her husband, but her head, for now, had to remain clear and focused.

She was tired. Her phone was out of battery and she hadn't been able to contact anyone, though Anthony would know that she was somewhere in the forest. It was dark and she was lost. She knew that the forest she was in was not a particularly dangerous one; at the end of the day this was England after all. There certainly were not any killer bears loose or lions or tigers that could creep up on her in the dark. She was thirsty, all of the walking had taken its toll and because she had only been taking her sons for a pee she obviously hadn't brought a bag of supplies with her. Oddly enough, trekking through the woods in the middle of the night hadn't been high on her list of priorities for the evening. She had a few pieces of gum in her pocket and a handkerchief, but she couldn't think up a particularly practical use for either of them right now as her nose wasn't running and her breath wasn't bad enough to warrant a mint. In any case, it was looking highly unlikely that she would be kissing anyone this evening barring a miracle. She took a deep breath and decided that staying put would be her best option for the night.

The more Jane thought about the way in which she had just gone stumbling through the woods, following a giggle and chattering that at this point she wasn't entirely sure she had really heard, at night was probably one of the worst and least responsible things she had ever done. Jane was a woman who, generally speaking, didn't make such rash decisions. Yet here she was, lost and alone in the forest. She hoped Anthony would have the sense to find a signal on his phone if he didn't have any and call rescue services by now and that they would be coming to look for her. She crawled over to the nearest tree, fumbling around across the floor, taking care to find the area where she had dug the arrow into the ground so that she wouldn't drag detritus over it. After a short period of time her outstretched right arm found the bark of a tree, and she moved the rest of her body close to it, before pivoting so that she could rest her back on it.

Jane closed her eyes, with the last thought she had before drifting off into an uneasy sleep being of her two sons, scrambling through the woods alone, being chased by creatures of the night.

Chapter Six

Dusk

Jane had drifted in and out of sleep all night. The sounds of the forest had made it nigh on impossible for her to fully relax, and the tree that she had been resting against compounded this. Its bark was thick and as hard as rock, digging into her back and scratching her every time she tried to adjust to make herself more comfortable. She was too nervous to lie down on the forest floor, not wanting to wake up with creatures crawling all over her face and body. More panic was the last thing she needed right now. She had considered trying to move to a different tree once her eyes adjusted to the darkness. The problem was that the darkness was so intense that her eyes hadn't been able to adjust. There was no light at all for them to try and adjust to. It was the blackest black she had ever experienced, and the last night in any forest she ever wanted to spend.

 Jane kept her eyes shut for a little longer, not ready yet to face the coming day. She was thirsty. That was the most worrying thing. She thought she would probably be very hungry too, but the fact was she was so thirsty that her stomach had decided to not make her life even worse by growling at her, which Jane appreciated greatly.

 As Jane sat leaning on the tree with her eyes closed, she began to drift off to sleep again. She saw a fountain spraying up cold, fresh, clear water into the sky, and ran to try and grab it in her mouth, but she kept just missing the water, and by the time it hit the ground it vanished into nothingness and she was left scrambling on the floor, digging at the dirt and praying for just a drop. Just a drop was all she wanted. Was that too much to ask? Not even a glass, not even a sip, just a measly drop of water. *Please God, please let me just have a drop of —*

The sound of a child giggling broke through her dream and pulled her back to reality once more. This time she did open her eyes, and was dismayed to find that it was still dark. She tried to pinpoint where the sound had come from, but determined that it must have just been a part of her dream. Her head must have willed the sounds of her boy's laughter into her head. She blinked furiously, trying to fight back tears that she wasn't sure she'd even be able to cry, given how much she needed water. As she continued to blink, the forest began to take up a dark, shadowy shape before her; the trees hanging ominously over her, judging her every movement. It wasn't dark like it had been when she had fallen asleep; she could at least see a very short distance in front of her. The early morning sun was beginning to rise and she imagined that if the forest roof hadn't been so dense with branches and leaves that she probably would have been able to see much more. She stayed sitting for a little while longer, giving her eyes as long as possible to adjust to her surroundings.

She was completely encaged by trees. The one she was resting on appeared to be in the middle of a circle of trees with trunks that were much thinner than that of the behemoth she had spent the night leaning against. Even so, the trees that were surrounding where she was sat were no less tall. She traced the height of one of the trees directly ahead of her with her eyes, and wasn't able to see the top of it without craning her neck at an almost 90-degree angle. The roof above her, made up of thick branches holding millions of dark green leaves, was beginning to let a little light through. The edges of the leaves themselves were glowing a reddish colour as the sun began its journey across the sky. Anne became lost in her own head just staring up into the trees, listening to the birds chatter to each other about what a nice day it was going to be.

Then she was brought back to the real world as the faces of her sons flashed across her mind. She realised that she was woozy with thirst, unable to concentrate unless she really focused her mind. When she did, Jack and Tom dominated her thoughts. A deep ache welled up inside of her, causing her to drop her head as if the pain she felt towards her missing sons was so great that she wasn't able to support her own body. She closed her eyes and begged with the powers that be for them to be safe and with their father. At this, her mind turned to Anthony. He had always been pretty rash when it came to her and the boys. He loved them all fiercely, to the point where he was apt to make very rash decisions. She remembered one particular occasion when Jack had broken his leg after falling out of a tree he had been climbing near their house. When Tom had come running in shouting that Jack was dying, Anthony had completely changed from the relaxed, story telling father that they knew and loved into a crazed, panicking mess.

He had run at Tom, swung him into his arms and shouted at him to show him where Jack was. Tom, shocked at his father, had begun crying and through his sobbing had been unable to say exactly where it was his brother had fallen, which had made Anthony doubly as crazed. Eventually, Jane had to take Tom off Anthony, who then ran out of the front door looking around wildly. Meanwhile Jane had gotten Tom to calm down before he was able to remember exactly where it was that Jack had fallen. Anthony had run off, apparently deciding to use his sixth sense as a father to find his "dying" son.

When Jane had found Jack with Tom, Anthony was nowhere to be seen, apparently having run off in the wrong direction. Jane had called an ambulance first and then rung Anthony, who answered with a series of panting and coughing as he attempted to get his breath back. She told him she had found Jack, who had hurt his leg, and that they were heading to the hospital and to meet them there. When he did turn up, it was the old, normal Anthony who arrived. Granted, he was much sweatier than he normally was, but his general demeanour was back to normal. He picked Tom up and hugged him, apologising for shouting at him earlier and explaining how much he loved them both and how worrying it would be if either of them ever got seriously hurt. Tom had laughed, but there had been apprehension in his face. Something Jane had never before seen from Tom when with his father. She just hoped to God that Anthony had managed to relax a little since then and wouldn't have done anything stupid. At the back of her mind, however, she knew that this was unlikely to be the case if the boys hadn't made their way back to camp quickly without her.

*

Jane's thirst was a seriously big problem and she knew it. She decided that now was the time to get going again and hopefully find her way back to camp. The longer she stayed sat in the forest the less time she would be able to walk before the thirst caused her to pass out. They had been camped near enough to the river that there should hopefully be a stream along the way, and if not she should be able to find the campsite in the light quickly anyway. She tried to heave herself up, but found that she had very little energy. She gritted her teeth, and using her legs, pushed her back into the tree, and then used her arms to lever herself up and onto her feet. Once up, she lent for a few seconds against the tree, catching her breath, and then she began to look around to find the arrow that she had dug into the forest floor the night before.

She staggered forward, feeling slightly dizzy from dehydration and a lack of food, before deciding she needed a little more time and stumbled back to the tree to catch her breath and regain her balance. Eventually, she felt ready enough to find the arrow again and recommenced her search. She knew she hadn't crawled for too long and so it wouldn't be too far from the tree she had spent the night against. When she couldn't spot the arrow straight away, a fresh fear welled up inside of her body. Had she really dug the arrow into the ground or had that been a dream?

Jane looked down at her hands; they were caked in mud, and her fear dispensed. The arrow was probably buried under some leaves that had fallen over night, or covered under detritus that animals or the wind had moved about. Not that she could remember feeling any wind, especially down here in the forest where all the trees would have acted as windbreakers. Still, there were plenty of animals about in the forest; she had heard enough of them last night. And leaves always fell off trees, so yes, she thought, it must just be buried under something.

Jane got down on her hands and knees and began gently brushing the forest floor, moving twigs and leaves and small insects this way and that, feeling the floor for any signs of indentation. After a few minutes, when she was sufficiently covered in mud and grime, Jane was feeling very uneasy. Maybe she had crawled further than she thought to reach the tree. After all, she had been very panicked and had lost her concept of time.

Could she have crawled 10 or even 20 metres? Had she crawled in a straight line or had it been angled? The arrow could be anywhere. She had begun to breath quickly and sharply without realising, but now she noticed herself doing it. Jane was hyperventilating and had to calm down. It was getting close to daytime; at least she could see a little, her sons would be fine. Positivity was the word for today. She just had to stay calm and make sure that she would be fine. Yes, everything was going to be okay.

    Jane tried to remember how long she had been moving before her phone had run out of battery and thought that it had been about half an hour. That meant she was probably 20 minutes from the edge of the forest and safety. She used all of these facts to bring her breathing back under control. She must have crawled pretty much directly towards the tree, and hadn't turned around consciously last night after she had drawn the arrow, which meant the arrow would have been pointing pretty much directly at the tree. So all she had to do if she couldn't find the arrow would be to walk in the direction of the tree. She'd give herself another 5 minutes or so to try and find it, and then use her logic to find her way back. Her logic had served her well in life up until this point, who's to say it wouldn't continue to her serve her well now?

    Jane continued to search, acting like a human brush to clear the floor around her, but soon came to accept the fact that the arrow was lost. If she hadn't found it by now, she thought the chances of her finding it were exceptionally close to zero.

As she was about to give up, something caught the corner of her eye, a slight dip in the ground. Hastily, she scrambled over to it and began frantically brushing a thin coverage of green-brown leaves off the indentation. She frowned. It wasn't the arrow, of course it wasn't. There was just a smallish circular dip that looked like it had been scratched into the ground, probably by a squirrel trying to either bury nuts or dig up nuts it had previously buried. Jane smacked the ground next to her in frustration. She was sure that she had found the arrow. It took her a second to realise that she had thumped her hand onto a sharp piece of rock and that she had cut herself. Jane cursed and inspected the cut closely. It would be fine; it wasn't de-

Underneath her hand and slightly to the right, where she had hit the ground, Jane noticed a second indentation in the earth. At first she thought it might have been hers, she did have small feet after all, but then she realised she hadn't been barefoot at all in the forest. This wasn't a boot print; it was an actual footprint. Jane stared at it perplexed. Looking at the size of it, it could easily have been Tom's, but then where were Jack's? And if it had been Tom's and he had gotten so close, why hadn't he found her?

Jane remembered how dark it had been and realised even if Tom had walked within a metre of her, neither of them would have seen one another. Plus, the noise of the forest animals had been so loud that it was unlikely that she would have heard his footsteps passing through. Jane nodded; they must be Tom's prints.

She got a wave of excitement as she realised she would be able to follow his prints through the forest to find him and began brushing the ground close to it to find the next footprint in the path. She couldn't find it. Maybe the next one had been on harder ground and hadn't made a print, so she decided to try slightly further away, but again with no luck.

Frustration began to rear its ugly head. Jane decided she would try and see where Tom had come from and trace the footprints back. She shuffled over to behind the first footprint and began brushing. Again, she found nothing and her frustration mounted. She went back to the first footprint to make sure that she wasn't just seeing things in the soil, but it was unmistakable. There in front of her in the earth was her son's right footprint. She was sure of it. Jane brushed to the left of the print to try and find his left footprint. After a few seconds, she caught the edge of his left foot and breathed a sigh of relief; she wasn't going crazy after all. He had definitely stood here. Once she had finished excavating, she stood up and viewed the footprints from about. Yes, they looked like Tom's, definitely. Except, she bent over and looked closer. The right foot was fully formed and looked right, but the left footprint looked strange. Jane couldn't put her finger on why. In the middle of the two prints was the dugout circle, and she frowned and looked back towards the tree she had spent the night against. It was probably seven or so metres away.

Jane looked back to the circular indentation, and it clicked in her head. Could this have been the arrow?

She looked back at the footprints, and realised immediately why the left foot had looked so wrong to her. Tom had all of his toes. This footprint was missing one.

Somewhere in the distance she heard a child giggle.

Chapter Seven

Forest

Jane ran from the four-toed foot, in the direction of the tree that she had spent the night under, for the first time running in the opposite direction to the giggling child. The sound that the child had made was not the cheeky noise that her boys made when they laughed; this was cruel in its delivery. More high pitched than her boys, and from a child younger than them, maybe one of six or seven. Yet at the same time the giggle sounded almost mature, as if the noise had been made thousands of times before. She had the feeling that something was chasing her from behind through the forest, which made her run even faster. She daren't turn back for fear of what she might see. There was something wrong with the forest; it didn't feel like the one that her family had trekked through yesterday. The birds were still chattering above her, but the noise wasn't as optimistic as it had been just moments before. It was more excitable, as if they were passing a great secret from one to the next.

"I'M HERE! I'M HERE! I'M OVER HERE!" Jane cried out as she continued to run away from the noise of the child, hoping beyond hope that there was a search party out for her and that they would be able to find her. She pumped her legs frantically fast, not wanting to slow down or turn around, knowing that if she did she would be caught. Her chaser would pull her to the ground, grab her legs and trip her up. Clamber all over her and feast.

She ran and ran, faster and further than she ever thought possible given her deep thirst, barely looking where she was going, barely managing to avoid trees. Her entire body existing purely off the adrenaline that was coursing through her veins. She left her thirst and hunger behind her; Jane was a being of pure instinct now, dashing her way through the forest with the single purpose of evading her pursuer. She felt that if she could just get to the edge of the forest, if she could just escape the confines of the forest, then she would be safe. Her chaser couldn't leave the forest; she felt it in her bones.

Eventually, though, the adrenaline began to run out. Frustration built inside her that couldn't keep her pace up. She told her feet not to stop, to stop meant death. She willed her body to give more, just a little more. Just let her get to the edge of the forest, to safety. Let her escape the creature. Her pace continued to slow and she was running through quicksand, desperately trying to keep her legs pumping but not seeming to travel anywhere. Jane accepted her fate, she would be caught and this would be the end of her. She would die alone, without anyone close by to hear her screaming. Jane slowed down to a stuttering walk and then stopped completely and bent over double, sucking in huge gasps of air, filling her lungs that had been screaming out so desperately for additional supplies of oxygen. They gratefully accepted the air as it flowed into them, and quickly transported it into her blood so that she could recover. She waited for the creature to catch up with her. To her right she spotted a thick piece of wood and she picked it up to use as a weapon. Finally, she plucked up the courage to turn around, fully expecting it to be the last action of her life.

She looked around, lifting up the wood ready to swing in attack, but found that she was still surrounded by forest. Only forest. There was no creature directly behind her, and she couldn't hear it running after her anymore. Jane tried to peer in all directions to see if she could spot movement between the trees, but the air between them was still.

As her breath became less ragged, she spat out some phlegm onto the earth. Her mouth was so dry that it didn't want the phlegm to leave her and it clung on to it, resulting in a long string of drool hanging out of Jane's mouth. She squashed her face together in disgust and wiped at her face with the back of her hand. She then bent down to the floor and picked up some fresh leaves, using them to wipe the phlegm off her arm.

Fear still dominated Jane's thoughts. She knew it wouldn't take her all day to find the edge of the forest if she just walked in one direction until she found the edge, but she was so thirsty she wasn't entirely sure how long she would be able to walk for. Running as she had done had been stupid; she had been like a kid who had to turn the downstairs light off whilst still downstairs and then run up them before the monsters in the dark could grab them. Of course there wasn't a scary creature out to get her, the footprints were probably left over from someone else who had been walking through the forest earlier in the day. Her arrow was probably under a patch that she hadn't cleared. It was all in her head. She was fine. It was all just in her head.

The forest was still relatively dark and Jane assumed that it was probably four or five in the morning. She was utterly exhausted, but knew that if she didn't continue now, if she lay down in the forest, there was a very high chance that she wouldn't rise again.

There was a giggle off to her left.

She twisted as fast as she could manage in the direction of the noise bringing up the wood in defence. Jane was too exhausted to run any farther, she knew that she would have to stand and face whatever it was that was coming for her.

"Hello?" She called out into the forest. "Hello? Tom? Jack? Can you hear me? It's mum! I'm here!"

There was no response, as there had been no response to any of her calls.

There was more giggling, this time behind her over her left shoulder. Jane twisted again still holding the wood aloft, her eyes darting all around trying to spot the source.

"Come on boys, this isn't funny! Come out from where you're hiding right now! I promise I won't be mad. Where have you been all night?"

Then the giggling came from all around her at once, it filled her head as if she was surrounded by hundreds and hundreds of children all watching one of their parents as they were about to sit on a whoopee cushion that had been cunningly placed underneath their seat cushion. The noise was deafening. Jane spun around and around on the spot madly screaming back at the giggling. She cried out in frustration as she twisted and turned and looked up at the forest roof and pleaded with it to reveal her children to her. And if not her children, then the creature that had come for her.

The giggling stopped abruptly, and she was left alone in the woods again with nothing but the sounds of the birds above her. Jane stood perfectly still. Her head was clear. It must be the thirst; she was hallucinating the sound.

Jane started walking again, she thought she must be going crazy, her brain turning the chatter from the birds into the sound of children's laughter. She had to get out of the forest and back to her family, fast.

She marched on, ignoring the complaints from her body, which was clamouring desperately for a drink. A new lease of life had burned up inside of her; her purpose was to get back to Anthony and her boys safely. She could have a big, long drink of water and cuddle them all and tell them about the horrible night she had spent all alone in the forest. She just had to get out of the forest, that was all.

Jane stopped dead in her tracks as she heard the giggling up ahead again. This time it sounded real, much more like her boy's than the one that she had heard earlier and run away from. They had found her.

She approached the area where the giggling had come from slowly, as if she didn't want to frighten her own children away from her. That a single loud noise might make them flee. She was too tired to call out to them in any case, her voice deserting her. Jane heard the giggling again, but this time it was slightly further away, and Jane began to increase her pace to catch up to it. There it was again, the light, cheeky sound. Again though, it sounded to Jane as if it was getting further away. She started to jog in the direction of it, when she heard the sound again it was about the same distance away as the time before, and so Jane ran. Jane ran towards the noise, faster and faster until she was sprinting flat out like she had been earlier when she had been escaping from the four-toed creature.

Then everything went black.

*

The sound of running water swept through Jane's head. She snuggled further into Anthony's chest, listening to the flow of the river, and began to daydream about the day before, when the four of them had been in the river in the afternoon, splashing each other and having a full on water war. Anthony had moaned that they had forgotten to put the fishing nets in the car and so Jane had suggested that they just hop in and use their hands to catch fish like proper adventurers would. Anthony had given the boys a suggestive look and they had run off toward the water, trying desperately to be the first one to strip down to their underwear, jump in and catch a fish. Anthony had run on in just behind them and Jane had been so caught up in their enthusiasm that she had found herself bounding down towards the water whilst stripping in a rather ungainly manner down to her underwear.

The fishing by hand had been extremely unsuccessful, with Anthony claiming that there weren't actually any fish in the river to be caught, for if there had been fish in the river, then he was skilled enough in the art of hand fishing to have caught them.

Jane, who had watched a rather large looking fish swim right through the middle of his legs as he gave his great "I am a big strong man so can catch fish" speech, merely laughed before pointing the fish out to the boys who had both told their dad off for not concentrating hard enough and splashed him for letting it get away. That sparked the great water war that would follow, lasting the best part of 20 minutes.

Jane wrinkled her nose as she became more conscious to the world. There was a metallic twang in the air that reminded her of the smell of old pennies.

She no longer felt thirsty or hungry, it must all have been a part of a terrible dream, she'd tell them all about it over breakfast. No doubt the boys would call her a wuss. Jane smiled to herself and stroked Anthony's chest, and was surprised when she found that it was sticky. Jane rolled her head slightly so that it was looking up at the sky and opened her eyes, squinting against the light as she looked at the hand that had just rubbed Anthony's chest. Jane did a double take then looked very hard at her hand, which was completely covered in blood.

Jane shot up off the floor and turned to her husband. The sight that greeted her would haunt her for the rest of her life. Anthony was dead, she could tell that right away. He was caked in blood. There were gashes all over his body, cutting through his clothes and going deep into his flesh. Around the edge of each gash was dried blood, whilst in the centre the blood was darker in colour, and looked almost glossy as if a thin skin had formed over the still runny blood below, like the skin of cream you get on the top of old milk bottles. His nose had been practically destroyed, with a huge chunk taken out of the centre of it that continued into his right cheek. His head was tilted away from the side that Jane had been sleeping on and his mouth was wide open, with a blood stain streak running down his chin.

There were further gashes across his chest and on his belly and arms, but Jane couldn't look any longer. She had been able to look for as long as she had because she thought she had been back in a dream and was curious about what was going to happen next in it. She was waiting for the monster to surface and come running at her and she had been bracing herself to get away whilst looking at Anthony's broken body but she couldn't take it anymore. She couldn't bear to see Anthony in this way for another second.

Jane pinched herself to wake up, a trick her mother had taught her when she used to have vivid nightmares as a young girl. The problem was, unlike the times when she had been laid alone in her small single bed surrounded by her dolls and cuddly toys that were standing guard ready to protect her from the evils of the night, this time Jane didn't wake up. She pinched herself, and then she did it again and again, each time she pinched harder and more desperately than the time before. Jane pinched herself so hard that she ended up screaming out loud as she continued to exist in her nightmare, her screaming turned into desperate crying. This wasn't a dream. She picked up Anthony's limp hand and pulled it into her chest, wailing at the air around them both. She put her head down into his cold knuckles and willed him back to life, shaking her head from side to side and whispering over and over, "Please don't be dead my darling, please don't be dead. Don't leave me my darling, please don't be dead."

When he still didn't move, she withdrew her head, and then noticed something odd on the tips of two of Anthony's fingers, she peered closer at them and saw that there were two holes gorged deep into them. She turned away from her husband's body and gagged aggressively.

Once she gained control of her gagging, she looked up toward the forest. Her eyes locked with a pair of bright green eyes. Jane froze on her hands and knees on the floor and stared straight back. Eventually, she blinked, and when her eyes opened again the green eyes had vanished, melting back into the forest.

She heard squelching footsteps running up behind her and turned as quickly as she could, fearing that the creature had somehow gotten behind her in the brief second it had taken for her to blink.

However, what was making the footsteps was not a green eyed creature, but a man wearing a full wetsuit. When he got close to Jane he stopped in the sand and stared wide eyed at her. He looked from her to the body and then back to her. She was completely coated in blood and mud. The man was carrying a paddle and was raising it above him in a defensive stance, facing Jane. But Jane wasn't about to pose a threat to him.

"Help me." She whimpered at him, and passed out.

Chapter Eight

Interrogation

Forensics took samples of the blood and mud off Jane's hands and arms, before taking her clothes in as evidence. She had then been taken into a private shower within the police station to be washed clean. All the while, Jane had been silent. Unable to speak. Unable to comprehend what had happened. She still thought she was in a dream, she was watching on as some other Jane in some other world was prodded and probed and swabbed by men and woman with their mouths covered, dressed from head to toe in white and blue overalls. She watched from afar as the water poured all over this other Jane, picking up notes of red and brown from her tangled hair before continuing down her body and streaking down her pale legs, between her toes whose painted nails had become cracked and broken from her trial through the forest. She watched as the reddish brown liquid swirled around the plughole in a vortex, eventually falling through it and into the beyond.

Jane didn't lift her hands up to wash her body, she just stood in the shower motionless, her head facing the floor, eyes open but unseeing.

The water slowly became clearer and clearer the longer Jane stood there as the majority of the mud and blood was washed off her. At last the water flowed clear, though Jane still did not move.

Her head could not compute what it was that had happened.

There was a bang on the door after an indeterminate amount of time, and a female voice called out to her to see if she had finished yet. Jane didn't reply, she wasn't entirely sure she could speak anymore. She was still waiting to wake up from this dream.

A couple of minutes passed, and then the knock was louder, as was the voice that accompanied it.

"You have two minutes then I am coming in to get you."

Jane continued to stand and stare and see nothing. The seconds ticked by, and she watched the water circle the hole, her head beginning to loll from side to side.

The cubicle door was pulled open, and a wrinkled hand appeared to Jane's right and felt around for the shower knob. Once it had found it and twisted it to the off position, a large white towel was draped around Jane's shoulders and she was led out of the cubicle, being told to mind the slight step on her way out.

The elderly lady who had helped her out then proceeded to rub the towel just a little too forcefully all over Jane's body, resulting in her pale skin going a pink-reddish colour. The lady handed her what looked like scrubs, but Jane just stood there and stared at the light blue clothing in her hands. The elderly woman huffed, before snatching the scrubs back and manoeuvring Jane into them.

Jane was led to a holding cell, which consisted of a low bed and a couple of chairs with a small table in the middle of them. The elderly lady took her over the to bed and sat her down.

"Would you like some coffee? Maybe some tea?"

Jane didn't respond.

"I'll just bring you some water, you have to drink something m'dear."

The woman shut the door with a click that sounded like a lock falling into place and went off to get Jane a glass of water. When she returned, it didn't appear to her as if Jane had moved an inch. The woman extended the cup out to Jane, who didn't take it.

"I'm not going to feed you, you're not a baby!" The woman quipped, before placing the cup on the table in front of Jane.

"I believe your interview will be taking place in around an hour, if there is anything you need in the meantime such as a book or magazine, or a different kind of drink then just knock on the door and someone will bring whatever it is you need. Okay?"

The woman had turned, not expecting a response from Jane, and she didn't receive one and so left, clicking the lock back into place as she went.

*

Over the course of the next hour, Jane didn't move from her spot perched on the bed. Her eyes were trained on the water in front of her; she was thirsty but did not have the energy to drink. She couldn't see the point of it now that her Anthony was gone and her children were lost.

The woman returned and said she would take her to the interview room, helping Jane up and leading her there.

The room was small, dark and empty when she was taken in. There was a large table in the middle that occupied the majority of the space, with two chairs on one side and one, Jane's, opposite. It was lit by a single light which dangled from the ceiling above the table, the bulb was old and needed replacing, giving out only the slightest glow of orange.

Jane was made to sit down and she looked blankly ahead.

The door opened and two men entered, each carrying a mug with steam drifting out of the top. They were both wearing suit trousers and a shirt. The one that sat down to Jane's left was in a light blue shirt, the other who sat to her right was in plain white.

The man in the light blue shirt spoke first.

"Hello Jane, my name is Inspector Jackson and this is my colleague, Detective Javid."

Jane did not look at either of them, she just kept her gaze looking straight ahead, almost directly bisecting the two men.

"This is just an informal interview, but we do have to ask if you would like a lawyer present for it. As you are aware Jane, you are under arrest on suspicion of the murder of Anthony Parkins. You do not have to say anything but it may harm your defence if you do not mention, when questioned, something which you later rely on in court. Anything you do say may be given in evidence. Do you understand?"

Jane gave no response.

"Jane, did you hear what I said?"

No response. Detective Jackson decided to give it a try.

"Hey Jane, did you hear what my colleague said? Do you understand that you're allowed a lawyer if you want one to be present in the room as we have this interview?"

Jane continued to stare straight ahead, not moving.

Javid looked at Jackson and shook his head at him. Jackson shrugged his shoulders back as if to say, "It was worth a try, but she is definitely not yet ready to cooperate!"

"Okay Jane, what we are going to do is take you back to the holding cell for a bit. Give you some more time. If you don't feel as if you can talk to us today then that is perfectly okay, we understand that you are in a lot of shock."

Jane's eyes shifted to look at Inspector Jackson.

"Do you understand me, Jane?" Jackson said, sensing some sort of breakthrough.

Jane nodded.

"For the benefit of the tape, the suspect Jane Parkins nodded to indicate yes. Okay good, we're going to call a doctor in to give you a once over, and they may be able to give you something to help alleviate some of the stress you are feeling. We are going to detain you over night and will interview you again in the morning. Would you like a lawyer present for that interview?"

This time Jane shook her head.

"For the purpose of the tape, the suspect has shaken her head to indicate no. Okay Jane, well we shall see you again at ten-thirty tomorrow morning. Interview suspended."

Detective Javid pressed the pause button on the tape and the two men got up. Jackson knocked on the door once, and it opened to reveal a uniformed officer.

"Hey Jake, can you escort Mrs Parkins here back to the holding cell please?"

Jake nodded his head and indicated for Jane to follow him. Jane found that she still hadn't gained full control of her body and couldn't get up on her own. Jackson looked back at Jake and then said a little more quietly so that only he could hear, "Might take more than a simple gesture to get her to move".

*

Jane spent most of the night lying on the bed staring at the ceiling. Every time she closed her eyes the image of Anthony's body penetrated her mind and it would take all of her strength not to gag and cry. As the evening had worn on, it had slowly but surely begun to sink in that Anthony was gone, that her husband was dead. As the numbness of that fact sank in and she wept the evening away, she remembered her children. Where were they? They hadn't been at the campsite and Jane hadn't been able to think about anything but the image of Anthony's body.

Jane tried to get out of bed to go and knock on the door to get someone's attention and to alert them to find her children, but her body was still in shock and was still fighting against her. She fought every inch of her body and willed it to get up. Eventually, with sweat streaming out of every pore, she heaved herself up and stumbled over to the door. She bashed on it as hard as she could, banging desperately until she heard the lock click out of its slot and the door push open. Jane was on the floor at this point and managed only two words.

"My children."

*

Jane was running through the forest, following a stranger's voice that was egging her on. "Come on Jane, get to me and I'll show you where your children are. Get to me and I'll protect your husband from all the evil in the world. Come on Jane I believe in you, you can make it Jane! Follow my voice I'll lead you where you need to go!"

Jane tried; she tried so hard to catch up with the voice but no matter how loud it would get and how close it appeared she kept falling agonisingly short. The voice was always a step quicker than her.

"Please don't give up Jane! I know you can do it. Come on, one last push Jane! One last big effort and you can make it! I know you can! Come on Jane!"

Jane ran as fast as she could, and when she reached her maximum speed, she tried to go even faster. She was getting so close she could feel it. Just a little more, just a little bit further and she would be reunited with her –

BANG-BANG-BANG

Jane's eyes shot open and she looked around confused, unsure about where she found herself.

BANG-BANG-BANG

The lock clicked and in walked the elderly woman carrying a tray with food on.

"Breakfast is served."

She laid the tray on Jane's lap.

"There's an omelette and an apple for you there, with some juice. Your interview is in an hour and I'll come back then to clear your tray and bring someone along with me who can take you to the room. How are you feeling this morning? Do you think you'll be able to communicate okay?"

After Jane had given out the warning about her children, the doctor had visited her for the second time that night. Dr. Andres was a jolly, short man with hair everywhere on his head except for the very top, which was shiny and looked as if it had been polished. The first time he had met Jane, he had given a thorough examination before determining that medication wasn't what she needed. All she really needed was some rest; she was in shock and would be fine in the morning. If she was unable to sleep, he had given the elderly lady a small packet that contained a single, mild sleeping pill to help her drift off. The best thing for Jane was, however, patience. Eventually the events would sink in.

The second time he saw her, he did prescribe her with an anxiety medication. Once she had taken it and had calmed down somewhat, Dr. Andres explained how the police had commenced a search for her children almost immediately after her arrest, when they had spotted there were two tents with one filled with children's belongings. The two officers were going to ask her about her children in the interview last night, but due to Jane's state they had been unable to do so and didn't want to risk worsening Jane's mental condition. The police had contacted the school that the boys attended and had them send in pictures, which were now all over the national news. Jane's extended family had also been contacted and had been informed of Anthony's death and Jane's current imprisonment. Jane had been relieved that the police had acted so swiftly in the attempts to find her children, but was mainly scared that they hadn't been found already. The idea that they might still be out there, lost in the forest all alone was heart breaking. Jane had wept for hours before she had eventually fallen into an uneasy dream about running through the forest, trying to find them.

Jane said she thought she would be okay to talk to the detectives, and the elderly woman seemed satisfied and left her alone, reiterating that she would be back soon to take her there.

Jane picked a little at her breakfast, but found that she could barely swallow the food. She managed most of the juice and before she realised it the elderly lady was back with a big, burly officer who had come with her to escort Jane to the interview room.

When she got into the room for the second time in roughly twelve hours, she found it empty again. She sat down and this time was able to look around a bit more. She noticed a glass mirror and wondered if anyone would be watching this from the other side. Jane was used to being in interview rooms, her father had been a lawyer and had taken her on countless tours of police facilities in the hopes of encouraging her to become one too when she was young. The two detectives came in a short while later and reintroduced themselves in case Jane had forgotten their names, which as it turned out she had.

"Now then Jane, you told us yesterday that you didn't want a lawyer present, but as you weren't in a great frame of mind at the time of my asking, I shall ask again. Would you like a lawyer present for this interview?" It was Jackson who spoke.

Jane shook her head. "No, I have nothing to hide from you. I want to cooperate as best I can and then get out of here and find my boys."

Javid smiled at her. "Excellent, then we can begin without haste."

Javid pressed the play button on the voice recorder.

"This interview is being recorded. I am Inspector Albert Jackson with the London Metropolitan Police force. I am joined this morning by my colleague, Detective Raj Javid. Would you please state your full name for the benefit of the tape."

"Jane Claire Parkins"

"And your date of birth?"

"8th of May, 1973."

"Thank you, Jane. Just to confirm that you have requested not to have a lawyer present with you at this time?"

"Yes, that is correct."

"Lovely, lovely. The date is Sunday 23rd July 2005 and the time by my watch is 10.37 in the morning…"

Jackson continued with the formal introduction to the interview, stating the room and reading Jane out her rights again and then stated that at the end of the interview the tapes would be sealed up, signed off and then stored in a secure place in the London Metropolitan police station. Jane nodded along. With the formalities completed, the interview began.

"Jane, you were found on Saturday 22nd July 2005 at around 6am next to the body of the late Anthony Robert Parkins. The man who found you, Richard Jones, had been kayaking on the river when he saw what he described as a 'horrific scene of unprecedented violence.' Upon watching you pass out, Mr Jones retrieved his phone from its waterproof casing and called the police at 6.07am. Officers and paramedics arrived at the scene at approximately 6.37am following difficulties in accessing the campsite. The search for your children commenced at 6.53am. Jane, could you please describe to us what happened that night."

Jane told them all she could remember, how she had woken up beside the body with no recollection about what had happened. The last thing she remembered was running first away from the four-toed creature and then towards her children's laughter.

"Your children's laughter?" Jackson inquired.

"I heard them laughing in the forest, I thought they were hiding so I tried to chase them but I couldn't catch them, they kept changing positions and running all around, I just couldn't get to them."

"Tell us more about what happened when you woke up. What was around you?"

Jane described her horror at seeing the state of Anthony's body and how she had been so relieved at first when she had woken up because she thought that her running in the forest had all been a bad dream. Then she stopped talking.

"Are you okay, Jane?"

"Green eyes."

"Sorry?"

"Green eyes. There was a pair of bright green eyes in the forest staring at me. Just looking right at me as if they could see right through me."

"Who did the eyes belong to, was it an animal of some kind?"

"No… I don't think so. I've never seen anything like it in my life. But no, they didn't look like any eyes I've ever seen, especially not animal eyes."

"So, you think they were human eyes? Did you see the body that these eyes were a part of Jane?"

Jane thought for a moment and then shook her head. "There were just these big, green eyes. I could see them from over where I was. It was some sort of evil creature, like one from a horror movie."

"Let me get this straight, you are trying to tell us that you think there was some sort of monster watching you from the forest?"

"I know what I saw. There was a big pair of green eyes, the brightest and biggest I have ever seen. I swear it to you. They belonged to the creature that killed my husband. I know it sounds mad but when I saw them I just knew in my heart what it had done. I knew it."

Javid spoke this time. "Jane, are you sure that is what you saw? It wasn't just a fox or something that caught your eye and your imagination ran wild? You were under a lot of stress."

Jane shook her head vehemently. "I *know* what I saw! Those green eyes will haunt me for the rest of my days and the creature that they belonged to destroyed my husband! Please you have got to believe me."

Javid gave Jackson a look, and Jackson looked at Jane.

"Is there anything else you can remember from that night? Are you sure you cannot recall anything from the period between you running, lost in the forest, to when you woke up on your husband's body and saw some green eyes? How did you escape from the forest, Jane? How did you get out in the end?"

Jane shook her head meekly, "I don't know."

Javid scratched his head. "Look, you've got to understand that from our perspective things don't look great for you, Jane. Hearing voices in the forest, forgetting how you escaped and yet conveniently waking up on your dead husband's body. And then claiming to see the green eyes of a monster? Surely you have to admit it seems pretty suspicious."

"But it's the truth." Jane whispered.

Jackson took in a deep breath. "Jane, I suspect that you are suffering with a type of post-traumatic stress and as such you are finding it hard to tell us the truth. I am going to arrange for you to have some one-on-one sessions with a psychiatrist. In the mean time we will have to wait for the results from forensics, but it looks pretty clear cut that the blood under your fingers and over your body was that of your husband Until that time, I am afraid that as a potentially dangerous and unstable citizen I cannot let you be released on bail, and so you will be transported to a nearby jail where you will be given your own cell."

Jane shook her head and began to shout at the two detectives. "No, you cannot do this! I saw it with my own eyes! A monster killed my husband! A monster with green eyes killed -!"

Inspector Javid shouted over her into the tape. "Interview terminated at 11.34am on Sunday 23rd July 2005."

Chapter Nine

Doctor

A water feature sat on Dr. Henrey's large oak desk in his mood lit office, though Dr. Henrey himself wasn't yet present. It was dark brown, with a rectangular cuboid of wood elevated at its centre. From it came a series of steps that spiralled down around it into a pool of water. At the top of the cuboid was a little shoot that was spurting water onto the first of the steps. The water then trickled with a delicate noise from that first step onto the next and so on until it reached the pool of water at the bottom, where, unseen to the naked eye there was a mechanism that sucked the water back up to the top of the cuboid so that it could begin its journey down once more.

Jane sat staring at the water feature from the leather sofa that she had been told by the pretty receptionist, with a warm smile and bright blue eyes, to sit at whilst she waited for Dr. Henrey. There was a beautiful low table in front of her that looked as if it had been carved out of a single piece of oak. Underneath the edges of the table on both the front and back (Jane had gotten up especially from the chair to check), were wonderful flowing patterns that curled and twirled their way around and down towards the bottom of the legs of the table. They looked like vines that you would expect to see in the finest vineyards in Italy or France, only much thicker and more textured. On the vinelike carvings veins were etched that were thick in the middle but then broke apart much like the ones you would expect to see on a leaf. The rest of the table was rather plain in comparison, but was a deep, dark brown colour and shiny, even in the dim light, from the varnish that must have been rubbed into it if not daily, then certainly weekly. On top of the table, at its centre, was a ceramic bowl filled with all sorts of fruit, from strawberries and grapes to apples and bananas. It looked like the fruit had been perfectly placed by an artist who wished to capture them working in harmony to create the perfect colour hit on the eye. Everything seemed so deliberate and well thought through.

Behind the desk that was supporting the water feature was a wall filled to the brim with books. Jane noticed a ladder in the corner attached to the wall, and then looked to the top and saw that it could be slid across the wall by hand as it was attached to a railing that reminded Jane of one she had seen in a very old, fancy bookshop in London a number of years before.

Jane leant back into the leather chair and stared up at the ceiling. In the middle of it hung a chandelier, its glass crystals motionless in the stillness of the room. No light was coming from it, indeed the only light in the room was coming from a couple of lamps, and the light from them was dampened by the dark shades that enveloped the bulbs. The ceiling was a slightly off white colour delicately textured with leaves surrounded by circles with double lines. Straight vertical and horizontal lines that met at a small circular dome sectioned off the leaves. The edges of the circles met to create curved diamonds that were filled with yet more leaves, resulting in an overall appearance that was simply stunning.

Jane was so lost staring up at the ceiling that she had failed to notice that a short man in a smart black suit had entered the room, perched himself on a chair behind his desk, and began to read from a collection of papers that he had pulled out of a brown envelope.

Jane eventually lowered her eyes from the ceiling to watch the water feature again and was taken aback when she spotted the head of the man looking back at her through spectacles over the top of the water feature.

"Oh sorry!" Jane said startled.

"Not at all, I should have announced myself when I came in!"

The man smiled warmly at her, his spectacles moving up his face ever so slightly as he did so. "My name is Doctor Henrey, though I am more than happy for you to call me Henrey, or Ray, or Doc for that matter. I'm not at all fussy. What would you like me to call you, Mrs Parkins?"

"Jane is fine, thanks."

"Lovely, Jane it is then. And how are you feeling today Jane? Did you have some of the fruit? It really is very good and I'd urge you to try a strawberry or two if you have not done so already! They are deliciously ripe; I've already had a dozen or so myself this morning alone. And with ice cream might I add! If you want some ice cream too with your strawberries, I would be more than happy to get Chloe out there to fetch some from my freezer upstairs for you? How does that sound?"

Jane did like strawberries, but wasn't really in the mood given her current situation, so she thanked Henrey for offering but declined, saying she might take him up on the offer later if she was feeling more up to it. Right now all she wanted to do was get down to business and prove to him that she wasn't insane like everyone else seemed to think she was.

Henrey went back to looking over the papers he had taken out of the envelope; Jane just sat in silence waiting for him to make the first move. When it appeared as if Henrey wasn't about to start proceedings anytime soon, Jane decided to take the initiative.

"How does this work then?" Jane asked him, the impatience clear from the tone of her voice. "So we just talk to each other for a bit and then you see that I am not insane and that I didn't kill my husband and I can go back to mourning him and help look for my boys?"

Henrey smiled gently at her. "I'm afraid it's not quite as simple as that, Jane. I, for one, am unable to prove your innocence or guilt with regards to your husband's murder - that is for a court of law and a jury to decide. My job is to determine your current level of sanity and then recommend to the judges and jury based on my professional opinion whether or not you are in a fit mental state to stand trial. If you are fit to stand trial, depending on how mentally stable I believe you to be, the next step is whether or not you do need to spend any time in a mental hospital in order to get yourself 100% straight. If I am fully convinced of your sanity, then you will have to stand trial for the murder of your husband, unless any new evidence surrounding the case is discovered. Have you followed everything that I have said so far?"

Jane nodded at him.

"Good. Now, what I would like you to do is lean back in the chair, like you were doing when I came into the room, if that's okay with you? I understand that you are currently under an awful lot of stress and this may make it difficult for you to remember certain details correctly. The techniques that we will use together will help to alleviate this, so that we are able to get to the bottom of what happened that night. By fully relaxing, I hope that you will be able to see events clearly. Almost as clear as if you were living them again. I stress that it may take us several days to get through all of the events, longer if the scenes that you will have to experience again are distressing to the point where you are unable to continue, which by the sounds of things they may be. I want you to take as much time as you like, Jane."

Jane nodded along with growing impatience. She wanted to get started as soon as possible. The longer she sat listening to this doctor drone on and on about how hard it would be to go through the details and how long it was going to take to get to the bottom of things was not what she wanted to hear. She had been expecting a single meeting, two at the most, where she would be able to show off how sane and mentally stable she was, go through the events, and show that she was innocent.

"Can we please just get started?" Jane cut in, her voice sharp with malice.

Henrey peered over the top of his spectacles with his eyebrows raised. "You have to take our work together seriously Jane, it is the only way. Every moment is important for you, your husband, and your children."

Jane continued to look at him impatiently, and Henrey realised there was no point in further delays to proceedings.

"Very well then. Rest your head onto the back of the sofa, keeping your back perfectly straight as you do so. Interlock your hands together, and rest them in the centre of your lap. Now, I want you to simply stare directly at the ceiling and begin tracing the patterns on it with your eyes."

Jane followed all of the instructions; her eyes began to slowly move as they traced the outline of the leaves in the ceiling. Her mind began to drift as she did this, and after a couple of minutes listening to the water feature trickle away as she traced, her eyes started to glaze over. She heard a distant voice echo through her brain.

"What happened to your Anthony?"

Jane closed her eyes and immediately saw the opening in the forest. The boys were bounding around excitedly in the midday sun, shouting about who would be first to go swimming in the lake. Jane began to speak as she watched the scene unfold in her mind.

"We arrived at around midday, the sun was really high in the sky and it was so hot. When we pulled up by the lake we realised that we'd have to walk through the forest a bit to get to the opening. I lathered the boys up in sun cream whilst Anthony unpacked the car. We didn't realise that we would have to walk quite so far to get to a good place to camp, and only had wheelie bags for the boys so they really struggled pulling the luggage through the forest. The floor was really bumpy as there were an awful lot of twigs on the ground and tree roots were actually coming out of the earth."

Jane continued to describe her journey with her family through the forest as she lived it almost in real time. She watched her children sweat as they dragged their bags through the forest and wished she were able to put down the tents and suitcases that her and Anthony were carrying between them and run up and hug them both, telling them that she loved them dearly. But she couldn't break free. She was viewing her own history and couldn't change what had happened.

She had started off playing herself in this vision, from a first person perspective, but then slowly her view began to rise up until she was seeing it all from a bird's eye perspective. In the real world, back in the room with Henrey, Jane was sat with her eyes closed stretching her hands out trying to get closer to her children again.

The scene crashed out of her mind and Jane broke down crying on the leather sofa. Her arms dropped back down into her lap and she was brought back into the room. Henrey got off his seat behind his desk and offered her a comforting arm around the shoulder, passing her some tissue, which Jane took and cried into.

"We'll take a short break; I'll make us come coffee. How does that sound? I'll bring biscuits in too."

Jane continued to cry as Henrey got up and left the room.

*

By the time Henrey returned, Jane had managed to reduce her crying to a quiet simpering.

"Here now." Henrey said, putting the cup of coffee down in front of Jane. "I wasn't sure how you liked it so I've brought everything in with me, I've got lots of milk and lots of sugar, what would you like?"

Jane wiped the tears out of her eyes and mumbled that she would like just a splash of milk. Henrey obliged and then picked up the cup and placed it in her hands.

"If you don't mind my asking, could you tell me what it was exactly that made you so upset?" Henrey asked gently.

Jane drew in a deep breath and let her sadness go. "It was like I could see them all in front of me, myself included, just walking through the forest. We had no idea what was coming, none of us. We were all so jolly; it was the start of another holiday. I just wanted so desperately to call out to them all and warn them about what coming. Force them to turn back, to go home. To never go camping again.

But I couldn't, I didn't have a voice. I could see it all but couldn't do a thing about it."

Henrey nodded slowly. "This is quite common with those who are recounting a traumatic experience from the beginning. We want oh so desperately to be able to alter the horrible events that we have had to endure, but you have to understand that the past is written, no matter how terrible. We cannot change the past, but what we can do is strive to make sure that the same mistakes are not repeated in the future. You've done really well so far Jane, I am impressed, it usually takes a session or two before people are able to go so deep, you're being really strong and I commend you for that."

Jane looked into the kind, grey eyes of the man sat next to her. He was giving her a soft look and she felt as if she had known him and trusted him for her entire life. They sat for a few minutes in silence, sipping on their coffees. Jane eventually regained full control of her emotions.

"Shall we continue?" She asked.

"Do you think you are able to do that or would you like a little more time?"

Jane nodded and said that she would try to continue, and that she was sorry in advance if she wasn't able to keep her emotions in check.

Henrey nodded appreciatively at her and then got up and this time took a seat next to the sofa that Jane was sat on after fetching his notebook.

"I want you to do the same as before, just rest your head back, you can lie on the sofa if it is more comfortable for you, and just listen to the water and describe to me all you can remember from that day."

Jane leant back and stared at the ceiling, listening to the sound of the water splashing into the pool at the bottom of the feature. Next thing she knew, she was watching her family, herself included, break through the trees and out into the clearing where they would pitch their tent.

As Jane was seeing everything in almost real time, it took her a long while to describe everything. She spent an hour alone describing watching Anthony put up the tents with a little help from her and no help whatsoever from the boys, who just ran around making a nuisance of themselves.

Eventually, just as she oversaw herself and her family returning from the hike they had taken through the forest in the mid-afternoon, Jane heard a rumbling noise. She opened her eyes and was transported away from her family and back into Henrey's office. Henrey was still perched on the chair near to the sofa with a notebook open in front of him. He smiled at her.

"There was a rumbling." Jane stated.

"Yes," Henrey chuckled, "It was your belly! I think now is a good time to stop the session and we can continue with this tomorrow. How does that sound?"

Jane realised just how hungry she had become and nodded.

"Excellent, I'll walk you to the door."

Henrey heaved himself out of his chair and offered his arm to Jane, who took it and used his strength to help pull her up from the sofa. Henrey walked her over to the door, opened it and then smiled at his receptionist, Chloe who returned the smile.

"Could you buzz the officers in please?"

Chloe nodded and pressed the buzzer. The door to the reception clicked open, and a few moments later two police officers entered the room. The larger of the two pulled out a pair of handcuffs and asked Jane to present her arms. She did so and he put the handcuffs on.

The officer motioned to the door, and Jane looked back at Henrey, who gave her a reassuring smile.

"See you tomorrow, Jane."

Jane mumbled a goodbye as the officers escorted her out.

Chapter Ten

Eyes

Jane couldn't sleep that night. Her cell was cold and the mattress was hard and lumpy. She could feel individual springs digging into her back and Jane wondered how many others had spent nights on this bed, unable to sleep, tossing and turning, waiting for the dawn to come. She wondered how many of the people who had spent the night on this bed had been innocent, as she knew she was. How many had been guilty? How many had been guilty but pleaded innocence for one reason or another?

"My husband beat me day and night, it was the only way out!"

"I didn't mean to kill her, I just wanted to teach her a lesson. I never wanted to kill her. You have to believe me, I loved her."

"I thought there was an intruder in the house, I was blind with fear. I didn't know what I was doing; I was just trying to protect my family. I didn't know my son had snuck out that night to see his girlfriend, when he came back in I just… I thought we were being robbed."

Jane continued to fidget in the slim hope that she would eventually find a semi-comfortable patch on the bed. Though, the more she thought about it and the more stories of people she came up with in her head, the more she realised that thousands of people would have fidgeted, moved, twisted, and turned all night long in the hope of finding a comfortable patch. After all this time and all of those people, every comfortable patch that this mattress had once provided would have been exhausted long ago.

Jane imagined the bed had always been uncomfortable. Prisons probably received old mattresses as donations and then from all the donations picked the nastiest, smelliest, most yellow stained with sweat and piss ones, before throwing them onto the hard metal frames of the beds in the holding cells. She thought that detectives probably asked for the vilest mattresses to be placed in the rooms of those who had just been arrested so as to prevent them having a good night's sleep. That way, in the morning when they woke up, or at least when the sun was high enough for them to no longer lie tossing and turning, they would be tired and weak from the night and would thus be more likely to give in to questioning and blurt out the truth, whatever it may be.

Hardened criminals were probably used to such treatment and the old mattress technique would be wasted on them. Jane saw in her head the image of a drug lord, with more golden teeth than white pearls in his mouth, a large chain around his neck. Big, thick broad arms sporting intricate tattoos. Crosses on his knuckles, each one representing a kill he had performed, and he had performed many as his knuckles were covered in them. His head was completely bald and his skin colour was a dark olive. He was surrounded by henchmen who all carried a variety of weapons;

one with a baseball bat, one with a gun slung over his shoulder, the last one with a machete.

At the end of the day, the drug lord would go to a secret location to sleep. In that location, he would have inserted the dirtiest, scummiest mattress ever seen. One that would put the prison mattresses to shame, so that if he ever were to be arrested, he would have the best night's sleep he'd ever had and be fresh as a daisy in the morning to deny all the charges set against him and get off scot-free.

As Jane continued to think about the drug lord and other criminals, and the techniques that they used to avoid jail time, she eventually drifted into an uneasy sleep. The sleep was made more difficult by the constant bubble of noise that came from the surrounding cells. There was chatter all around her, one person was even humming a merry tune off somewhere to the right. Over to the left, another was sat banging on the door. Not in a particular pattern, which Jane would have been able to ignore, but just every now and then. Irregular enough to always be a surprise and always break through into Jane's troubled mind.

The worst noise, however, was none of these. It was the snoring. Due to the uncomfortable nature of the mattresses, it meant that the inmates were forced to lie on their backs, which resulted in the vast majority of those who did manage to catch some winks snoring intensely. Jane had never heard anything close to it. Anthony used to snore on occasion, and Jane would nudge and push him until he moved onto his side whilst still asleep, which always seemed to stop the snoring, or until he woke up grumbling in annoyance. Jane had managed to master the art over 15 years of marriage so that she was delicate enough with her prodding that Anthony didn't suspect that he had been woken by her, but firm enough to actually wake him and stop him snoring. She had been proud of that achievement, though realised now that she would never be able to stop him snoring again, his sleep would be soundless from now on.

Eventually, the snoring drew quieter and quieter until Jane thought that she might stand a decent chance of getting some sleep in, but then there was a knock on her cell door and the window about three quarters of the way up it was slid open. A face appeared. It was the taller of the two officers who had taken her to see Henrey yesterday.

"Half an hour until we leave." He said, "Breakfast will be delivered in 10 minutes, please eat quickly. We don't want to be late for Doctor Henrey."

He slid the window shut and Jane realised why the snoring had died down, as everyone was being woken up. The sun was finally high up enough in the sky to stop the tossing and the turning.

*

She ate very little of the breakfast that had been brought into her. It had consisted of a small bowl of tasteless porridge and a banana. Jane had pushed the porridge around her plate, but had eaten the banana. She had considered mashing it up into the porridge to give it some flavour, but had worried that the blandness of the porridge would have neutralised the bananas flavour and decided she didn't want to risk it. She could always take some fruit from Henrey's bowl later if she was feeling hungry, and might take him up on his offer of strawberries and ice cream if it still stood.

About 25 minutes after her breakfast had arrived, the taller of the two officers returned with his colleague. They entered the cell and asked Jane to present her arms so that they could cuff her. She obliged, and once the handcuffs were in place, they walked her out of the cell and down the long corridor towards the exit at the end of the hallway. There was almost no noise now coming from the cells as the inmates ate their breakfasts. Jane was in a wing full of others who couldn't afford bail and were awaiting trial, or who were being medically examined, as she was, to determine whether or not they were sane enough to stand trial.

The taller of the two officers typed a code into the keypad by the side of some elevator doors, and then pressed a button that called the lift up from below. As they waited for it to arrive, Jane looked back down the corridor and realised what a dreary place prison was. She couldn't imagine being an officer in a place like this and having to come into work each day and walk up and down the drab corridors with their neutral colours to deal with people who had broken the law. She figured that the officers would know which crime each inmate had committed, or at least was charged with committing, and wondered how they maintained their professionalism when dealing with people who had raped and murdered and stolen. She did admire the men and woman whose jobs it was, but she did not like them particularly. Especially not these two; they wouldn't speak a word more than necessary, and wouldn't even update her on the search for her children, which was still on going. There was a detective who would come in and see her and provide her with any updates in that case. So far there had been no change; her boys were still lost.

The three of them went into the elevator, an officer on either side of Jane as it descended. Once it reached the first floor and the doors opened, the officers marched her along a series of corridors. They had to stop every now and then so that passwords could be entered and fingerprints could be scanned to open the doors ahead of them. When eventually they reached the police car that would take her to see Henrey, she had to wait a few minutes whilst the officers thoroughly checked the whole vehicle. Once satisfied, they let her in and got into the front seats. The taller man spoke into his radio, and the doors to the large garage opened.

They drove into a holding pen, whilst the door to the garage behind them shut. Once shut, the doors ahead of them opened, and the officer put the car into gear and drove off.

*

After an uneventful 20-minute drive that had consisted of the three of them sat in silence listening to the police radio, the car pulled in to Henrey's practice. The officers jumped out, and then got Jane out of the car.

The three of them walked into the building, and then the tall officer pressed on the buzzer and spoke into it.

"Hello this is Officer Paulson; we have Jane with us."

"Hello! I'll buzz you right on up."

There was a loud buzzing sound following by a click, and the door to the elevator opened. The three got in and were taken up to the reception area where Chloe was sat with a warm smile on her face waiting for them.

The officers removed Jane's handcuffs and then said to Chloe that they would wait downstairs again like they had yesterday. Chloe smiled brightly at them and waved as the elevator doors closed with the two officers inside.

"You can go straight through, he is in there already, on time for once!" She quipped as Jane pushed open the door to Henrey's office.

The office was as immaculate as it had been yesterday, and the lighting and the sound of the water feature instantly soothed her.

Henrey lifted his head up from the desk where it had been buried in the papers neatly piled up in front of him.

"Jane! Hello! Good to see you again! How are you this morning?"

"I'm okay, a little tired really. The mattress at the prison is awful."

"Ah yes, I have heard that they are ghastly things. Truly ghastly. Well, why don't you sit down there on the couch, which I hope is a little more comfortable for you! Would you like a snack? Some fruit?"

Jane nodded and took a few grapes and strawberries from the fruit bowl that she had been so struck with yesterday. She popped a grape into her mouth and bit down on it, relishing the taste of the juice as it exploded under the pressure from her teeth.

"Good, good." Henrey said cheerfully, before pulling open a drawer and producing the notepad he had been using yesterday along with a pen. He got up from his desk and resumed his position on the chair nearest to the sofa that Jane had just laid down on. "Right, I'd like you to carry on as best you can from where we got to yesterday, if I recall correctly you and your family had just returned from your hike through the forest. Why don't we go from there?"

Jane nodded and rested her head back on the arm of the sofa, looking up at the patterned ceiling and tracing the outlines of the shapes. She closed her eyes and after a few minutes of searching found her and her family breaking through the clearing, all with large sweat patches under their arms and around their necks from their long walk through the forest.

Jane continued to describe the rest of her day after that. All four of them had gone for a dip in the river following their walk to cool off and wash the sweat from their bodies. The water had been very cold, colder than they had expected it to be for that time of year, but the temperature had been welcome after the heat of the day. She watched from her bird's eye perspective as, after a few minutes in the water, the boys started a splashing fight that turned into a full scale splashing war with bother her and Anthony joining in.

Henrey observed Jane laugh out loud whilst describing the scene that was unfolding before her, occasionally jotting down a note or two. He paid careful attention to her facial expressions and the way she described herself and her family.

Eventually, it began to get dark in Jane's world. The sun got lower in the sky as she cooked sausages on their portable BBQ that the boys and Anthony had carried between them through the forest whilst Jane had been relaxing and reading her book. Jane had put the sausages into hot-dog buns and passed them around. The boys had wolfed them down at close to light speed, and she forced them to have some salad before they were allowed their second ones.

As they all settled down around the fire for the evening, the boys asked Anthony to tell a scary story. Jane had been a little wary of him telling one, as she wasn't sure the boys should be getting ideas in their head, but she decided that as they were on holiday it would be okay.

She recalled the story about the great Count Dracula that Anthony had told them, and had even lapsed into a poor excuse of a Transylvanian accent as she did the Count's speaking parts. About three quarters of the way through the story (Jane knew this because she had heard Anthony tell it before when they had been kids and had gone camping together with their families), Anthony had noticed that the boys were a little cold and realised that he had left the blankets in the car. He told them that he was going to fetch them and would finish the story when he got back. In the mean time they should all get ready for bed.

Jane watched as her old self asked the boys if they needed to go to the loo before bed. Both of them had nodded and so she stared hopelessly as they were taken off into the forest.

Jane opened her eyes, which had started to tear up again. Henrey was busily scrawling on his notepad, and he looked up when he realised Jane had stopped describing what she was seeing.

"Are you okay, Jane?"

"That was the last time I saw Anthony alive." She stated, not quite being able to absorb the fact. "He was wandering off to get blankets, we were all happy and together and then we split up and he went off and we went off, and he died and the boys vanished." Jane was staring up at the ceiling, trying to take in the words that were coming out of her own mouth. She was unable to comprehend the fact that her husband and children were gone, with her husband confirmed dead and her children at best lost out in the forest, at worst… Jane began to hyperventilate.

"Now try and stay calm for me Jane, I know this is extremely difficult for you and you've been so, so brave. I really am very impressed with all you have been able to recall. Take some deep breaths for me, Jane. That's good, excellent. Slow, deep breaths. You're doing amazingly. Let's take a short break, I'll get us both some coffee. Just a splash of milk, isn't it?"

Jane managed a nod but was no longer in the room; she had calmed herself by rewinding her story and was back in the river having a splashing war with her boys and Anthony. Anthony picked her up by her waist and flung her away into the water and she laughed gleefully, her boys rushing in to splash her from both sides.

*

Henrey returned with the coffee a few minutes later and Jane took a few sips. Henrey looked at her like a stamp collector might look at one of his favourite stamps.

"We're getting very close now, aren't we Jane? To where you lost your children and when you found Anthony's body."

Jane nodded at him.

"This will be extremely upsetting for you, and I don't mind if we have to take a lot of regular breaks. If you want to continue tomorrow, that is also okay."

"No, I want to get through this today. If I wait another night I'll just spend the whole time crying over it. I need to just get it all out of my system I think. I'll try as best as I can."

Henrey nodded as if accepting some great long lost nugget of information, and then motioned for Jane to lie back on the sofa and continue.

She could no longer see Anthony, who had gone off in the opposite direction to fetch the blankets from the car. Anthony's mum had thrust them upon them just before they left. Jane thought they were extremely ugly things, but then a blankets main purpose is to keep you warm and not to be some sort of great fashion statement. Still, it would have been even nicer of Anthony's mum to give them a nice looking, warm blanket!

She didn't take the boys too far in the forest as she had forgotten to grab a torch from one of the tents, however there was still just about enough light from the sun for them to get to the forest without falling over anything. As they stepped into the forest it got significantly darker, as if God had just decided that enough was enough and turned the lights off for the day. The large trees blocked out the majority of the end of day light that the sun was still desperately trying to give off.

Jane had left the boys by one of the large trees and told them not to move a muscle while she went just a few metres away to check out a rustling in the leaves.

Henrey noted down as Jane winced at recalling how she couldn't see her children when she went back to the tree. How she thought that they were just playing a big trick on her like they liked to do every now and again. But then the fear slowly overcame her as the time went by and they didn't jump out at her. She remembered running and running. So much running. Stress began to transfer from the dream state into Jane's reality with Henrey. Sweat poured down her face and it became harder for her to concentrate and see what was happening.

Back in the dream she was so tired and had to stop. Then she was running again. The memory was fuzzy and whirred past her vision in a blur.

The picture in her brain went black and Jane saw nothing. She opened her eyes and looked at Henrey, confused.

"I can't see anything, it's all gone black. I was running in the forest and then everything just went black, as if someone turned off all the lights and drew all the curtains. I can't see anything; I can't remember it."

Henrey nodded again, noting everything down now. "Rewind to the very last thing you remember, try and explain it in great detail to me if you can."

Jane closed her eyes and tried to go back a bit, she saw the big tree she had left her boys at just moments before, and described in great detail her search around it. Jumping from behind it in order to scare them before they scared her. The slow realization that they were gone. And then the running, scrambling through the trees looking left and right. And… and… the giggling. She had forgotten about it the first time she had described it, but now she could hear it coming from a direction away from her.

"Giggling?" Henrey enquired.

"Yes, there was… there was this laughter. That is why I thought it was the boys playing a trick on me. I followed the giggling; it was coming from the trees. No matter how close I thought I was getting to it, the noise was just out of my reach. Moving farther and farther away, as fast as I could run if not faster."

"Can you explain the giggling to me, what exactly did it sound like would you say? Was it happy as if someone had just told a rude joke?"

"No, it wasn't particularly happy I wouldn't say. It was light and airy, as if the laughter had been caught on the wind and carried to me. It was definitely a boy's giggle, closer to cheeky than anything else. That is why it had to be one of my children, they were always laughing like that when they were about to do something they shouldn't."

"Would you say you had heard the giggle before then? Before that night? Was it one of your sons?"

"No, I don't think so, no. I think I was just scared that I had lost them. I'm not even sure if the giggle was real in the end. I didn't find them, did I? If it had been real surely I would have found them?" Jane started to cry. "I just want my sons back. Please help me. I just want them back!"

This time, Henrey did not move from his chair to comfort her, he sat and watched and made notes of everything. After a couple of minutes, Jane managed to regain some of her self-control and wiped the tears off her face. Henrey did offer Jane some tissues that she accepted them and blew her nose.

"There are great scores of people out looking for your boys, Jane, and I promise you they will find them. People are walking in great long lines through the forest using sniffer dogs and recon surveillance of the area. Police are also checking local CCTV footage just in case the boys broke free of the forest and couldn't find their way back to camp and so instead headed for one of the local towns. They will be found; of that we can be certain." Henrey stated in an attempt to reassure Jane.

Jane nodded meekly though didn't give off the impression that she believed a word he was saying. She had seen the eyes of the creature that had brutalized her husband's body. The monster that could do such a thing to an adult, to a father and a husband, would have no qualms in its head about killing two boys as well, of that Jane was certain.

When she finally looked up at Henrey, she was no longer crying, her face was stern and set with total fury.

"I have seen the creature that ripped my husband from this world. I saw the eyes of the monster. I need you to confirm my sanity, because I swear to you that I am not insane. I need to get out of jail and help the search for my sons. Once they are found, I will begin a second search – one for the monster that has torn my family apart."

"I am afraid that I have a strong professional code that I have to stick to. I cannot clear you of insanity without spending more time with you. Once you have described to me fully all that you can remember from that night, once I have asked you questions and we have managed to clear up any loose ends, once I have carried out a series of tests, which you are required to pass in order to be deemed sane in a court of law and your innocence is proven, then and only then will you be able to either join the search for your children if they have not already been found by such a time, or pursue this monster that you claim to have seen. Do you understand that, Jane? In order to be able to move forward you need to have a degree of patience now. We are dealing with a man's life, your husband's life, can you understand that all due diligence needs to be followed? If the police were holding another man who claimed to have seen a monster far, far away on the other side of a forest, would you want him to be released just because he himself claimed that he was sane?"

Jane shook her head weakly, feeling at once that Henrey desperately wanted to believe her story, all of it. She could hear it in his voice. But at the same time as a professional psychiatrist he had a duty to his profession and to the justice system to make sure that she wasn't insane, and to find out as much as he could about what went on that night so that he could get a feel for what she had experienced. Jane let out an exasperated sigh.

"Can I continue?"

"Yes of course. You were saying about the giggling…"

Jane lay back down and looked up, tracing her eyes as part of the movement that she realized had become almost second nature to her already.

"I followed the giggling, I thought if I could only just run that little bit faster, only just stretch my legs that little bit farther then I would be reunited with my boys. But even at the time, I didn't think the giggling was real. I had this suspicion that it was actually just my head playing tricks on me because if it were really real then I would have caught up with the voice. It was a child's voice, and I am certain I am quicker than any child that produced the giggle could have been. I am certain of it."

Jane remembered everything else she possibly could right up to running as fast as she could through the forest, following the giggling, and then her mind went completely black again and she stopped and opened her eyes, at a loss as to what to do. She didn't know how to break through the black cloud that was masking her past from her current self, and she said as much to Henrey.

"How about this, try and look forward past the blackness and to the next thing that you remember. Where are you at the end of the blackness? What time of day is it?"

Jane closed her eyes again and tried to skip on past the black area in her mind. She fast-forwarded all the way to waking up on her husband's body and then tried to go back from there. She found that she couldn't. Before the time that she was knelt clutching Anthony tightly, hugging his violated body to hers and crying into his blood soaked chest, she couldn't see anything. She couldn't remember a damned thing. She played the scene out in her head from the point where she was clutching at his body, to the moment where she pulled herself away slightly to see two big, green eyes shining back at her from the opposite side of the forest.

"What did the body of the creature look like, Jane? What physical form would you say it most resembled?"

"It looked like…" Jane squished her face together as she delved back into her dream and tried to see the creature again from her bird's eye view. She strained as hard as she could then gave her conclusion to Henrey. "It looked like a human. Though, more like a blob actually, as if it was wearing a big cloak. I couldn't really make out any limbs, it was quite far away from where I was with Anthony, but I would say height wise it was about the height of a man. But the eyes, I'll never forget those eyes. I could see them as clear as day from right across that open space, it was as if they were part of me. Like they were inside of me they were so, so clear. They were so clear they made the rest of the creature look even more faded in comparison."

"You say the eyes were so clear that you felt as if they were in your head? Are you one hundred percent certain that the eyes weren't in your head? That they were attached to a live body on the other side of the forest? Are you sure that the shadowy figure that they were attached to wasn't just a bush?"

Jane looked as if she had just been slapped across the face. He didn't believe her. Henrey had been nice and kind and generous and had nodded at all the right moments and looked sad and empathetic when she was crying, but as she looked at him now, although his face gave nothing away, she could almost sense it in the room. His disbelief of what she was saying. His deep scepticism. And she went back over her story and realized that she didn't blame him one bit. She was trying to prove her sanity and yet she had gone on and on about giggling voices in her head and green eyes that she could see as clear as day across a large distance when she had admitted that she couldn't really make out any other features other than a blob that the eyes were attached to. Jane tried not to show the panic that was bubbling up inside her that the man in front of her was going to give her an insane verdict, and swallowed a lump that had been steadily building in her throat and cleared the look of panic that had crept onto her face. She had to try and think of a way out of this.

"I know what I saw, they were not a part of my imagination. Look I get that I was completely devastated by the state that I found Anthony in, but how many other people have you come across that see bright green eyes at a murder scene that they have just arrived to? If it were a stress-induced thing, surely everyone who discovers a body would experience something similar. The eyes were real, they existed and they still exist. Whoever they belong to is out there and is probably going to kill again. When you find another body that looks like my husband's, and you have locked me away because I am insane, then you will know the mistake you have made. Please, let me have another chance to look at the creature, I know I can remember more of what it looks like, I just need a minute to relax."

Henrey sat patiently and watched as Jane closed her eyes yet again, he could see the desperation written all over her face. He watched her lie there motionless for almost 10 minutes, and observed her face relax and become becalmed. Just as he was suspecting that she might have drifted off to sleep, she opened her mouth and began to describe the creature that was fleeing the murder scene.

"The eyes were far too big for the head, it was as if they were perhaps six or seven times bigger than a normal person's eyes, and much, much brighter. That is why I think I could see them so clearly from so far away. They remind me of green emeralds, a really pure green colour. It's hard to explain. I can't make out the creature's hands or feet exactly, but it's certainly as tall as a man, probably around six feet. It's just far enough away that I can't really tell, it might be as tall as seven feet, or as short as five. It's wearing some sort of cloak. I can make out that it does have limbs, probably the same as a human, but its clothes are so loose and baggy it sort of just all merges into one blob like thing." Jane opened her left eye very minutely to try and catch a glimpse of Henrey's expression, to see if this added, made up information had persuaded him at all about what she had seen. His expression was unreadable and he was just jotting down yet more notes.

Jane opened her eyes fully and looked at Henrey, expecting him to probe her with more questions about the creature. Henrey considered her for a moment and then surprised Jane by tracking back to her black outs.

"I believe you cannot see any further because what you witnessed past the point of you running was so horrific to you that your brain is trying to block it out. Now I know you have already told me that you didn't see your children again after you left them, but something you saw or something that happened to you in the period between you running and you discovering the dead body of Anthony has made you so shocked, and your body so horrified, that it has decided to erase it or at the very least hide it from your memory. You have to dig really, really deep Jane. Find out what it was for your sake as much as your family's. I am going to be honest with you now, and you are not going to like what I have to say. I am only telling you this because I need you to really want to dig deep, to really break through your blackout."

"Based on the information that you have given to me so far, I will only be able to give an insane recommendation to the courts. Now, I would accept the argument of extreme trauma for your blackout. God knows if I saw my wife in the state that your husband had been in when you found him, I would be in a state of complete shock and certainly wouldn't want to remember it. But therein lies one of the issues – I wouldn't want to remember seeing my dead wife, as you wouldn't want to remember seeing your dead husband. But you do remember seeing your dead husband, you remember it perfectly. This means that whatever traumatized you, to the extent that your body is rejecting the memories, must be worse than the vision of seeing your husband's body in the state that it was in. I have to ask the question to myself, what could possibly be worse than that sight? My second issue, and this is more closely linked to your level of sanity than to your loss of memory, is the voices in the forest. The giggling that you heard. From what you have told me, you only heard one voice, and yet you have two children. Surely you would have heard both children giggling if they were trying to hide from you? If you only heard one then we can either assume that your children had separated from each other and were lost, and that one was still trying to play a game on you, perhaps unaware in the dark that they had lost their brother. Or, the voice didn't come from your children; it came from inside your head. Now, carrying that forward, if I were to assume that you had heard a voice giggling in your head, surely it wouldn't have been any harder for you to conjure up the image of eyes off in the distance running away from the scene of the crime?"

"So this is the crossroads we find ourselves at, because here is the great, final dilemma that I have. It is extremely common for people to have large areas of their memory missing due to traumatic events that they have experienced… or taken part in." As Henrey spoke the last four words his face darkened. "These blackouts are most common in two types of situations. The first is by those who are unfortunate enough to witness someone they love being killed. The second is by those who have committed an atrocity, such as murder, who cannot bear to live with the memory of their crime. From what you have described to me, from all that you have said, unless you can convince me that you can break through the black void that you have in your head, I am inclined to believe that you are in the latter category. If the police have sufficient evidence to take you to trial, which I believe with your fingerprints alone all over the body they most probably do, then you will be convicted of murder. However, should you be tried tomorrow, based on the evidence you have given me, I would present the case that you are legally insane, or at least were at the time of committing the murder. So you see Jane, this is why I need you to fight your blackout. I need to know what else happened that night, what else you saw and did. How you got out of the forest and when you got out of it. I need to know it all. Otherwise, if you cannot provide sufficient evidence to the contrary, I will be obliged to believe that you killed your husband, and that you are legally insane."

    Jane's mouth had dropped halfway through Henrey's speech, and had continued falling throughout the rest of it. She had been right in believing he thought she was insane, but had no idea that her blackout could be because she was trying to protect herself from memories of killing her own husband. She searched her consciousness and pleaded with it to reveal to her what was hidden in the black space. But the more she tried, the more her head resisted, and the more uneasy she felt. It began to dawn on her that perhaps

Henrey was right; perhaps she was completely insane. That she had lost her mind whilst running in the woods, lost it to the extent that she began to hear voices. Began to hear children giggling. Began to see the dark green eyes of a monster that did not exist in the real world. One that lived entirely within her own head escaping the murder scene. A scene that was her own doing. It all made sense to her too, that was the worst part. It made perfect sense that she would lose her head in a crazed panic after losing her children in the forest and that she would start seeing things to blame their disappearance on. It made sense that when she did finally break into the clearing and saw a man by the fire on his own without her boys there that she would see the green eyes on his face. She loved her boys oh so dearly, oh so deeply and completely, that it made sense to her that upon seeing the green eyes of a monster that she thought had taken and killed her children, even if they were part of her own husband's body, that she wouldn't hesitate in destroying whatever it was they were attached to.

Jane sat on the comfortable leather sofa, in the dimly lit office with the water feature and the wonderful book shelf behind the lovely big oak desk, and slowly but surely became more and more convinced that on that night she had gone insane.

She drew up the image of her wedding day, when she and Anthony were stood looking into each other's eyes and saying their vows. It had never quite struck her until that moment in her life just how beautiful his eyes were. His beautiful, bright green eyes.

Chapter Eleven

Blackout

The following day Henrey had to attend to an emergency and was unable to see Jane, much to her disappointment. Seeing Henrey seemed to be the only way that she could see her family. Reclining on the leather sofa, listening to the trickle of water and losing herself in the patterns above on the ceiling seemed to unlock her mind in a way that she couldn't unlock it on her own.

When she had found out that Henrey wasn't able to see her, she had tried to recreate how she felt whilst lying on the sofa and looking up in his office in her cell. She had moved her horrible mattress off her bed and into the middle of the floor. Next, she had tried to recreate the sound of the water feature using the small hand basin in the cell. She had spent over half an hour adjusting the pressure of the water, lying down on the mattress and looking up, listening for a minute or two as it trickled into the basin, before getting up and adjusting it slightly up one time and then slightly down the next, trying desperately to strike the perfect balance that the water feature in Henrey's office was able to.

Once she had gotten the tinkle of the water just right, she tried to relax her body and stare at the ceiling. The ceiling in the cell was juxtaposed to the one in Henrey's office. It was almost grey in colour and was going yellow in the corners where damp and old age had taken its toll on the paint. There were no patterns painted into it, no lines that Jane could trace with her eyes until they turned into tents surrounded by forest on three sides and water on the other. It was just one solid block of misery.

Jane tried to close her eyes instead, figuring that maybe the water alone would be enough to get her back to her family. She listened to it as it splashed down into the basin, and for a split second she was back in Henrey's office hearing the beautiful water feature. She was lying on the sofa, her eyes closed, and down below her now from her bird's eye view was herself with Anthony and the children splashing about in the river, the sun shimmering off the surface and into their eyes, blinding them for a moment if they caught the reflection off the surface at too strong an angle. But almost as soon as the wondrous scene entered her head, it was gone. A spring in the mattress dug deep into her back, causing Jane to cry out in frustration. Tears fell down her face and she attempted to squeeze her eyes shut and will herself back towards her family but she knew the attempts would be hopeless.

Jane pounded on the mattress with her fists; bashing them harder and harder into its stupid springs and its sweaty, stain filled uncomfortableness. She pounded and pounded, feeling nothing but bitter disappointment with herself as much as the mattress itself. She cried out agonisingly and screamed as she continued to attack the mattress, shaking her head violently as she did so. She tried to rip the mattress apart, leaning her face down into it and getting a whiff of the hundreds of bodies that had sweat into it before it had been her turn to sleep on the mattress. She bit into it and tore, an acrid taste filling her mouth, bitter on her tongue. Her teeth strained against the material, but she eventually managed to create a hole in the mattress, which she burrowed her hands into, spitting the vile piece of fabric from her mouth. She put her hands into the created hole and yanked them apart, trying to split the mattress in two. But this time, the mattress didn't give in; it fought back and wouldn't let her destroy it that easily. Jane cried out again in an anguished frustration and tore and bit and shook and screamed. This time when she dug her hands into the hole, she heard the mattress begin to rip as she gripped the sides of the hole and pulled her hands apart as hard as she physically could in opposite directions, letting out a huge battle cry as she did so.

Suddenly, she was being pulled away from the mattress. Jane screamed again and kicked out, swinging her feet wildly about her and flailing her arms, connecting them with soft flesh. Some of the hands fell away from her, but more quickly took their place.

"OH YOU'VE GOT FRIENDS, MATTRESS, HAVE YOU?! OTHER MATTRESS BUDDIES? WELL I'LL KILL THEM ALL. I'LL DESTROY THEM TOO LIKE I DESTROYED YOU. YOU WON'T STEAL SLEEP AGAIN! FUCK OFF! GET OFF ME

YOU FUCKING CRUEL BASTARDS. ALL OF YOU! FUCK OFF!"

She spat out froth as she shouted the words as loud as she could at the mattress that she had been tearing apart, giving it wild evil eyes as she did so and continuing to struggle against the arms that were dragging her away from it.

"THIS ISN'T THE END I WILL FINISH YOU I FUCKING SWEAR IT! GET OFF ME!"

Jane continued to cry out as she was dragged out of her cell and into the long corridor that she had walked down with the two police officers yesterday.

Her limbs were flying all over the place, but the speed at which they were flailing was slowing significantly. Her vision began to blur and she lost the strength in her body, which seemed to be closing down. Jane tried to cry out but could only manage a muted exhale of breath. Her head lolled to the right, her neck no longer able to support it, and her eyes caught the faintest glimpse of a needle sticking out of her thigh before her vision went entirely black.

*

Jane saw a bright white light and tried to walk towards it. *This is it, this is the end* she thought to herself. *I'm coming for you Anthony, I'm coming.*

The bright white light seemed to get stronger, and she went towards it. She knew in her heart that if she could just get to it, just reach out and push her hand into the light then she would escape this world. She would escape the police officers that came for her and trapped her in handcuffs. She would escape the questions from the police and from Henrey and from everyone else who she had spoken to since she had been found. She would escape to Anthony and to her children who were now all surely waiting for her, looking down and watching her suffer, wishing that she would leave the world and come up and join them. They could splash about in the pools in heaven for the rest of their days, the happiest family that the world had ever known, reunited once more. She could cook them sausages on a campfire every night and they could eat them as hotdogs. She wouldn't even force her boys to eat salad if they didn't want to, if it meant that she could just see them again.

Jane reached out for the light now, stretching as far as she could, reaching... reaching... reaching...

She heard the beep of a heart monitor and realised that the white light wasn't from some divine power, it was coming from the outside world, the real human world where her husband no longer was.

Reluctantly, Jane popped her left eye open slightly, then shut it again almost instantly as the light that greeted it was a shocking, blinding white. One of the nurses had spotted the eye open and called out to a colleague that Jane was conscious. Her colleague came over, and she could smell the perfume of the woman, which was light and flowery.

"Jane? Can you hear me Jane? You are in St. Paul's hospital just as a precautionary measure and are in good hands. Take your time to open your eyes, I know it will seem extremely bright to you at first and it'll take them a few minutes to adjust."

Jane was in a hospital. She wasn't in the prison anymore. It suddenly occurred to Jane that she might never have been in prison, that it had all just been one terrible nightmare. She must have fallen over whilst looking for the boys when they got lost in the woods. Anthony must have found her and called an ambulance and she'd been brought here to recover. She opened her eyes quickly hoping to see Anthony perched on the end of her bed looking back at her, concerned. Her eyes burnt from the glare of the light and she couldn't see properly, but she would accept the pain in them if she could capture a glimpse of her husband.

She moved her head around, much to the dismay of the nurse who told her to keep it still. The nurse explained that she had taken a very heavy blow to the back of her head. And Jane almost jumped with joy at the news. A blow to the back of her head? She must have fallen in the forest! That is why she was having a blackout in her dream with Henrey after all of her running to find the boys! Yes! She scanned the room, ignoring the nurse's orders and there! There! Stood over by the door was her Anthony. He was the right height and was bald, she could tell that even through the haze. She lifted up her arms willing him to come over to her and embrace her, to tell her that everything was going to be fine. That her boys were fine. She willed him to come to her and called out his name.

"Anthony! Anthony!"

The figure moved further into the room towards the bed, and now Jane was sure. It was her Anthony. She stretched out her arms as far as she could toward him, but then Anthony stopped approaching the bed and turned to one of the nurses. Jane couldn't understand what he was doing, why wouldn't he just come to her? Maybe she was too fragile, she thought, but she didn't care about her fragility. She just wanted to be back in Anthony's arms.

Her vision slowly began to improve, and as Anthony came more and more into focus, the less and less like Anthony this Anthony became. Yes, this Anthony was bald, but his skin colour was wrong. This Anthony was the same height as her Anthony, but he wasn't wearing a checked shirt like her Anthony would have been, he was wearing a plain blue one.

Jane's vision fully returned to her, and her stomach dropped as she realised that this Anthony was no Anthony at all. It was the tall policeman, Officer Paulson, and he was in conversation with the nurse who had first spoken to Jane when she had woken up.

Jane started shaking her head as she was thrust back into the reality that she didn't want to be her reality. She began shaking her head from left to right, slowly at first. Whispering, "No, no, no, no," over and over again. Her body and her brain trying to reject the room she was in and the situation she was suffering through. It had been peaceful whilst she had been asleep. She hadn't even really existed. There was no Anthony, no boys, no Henrey or police officers in the sleep that she had been having. There was just peace. Peace from everything.

Paulson looked over at her as she sat shaking her head and whispering her no's with a concerned look on his face that she had never seen him give her before. He gave the nurse a quizzical look, and she went over to Jane's bed again.

"It's okay dear, I know it can be quite a shock waking up in an unfamiliar environment with no idea what is going on, but I just need you to relax. You are safe in here. Would you like some water? You must be thirsty. And after we can see if you can stomach a little solid food. How does that sound to you?"

Jane didn't want food or water; she wanted to be asleep again. She wanted to fall asleep and never wake up. She wanted to follow the true white light up to her Anthony and to her children. Her children. She snapped back to life.

"My children." She just stated the words at the nurse, who understood immediately the question behind the statement.

"I'm sorry to say that the search is still on going for them and that's all I know, I think Officer Paulson will be able to give you a few more of the specific details but I'm afraid all I know is what has been on the news." The nurse gave her a sympathetic look and then went off to fetch Jane some water.

Jane shot her eyes towards Paulson, who took this as his cue to get closer to the bed.

"Unfortunately, Nurse Linda is right. Sadly we have not yet found the boys, though efforts are still in full swing. The CCTV footage that we have reviewed from Beaulieu and from Bucklers Hard hasn't returned anything of note and so it seems as if your boys did not pass through either of the towns. It is very possible that they made their way to a main road and were picked up by strangers, though if this were the case we would have expected them to turn up soon afterward. Today, sniffer dogs will continue to search the nearby forests, and we have also sent divers into the river."

Jane was taken aback.

"You think they're dead."

Saying it out loud made her very hollow, it made it almost real. She had suspected from the moment she had seen her husband's body by the campfire that her sons had also suffered a similar fate, but whilst they had still not been found she had pushed that thought to the back of her head, buried it as far down inside her as she was physically able to. Now the thought surfaced and broke through her defences, swimming across her moat and pounding her high walls down.

Something else bubbled up inside her, and an image of her two boys floating down the river face down with their bodies sliced and mangled like Anthony's filled her head. She shook it, trying to get the image to leave her mind. It wouldn't leave, and the next thing she knew she twisted in the bed and threw up onto the pristine white floor beneath.

Paulson jumped backward once he had realised what Jane was about to do, and he quickly moved for the panic bell and rang it. The nurse had been just outside the door carrying the water back and she burst in, saw the sick and Jane leaning over the side of the bed, and then turned and called into the hall for assistance.

She went into the room and gently rolled Jane over so she was on her other side and facing away from the mess she had just made all over the floor. She walked round to the other side of the bed so she was facing Jane and asked her to take a few sips of the water. Jane lifted herself up a little so that she could drink and took of couple of short sips, before lying back down. Meanwhile, two more nurses had entered the room and had begun cleaning the floor. Paulson had retreated out into the corridor and was explaining what had happened to his colleague, the shorter officer.

Jane groaned as all of this went on around her, and could taste the sick and the bile in her mouth. She purposefully tasted it a second time, the bitterness seemed to stop the horrific image of her two sons from entering her head, if only briefly.

The nurse who had given her the water had left, but came back now with a toothbrush and asked Jane if she was okay to sit up, so that she could brush the horrible taste away. Jane lied and said that she wasn't, and if she moved she thought that she was very likely to throw up again as she was fearful that if the horrid taste of sick left her mouth, the image of her sons would return to her and she couldn't cope with that.

The nurse said she would leave it for a few minutes, but that it was best to brush as soon as possible.

The other nurses finished cleaning the floor, and as they exited Paulson came back in and stood guard by the door. Jane had rolled onto her back and looked up at the ceiling, praying that she would see her sons alive and well again.

Chapter Twelve

Solitary

Jane spent a night at the hospital whilst she continued to recover from the episode in her cell, all the time being closely watched over by nurses and officers. Two that Jane hadn't seen before had replaced Paulson and his shorter friend after a few hours, and she didn't see much of them now as they both chose to sit outside the room.

Jane ended up having a very good night's sleep, and she suspected it was down to the mattress that she was on as much as anything else. The mattress was in stark contrast to the one that she had set about destroying. It moulded around her body, gently spooning her to sleep.

In the morning, after the nurses had carried out some checks, she had been given the all clear that she could return to her cell. Paulson had returned in the morning, and he and the shorter officer escorted her to the police car before driving her back to the prison. She asked them if she would be seeing Henrey, but Paulson replied that he was still out on his emergency call and she wouldn't be able to see him now until after the weekend. That meant that Jane had to endure another three days without being able to see her family alive and well, and would have to suffer three more days on a shitty mattress in the meantime. It had taken only two nights for her to be driven to destroying the first one she had been given, and she wasn't sure she still possessed that level of restraint.

It occurred to her that perhaps she shouldn't try to exercise any restraint whatsoever. After all, it was her attack on her mattress that led to her being drugged and the best night's sleep she'd had in as long as she could remember. Not to mention the blanked out state where she had felt nothing. Jane decided then and there that she would wait a couple of hours in her cell, and then attack the second mattress that would be on her bed. She would kick and scream like she had done before and force them to drug her and take her back to hospital. She would continue to do this until she could see Henrey, and hence her family, again.

They arrived back at the prison and caught the lift up to Jane's floor. They walked down the corridor towards Jane's room, and stopped outside of it as Paulson got the keys out and unlock the door. He opened the door and Jane went to enter, but the shorter officer put his hand on her shoulder and stopped her from going in. Paulson looked down at her and shook his head.

"We're just picking up your stuff, you're not staying in this cell anymore. Your antics the other day mean that you are being transferred to one of the solitary confinement units, where everything is fixed to the floor to prevent you from damaging any more prison property."

Anne couldn't say that she found this revelation completely shocking, for she would have done the exact same thing as the prison authorities if she had been in their position. After all, she had been planning on destroying another mattress that night.

The shorter officer went into the room and grabbed Jane's toothbrush and the few other bits and pieces such as her pyjamas that she had been allowed in the cell.

They marched her down to the other end of the corridor, where they went through a set of large doors following a fingerprint scan. The doors opened onto a much smaller corridor. There were only four doors coming off it, supposedly into four solitary confinement units Jane thought. They went up to the second door on the left, and Paulson entered a passkey into a panel on the wall. The door slid all the way across, and he motioned for Jane to enter.

She walked into her new surroundings, before turning so that the shorter officer could take her handcuffs off. Once removed, the officers left her and the door slid closed.

The room was significantly smaller than her previous cell. There was a small silver basin, similar to the one that had been in her other cell, with a small dull silver tap. She inspected it closer and saw that it was only for cold water. The floor was made of lino that was a muddy red colour and overlapped up the wall. There was a tiny window, just about the size of Jane's head that let in a cylinder of sunlight which landed close to the middle of the muddy red floor. There was a metal seat that was attached to the wall underneath a metal desk, which was also jutting out from the wall. The table was horribly scratched with what looked like claw marks, probably from the nails of the people who had spent time in the room before Jane. These features were dull and drab, but they didn't overly concern Jane. What did concern Jane was the bed. Like the other features in the room, it was fixed to the wall, but unlike the bed in the cell, the mattress was a part of it. She tried to pull it up, but it wouldn't budge. At one end, the mattress had slightly more padding resulting in a low hump that Jane assumed must be the pillow. On the other end was a neatly folded plain white sheet that she assumed would act as her duvet.

Jane went to the sink and splashed her face with water, which turned out to be a tepid temperature rather than cold. She turned around and noticed that there was a small black camera pointing at the bed from the top right hand corner of the room.

Jane went to change her clothes, but found that her belongings hadn't been left in the room and banged on her door, calling for the officers. Like her other cell, there was a window in the door that could be open and closed only from the outside and through which she would be given food. As she called out, it opened and an unfamiliar face looked in at her.

"I think the officers forgot to leave my stuff in here."

"You're not allowed anything in the room that wasn't in the room when you arrived." The stranger replied to her.

"What? How am I going to brush my teeth?"

"There is an on hand nurse who will come in at 8am after breakfast and again at 8pm after dinner. She will bring a toothbrush with her which you will use under her and an officer's supervision."

The stranger shut the window with a metallic clang and Jane was left alone again thinking it very odd that they wouldn't even let her have a toothbrush, all she did was tear up a mattress a little.

*

After an excruciatingly long half hour during which Jane had been left to her own devices, the window opened again. The stranger asked her if she would like a book. She had a choice of two, neither of which Anne had read before and neither of which she particularly wanted to read now, but she couldn't stand sitting in silence doing nothing but think about her family any longer and picked the second one. It was a Stephane Stephens novel and seemed to be about an unfortunate man who had had a car accident and then been found by a group of young children who weren't what they first seemed. Jane wasn't really following the story too closely and her eyes kept wandering over the words on the page, the letters jumbling up in her vision.

After a couple of hours, when she realised she had been staring at the same page for close to twenty minutes, she folded the top corner and set it down. She had been sat at the metal chair at the desk, and decided it was time to try out the bed.

As it turned out, because the mattress that was ingrained into the bed was very thin, it was actually too thin to have springs in it and was more like the matts that you would use at primary school during gymnastics.. Jane closed her eyes and was soon fast asleep.

*

BANG-BANG-BANG

The knock startled Jane awake. The window opened and a plate of food, which Jane took to be her supper, was slid through the gap, before the window was quickly shut behind it.

Jane got out of bed and walked the few steps that it took to get from the bed to the door. She picked up the tray and put it down on the metal table before bending herself down onto the chair.

The tray was divided into three different sections. In the largest section there were a couple of slices of what looked like processed meat, some overcooked broccoli and 3 soggy potatoes with a handful of carrots. In the other two sections there was a small plastic cup filled with orange juice and yoghurt. She hadn't been given any cutlery to eat it with.

The processed meat was perfectly inedible, but the vegetables were okay and the yoghurt was actually a nice mango flavour. Once she had gulped down the juice, she returned the tray to the window and knocked on the door. It took a few minutes for the window to open again, and when it did it was only open for the brief time it took for a hand to grab the tray and pull it back out of the room.

The nurse came in about an hour later with Paulson, and they stood either side of her as she brushed her teeth. Once she was finished she handed the toothbrush to the nurse and watched as they both left the room. She picked up the book and read it for another 20 minutes, before deciding to turn in for the night.

*

Jane had to endure two more days of the rigid routine of being woken at 7am with breakfast, followed by the nurse at 8 to do her teeth. She was let out on her own in the yard at 10 accompanied by two officers; the two officers were different on both days. After going for a long walk around the yard, Jane would return to her cell and read for a little while before lunch slid through the window at precisely 12. Once her lunch tray had been taken away, the endless afternoon would begin. Jane had found that she couldn't concentrate on reading for more than 20 minutes or so at a time, this meant that she had long periods where she was left with nothing but her own thoughts, and her own thoughts were dark.

On the second afternoon, Jane was sat on the hard bed, staring at the door. In her mind all she could see was the vision of her family, all three of them dead, floating around drifting from one location to the next. One time, they were back at the house, Anthony had just come in from work and they were talking about what they were going to do with some money that they had just inherited. Jane wanted to buy a new car as their old one was getting ragged, but Anthony loved it and was arguing it had great character and you should never get rid of something that has great character. They had both gone out to inspect the car when Anthony had started shuddering. His face went blue and blood started pouring out of his eyes and nose and ears. Cuts opened up all over his body and green slime oozed out of them. Jane tried to look away from the scene into the car window, pressed up to the window of the back seat was a small hand covered in blood and slime. Jane took a few steps closer and peered in to see her two sons, eyes wide open but unseeing, staring into nothingness. As she watched, their eyes began to glow green.

Their bodies began to move, and laughter shot out of their mouths aggressively. A high-pitched giggling. Jane stumbled back, away from her sons. But the car doors opened and they got out and started dragging their broken bodies towards her. Giggling together as one.

Jane shook her head and opened her eyes into the cell. She looked at the cell door with relief. But then the giggling started up again. Jane screamed out as the noise got closer and closer. She cried out for help. Begging someone to come in.

"IT'S HERE! IT'S IN HERE! THE CREATURE IS IN HERE!"

The giggling continued to get louder, pounding on her head and forcing Jane to her knees. A piercing scream left her mouth as Paulson ran into the room to see what was going on. The giggling immediately stopped, but Jane continued to whimper.

*

Jane accepted her insanity. She believed that she had lost her mind out in the forest and had begun seeing things. She was plagued by voices in her head that giggled and tormented her. At night the sound of the laughter crept into her cell and became deafening.

She believed that when she had finally broken through the forest and had seen Anthony by the fire her hallucination had transformed him, starting with his eyes, into some sort of demon. In order to protect herself, she must have picked up one of the sticks and bashed him with it. It must have been sharp and that is why his skin had been covered in deep gashes. She even thought that the reason there was no murder weapon was because she had then thrown the stick onto the fire and that had destroyed that evidence. It all made perfect sense to her.

She accepted that she was insane, and wanted to die because of it. Jane would lie for hours and plan how she would give her own life, to make up for the one that she had taken out in the forest. The only problem was the security camera; she was constantly being monitored and didn't think she would be able to kill herself quickly enough before she was swarmed with officers armed with needles that would knock her out in a matter of seconds. She couldn't hang herself as there was nothing to hang off of, and she didn't think she could create a rope like object strong enough from the sheet she had in order to hold her up anyway. The washbasin didn't have a plug, so attempting to drown herself was out of the question too. She had considered bashing her head on the wall, but felt like this would only knock her out and wouldn't kill her. Then she would wake up in a hospital, bandaged up, and probably put into one of those insane peoples zip up bags so she couldn't do anything but roll around like a slug.

No, she had come to the conclusion that she would just have to live with the guilt. Live with what she had done until such a time as death presented itself to her through an easier route.

Besides, tomorrow she was seeing Henrey again, which meant that she would be able to see her family alive and well. Tomorrow she would see her Anthony before she had killed him.

Chapter Thirteen

Barking

"Hello Jane." Henrey spoke not in his usually cheery voice, but in one that was heavy with exhaustion.

"Did you manage to sort out your emergency?" Jane asked, genuinely concerned after hearing the strain in Henrey's voice.

Henrey ignored the question. "We are here today to discuss your present situation. I hear that whilst I have been away you have been in a lot of trouble Jane, an awful lot of trouble." Henrey tutted to himself as he read over his notes.

"You destroyed prison property, assaulted two police officers, spent a day in the hospital recovering from a shot of morphine and have spent your time since in solitary confinement, where you have been hearing voices." Henrey tutted again, shaking his head slowly. "Do you have anything to say in your defence?"

Jane sat looking at him for a moment, there were deep black bags under Henrey's eyes and his face was grey and forlorn, as if he'd seen a ghost. She suspected that he had lost someone very dear to him. She reasoned it probably wasn't one of his parents; he seemed too old for them to have still been around. Perhaps it was his wife, or maybe a child.

"I was trying to recreate your office in my cell." Jane tried to explain. "I wanted to see my family again, alive and well. I wanted to be with them, so I put the mattress on the floor and lay back like you showed me how. I even set the tap running to sound like your water feature, I had everything perfect. I could see them again, we were in the river, you know like I told you, in the river splashing and having fun, it was the best time of my life… only… only then the mattress spring dug into my back and I lost it all. I lost my family yet again. I can't keep losing them. I was so angry; I was blind angry. Have you ever been that angry Henrey? So angry that you're not even yourself anymore, you don't see or feel anything around you? Well that is how angry I was. I just wanted the mattress to be good for me, but it wasn't being good so I had to discipline it. I had to make it pay for losing my family, you see? You understand don't you Henrey? You know exactly what it's like to lose someone you love. I can see it in your face. That was your emergency. You lost someone you love and now you feel the white anger too. You know it's real! I can see you know it is!" Jane was speaking excitedly at Henrey, tripping over her words as she struggled to keep her mouth up with her brain, which seemed to be working in overdrive.

Henrey shook his head again slowly. "I am not angry, Jane. I am far from angry, I am upset and I am broken and sad, but one thing I am not is angry. I am deeply worried about you Jane, this attack on your mattress and subsequently on the officers that rushed in to restrain you, coupled with what you have just described to me about not knowing who or where you were..." Henrey tutted to himself again and continued to shake his head slowly. "You think that you killed him, don't you?" He asked, almost casually.

Jane didn't reply, but she didn't have to. Her tears said it all.

Henrey nodded to himself and jotted down a note. He leaned back in his chair and observed Jane from the new position.

"I am going to finalise the details of my report, and then submit it to the courts. Jane, I do believe you to be legally insane. Both at the time of the murder, and now. I am going to recommend to the judge that you be admitted into a mental hospital, where they can look after you and make you better again. It is my professional opinion that you were not yourself when committing these vile acts, that you had become overwhelmed by another part of your brain that turned you into a monster. This monster within you has the capacity to surface again as was demonstrated the other day. It will be left to a judge and jury to determine the minimum amount of time that you will have to spend in an institution, though if there is no significant improvement whilst you are there then you will have to remain indefinitely."

*

About a hundred miles from Henrey's office, a much reduced team of sniffer dogs and searchers were exploring the last few hundred square feet of the forest that had yet to be searched in the look for the two missing Parkins boys.

The diver's efforts in the river hadn't returned anything, and although people had continued to search the forest, it was becoming more and more in vain. Many of those from the local villages had stopped looking and gone back to their day jobs, with the gossip being that the boys must have been kidnapped, or their bodies had floated down the river and out into the sea where they would never be found.

The team of four officers and three sniffer dogs that were left searching the very far reaches of the forest were all beginning to get hungry as supper time approached.

Charles looked across at Amy, who rubbed her tummy theatrically and gave him a look that told him she would positively pass out if she didn't get something to eat soon.

"Ten more minutes and then we'll stop for food." Charles called out to the others, who perked up at this.

They continued to walk slowly through the forest, the dogs sniffing the ground all around them trying to pick up some sort of a scent. They had taken the dogs to the Parkins house and into the boy's room to allow them to smell their toys and clothes so that they would be able to track them, but so far it didn't seem to be working. The dogs hadn't been able to pick up a scent of the boys past the tree that they were left peeing at by Jane.

One of the dogs started barking, and Charles looked up sharply from the bush that he had been knelt searching through.

"What is it, Amy? Anything?"

Amy was closest to the dog and went over to it. "What is it, boy? You found something?" Amy knelt down next to the dog, which was wagging its tail excitedly. She called out to Jen for a brush, and Jen went over and passed her one. Amy brushed the leaves off the floor. There was nothing but dirt underneath.

"Doesn't appear to be anything, must just be a false alarm."

Amy turned to walk back to the area she had been searching, when the dog barked again, this time digging its paws into the dirt in the opening she had just created by brushing the leaves aside. Amy gave Charles an uneasy look.

Charles lifted his radio to his mouth. "Base, this is Charles requesting a dig team in the forest, I repeat a dig team in the forest, over."

"Charles this is base, we copy you and will send the team out right away."

Charles looked at his small team who had gathered around the dirt patch, each of their faces were pale. He decided not to suggest lunch whilst they waited; no one was feeling hungry anymore.

*

The dig team arrived about half an hour later and began their excavation of the site.

After an hour of carefully extracting the soil, the lead excavation officer called Charles over.

"We've found two bodies. They are covered in soil and dirt, but they are roughly the right heights of the missing boys, and by the looks of things they suffered very similar injuries to Anthony Parkins. Shortly we are going to look to pull them out and transport them to a coroner, where they will be cleaned up and identified. I would recommend that you cease your searching until the bodies have been identified, in the meantime debrief your team and thank them for a job well done."

Charles thanked him for coming out so quickly and finding the bodies, and then turned and headed back over to his team.

"They have excavated two bodies from the area and they are pretty much 100% the missing boys, all that is left is the formal identification once the bodies have been moved out and cleaned up. I would like to personally thank all of you for your hard work these past few days. I know these searches can be very hard on the searchers; no one really wants to be the one to look into a bush and find the bodies. It is the hardest job in the world and I truly commend you for your great service. Those boys will be able to rest now and can be given a proper burial. I want all of you to have the rest of the week off. Go and spend it with your families, get out of town for a few days and refresh yourselves. That's all I have to say, let's get to the van and go home."

The four of them led the dogs out of the forest and back to the van which was parked a good mile from where they had found the bodies. They took the entire walk in silence, and even though none of them had seen the bodies, they all remembered the picture they had seen of Anthony Parkins and from it each had a picture conjured up in their heads about what those two poor boys would have looked like, caked in blood and mud and dirt, all alone, buried in the forest floor.

*

For the first time since Jane had returned to her solitary confinement cell, someone other than Paulson or the teeth brushing nurse entered the room.

The man who came in was wearing a large black trench coat, which was extremely dark around the shoulders before becoming lighter past the waist with only the occasional darker smudge and Jane realised that it must be raining heavily outside.

"Hello Jane, my name is Inspector Stephens. I have some news for you and it's probably best that you sit down."

Jane knew exactly what was coming before he said it, the only reason anyone would be allowed to visit her in her cell, especially anyone like a detective, would be if there was news of her children. Based on the expression on the Inspectors face, the news he had brought her was not good. She collapsed onto the bed and broke down into tears as he continued.

"At around midday yesterday, our officers were alerted by sniffer dogs to a burial site. Excavation officers were called to the scene and recovered two bodies." Jane let out a hallowing scream that was so piercing and filled with agony that it would haunt the Inspector for the rest of his life. The inspector steadied himself before continuing.

"The bodies were taken away and cleaned, before being identified as your sons, Jack Parkins and Tom Parkins. The nature of the wounds they sustained is all but identical to those found on the body of your husband, Anthony Parkins."

"Jane Parkins, I am arresting you on suspicion of the murders of Jack and Tom Parkins. You do not have to say anything, but it may harm your defence if you do not mention when questioned something you later rely on in court. Anything you do say may be given in evidence."

Part Three

Asylum

Chapter Fourteen

Hell

A clock ticked away in the background as the air was thick with the screams of the insane.
Tick-tick-tick.
Counting the seconds away.
Tick-tick-tick.
"Stop the voices, STOP THE VOICES!"
Tick-tick-tick.
"CAN YOU SEE THAT PERSON? CAN YOU SEE THEM? ARE THEY THERE?!"
Tick-tick-tick.
"They're trying to kill me. Look at that whore, she's trying to kill me."
Tick-tick-tick.
"Please? Can anyone see that person? By the door? Can anyone else see that person?"
Tick-tick-tick.
"I DON'T WANT YOUR POISON! SHE'S TRYING TO KILL ME, SOMEONE HELP! GET THEM OUT OF MY FUCKING FACE I DON'T WANT YOUR FUCKING POISON! SHE'S TRYING TO POISON ME TO DEATH. PLEASE, PLEASE HELP, SHE IS TRYING TO KILL ME."
Tick-tick-tick.
"HAHAHAHAHAHAHAHAHAHAHA."
Tick-tick-tick.
"Rosie, Rosie, had a little posie."
Tick-tick-tick.

"Can you see them over by the door? Please…"

Tick-tick-tick.

"Rosie, Rosie, watch her as she's dozy."

Tick-tick-tick.

"PLEASE SOMEONE HELP ME SHE WANTS TO KILL ME."

Tick-tick-tick

"Drip, drip, Rosie what's that on the floor?"

Tick-tick-tick.

"KILL ME, FUCKING KILL ME."

Tick-tick-tick.

"Drip, drip, Rosie why were you a whore?"

Tick-tick-tick.

"HAHAHAHAHAHAHAHAHAH."

Tock.

*

"Open up."

Jane shook her head.

"Open up, now."

Jane clamped her mouth shut as tightly as she could.

"Jane, don't make me ask you again."

Jane continued to refuse.

The nurse pinched her bicep sharply and Jane's mouth opened in her pain. The nurse took the opportunity and thrust her non-pinching hand deep into Jane's mouth before releasing the pills into the back of her throat. Jane bit down as hard as she could, but the nurse's hand was back out of her mouth as quick as a flash and her teeth made a loud tocking noise as they came together. The nurse grabbed Jane's jaw and held it shut tight so that she couldn't spit the pills out. Jane struggled against the nurse and shook her head violently from side to side trying to dislodge the grip so that she could get away. But the nurse was strong and wily, this wasn't the first time a patient had struggled against taking a pill and it certainly wouldn't be the last. It probably wouldn't even be the last time that day. The energy drained out of Jane and she conceded defeat, swallowing the pills down.

Her body slowly began to relax, and the nurse let go of her jaw.

"Now then, that's better isn't it?" The nurse spoke clearly, but it sounded like a distant echo to Jane who had exited her own body and was drifting away up towards the roof.

*

Tick-tick-tick.

"What's that Rosie comin' through your lips?"

Tick-tick-tick.

"NA-NA-NA-NA-EEE-OOOOOWW-EE-OOOOOWW"

Tick-tick-tick.

"Blood red, blood red, down onto your hips."

Tick-tick-tick.

"WHO'S THAT JUST COME IN CAN ANYONE ELSE SEE THAT MAN? WHO IS THAT?"

Tick-tick-tick.

"Drip, drip, Rosie what's that on the floor?"
Tick-tick-tick.
"IT WANTS TO SCRATCH MY EYE BALLS OUT SOMEONE HELP IT'S TRYING TO SCRATCH MY FUCKING EYE BALLS OUT!"
Tick-tick-tick.
"Drip, drip, Rosie why were you a whore?"
Tick-tick-tick.
"HAHAHAHAHAHAHAHAHAHAHA."
Tock.

*

Jane returned slowly to consciousness, floating down from the ceiling back towards her body.. She brought her forehead down onto the forehead of the sleeping version of herself, and found that her head began to absorb into her sleeping version as if she were made of water and her sleeping version of sponge. She absorbed herself fully and then came to, gripping the bed sheet tightly around her neck. Sweat was pouring down her face and there was an acidic smell that made her nostrils burn. She blinked and her eyes instantly began to sting as droplets of sweat found their way into them. She released her grip of the bed linen and brought her hands up over her face, wiping at the grime and trying to clear it away. She pulled her hands away and looked at them, they were caked in dirt and wet with sweat. She wiped them over the front of the linen and rubbed into it hard as she tried to clean her hands. Her hands dried of the sweat, but remained dirty. They left two circular patches of a grey-brown colour on her white linen where she had just rubbed them.

Jane raised her body up, straining against a sharp pain in her side, which made her yelp out as she moved. She shuffled up the bed until she was sat bolt upright, leaning on the wooden headboard.

As she sat she started to daydream about her wedding day with Anthony. Her dress had been ripped as she tried to get into the car that was taking her to the church, and she had desperately tried not to cry in order to protect her makeup from running down her face. She had taken a pregnancy test that very morning, after feeling very ill the past couple of days when she had woken up, and it had displayed a blue cross, indicating that she was pregnant. She had wanted to ring Anthony straight away to share the news with him, but had decided against it and to wait until that night after the wedding had taken place. As good a man as he was, and despite the fact he was marrying her, Anthony had always been scared of commitment, and Jane felt that revealing her pregnancy may have tipped him over the edge and caused him to run out on their wedding. No, she had decided, she'd make sure they were husband and wife before she revealed the truth about their child.

As she walked down the aisle to the Bridal March, Anthony had sneaked his head round to catch a glance of her walking down, and she caught the smile in the corner of his face when he saw how she looked. Whenever she had been sad from then on, she had always remembered that smile and how it had made her radiate for the rest of the day. It was a smile of unconditional love and she had realised in that moment that Anthony wasn't going anywhere, she could have rung him that morning and told him that she was pregnant and he would have been waiting for her that afternoon in the church like he was now. It was a smile that told her he was finally ready to commit to her after all the years of waiting. It was a smile that told her he loved her unconditionally and would continue to love her unconditionally until death made them part.

Silent tears rolled down over her cheeks and fell onto the bed linen, mixing with the dirtied marks that her hands had made on it.

She continued to let the memories of her wedding day with Anthony wash over her She closed her eyes and listened to the softness of his voice as he recited his vows to her, promising that he would turn into an old man slowly and wouldn't let his figure go until at least 6 months into their marriage. Jane laughed at the memory as more tears streaked down her cheeks.

The two of them had choreographed a first dance to try and wow their friends, and had created a mix that started with a slow dance before slowly transitioning to a grand finale that involved some rather raunchy moves and butt slapping. It was the worst and best dance that she ever had. Their families and friends had roared with laughter come the end, though she hadn't been entirely sure whether they were laughing with them or at them. Anthony, after all, had been an appalling dancer, though he wouldn't admit it himself and claimed he could have made it as a professional if he had the will power to dedicate his time to dancing.

There was a brief knock at the door. The nurse who had forced the pills down Jane's throat came in without hesitating for a reply from Jane. She was carrying a tray of food and put it down on the table next to Jane.

"You're not normally up at this time." The nurse stated bluntly, but really she was relieved that she didn't have to wake up Jane to give her the food. She had always been creeped out by the way that Jane awoke, it was if she wasn't in the room, she was some place else, she could almost feel her spirit re-entering the place as she woke. The nurse found it eerie, and that was coming from someone who had spent nearly 30 years working in the mental hospital. The nurse left her to eat, and Jane waited until the door was pulled shut behind her before reaching for the tray.

She despised the nurse, everything about her from her plain white plimsolls to the nest of hair that sat on her head. She detested the way the nurse looked at not only her, but also everyone else in the place, as if they were filthy animals caged up in a zoo. Jane had seen her sneer and laugh as she turned away from the patients in the hospital on more than one occasion. She didn't think the nurse was better than any of the patients in the place.

The tray of food was almost identical to the one that she had in prison. There were a few vegetables and some processed meat that looked like it had come from about four different animals, and Jane didn't doubt for a second that that wasn't the case.

She picked at a few of the vegetables and drank the small glass of water that accompanied it. Jane had lost her appetite since arriving at the mental hospital. She wasn't entirely sure how long she had been there, but assumed it must have been close to three months by this point. She slept away most of the days, because she hardly ate anything she didn't have the energy to do anything else.

In the first few days and weeks that she had been in the hospital, she had continued to try and break through her blackout, but it had been to no avail. She had been given a 10-year sentence in the institution after having been found mentally insane by the jury, who had believed unanimously that she had killed her family. The dirt in her nails and all over her hands had been a perfect match to the samples taken from where the bodies of her children had been recovered.

Jane hadn't been able to process the fact that she had killed her entire family, and it still didn't make sense to her without the explanation that she must have been insane, so she had accepted that she was exactly that. She had lived in hope at the beginning of her sentence that she would still be able to break through her blackout and discover the truth of that night, no matter how painful it was, but Henrey had told her that breaking through it would be nigh on impossible. He had likened it to when you reset your computer to factory settings. All of the data is erased and is unrecoverable, as if it never really existed on the computer in the first place. It was gone, and there was nothing that anyone could do about it. But Jane hadn't accepted that at first. Anthony was an IT whiz and had taught her a thing or two along the way; she reckoned that she could give recovering lost data a good crack.

The search into the blackout had been torturous for her. Every day she had to witness the state of Anthony's body, hear the giggling in the woods as she searched desperately for her lost children. Every attempt ended with her seeing the bright green eyes off in the forest, and every time she saw those eyes her resolve reduced. She had slightly less strength. She wanted to look back to that period less. Until eventually, after about three weeks of trying to get through the blackout she had fainted, exhausted and defeated. That is when the nurse had begun giving her more pills a day, including the one that knocked Jane out cold, which she received every day at 2 o clock. It kept her out until dinner and she hated it. She hated how it made her sleep, her conscious self feeling as if it was leaving her body and floating up and away. She feared that if she was ever given the pill outside, that she would never be able to return to her body and that her consciousness would just keep floating up and up without a roof to stop it from escaping.

Once she had stopped trying to break into her blackouts, she found that the days became much shorter and they all began to blend into one. She had tried to forget the sight of Anthony's decimated body and had tried to stop thinking about him and her family all together. She had closed off her mind during her waking hours, but sometimes when she slept she would find herself thrust back to that night once more, suffering for hours before her body would allow her to wake.

*

Tick-tick-tick.
"OOO-AAAAHHH-KAAAA-BLAAAA-SHEEK-SHEEK."
Tick-tick-tick.
"Darling Rosie smell my prick."
Tick-tick-tick.
"I KILLED HIM! I KILLED HER! Dead. Dead. Dead-edy dead."
Tick-tick-tick.
"Why I heard you love men's dick?"
Tick-tick-tick.
"Hello? Hello? Is anyone there? I think I've lost my mummy. Hello? Can someone help me please I was by the bread and I lost my mummy. Where is my mummy? Can you help me find her please?"
Tick-tick-tick.
"Drip, drip, Rosie what's on the floor?"
Tick-tick-tick.
"Can anyone else smell that? I think there's a gas leak! Someone please help me get out of here! THERE'S A GAS LEAK! SOMEONE PLEASE HELP ME? I CAN SMELL IT THERE'S A GAS LEAK! I'M GOING TO DIE! SOMEONE

SAVE ME, HELP ME, OH GOD PLEASE ANYONE HELP ME."

Tick-tick-tick.

"Drip, drip, Rosie why were you a whore?"

Tick-tick-tick.

"HAHAHAHAHAHAHAHAHAHAH."

Tock.

*

Jane had to spend an hour a day in the common room with some of the other patients. According to the psychiatrist that she had to see three times a week, spending time with other people regardless of their mental condition was good for the human brain and kept it healthy and fresh.

Jane hated these hours, which often felt like an awful lot longer than 60 minutes. The common room felt like an old people's home, and smelt worse. Most of the patients did not clean themselves unless they were forced to clean themselves. A lot of the patients seemed to be in a far worse mental state than Jane was, to the point where they were unable to look after themselves at all. There were a team of nurses who worked day and night looking after everyone, and some were better than others.

They tended to work in teams, with kind nurses paired with the harder, unforgiving ones. Jane wasn't sure whether it was done to make the kind ones harder or the hard ones kinder, but she suspected it was not the latter of the two. In any case, she had noticed that the kind ones tended to be younger and new to the job. They perhaps went into the profession because they cared about people who had lost who they were and had great visions of bringing them back from the brink, being surrounded as they did so by cheering academics who lauded them for their ground breaking work. But soon they would be battered down and beaten, like the older nurses who were so hard on every patient. Soon they would discover that some people are just too far gone. That the patients that winded up in this place were the worst of the worst and the reason they were here was because there was no saving them. There was nothing to be saved. The patients in this hospital were born different from other humans. They had no concept of right and wrong. Some of them saw dead people; some of them saw strangers in the corners of rooms that were there to kill them. Many had multiple personalities. Some cried out that there was a dog telling them to kill everyone in the room in the name of God.

Jane sat where she usually sat, in an armchair in a corner away from everyone else. No one else had previously sat in the armchair next to her, and she preferred it that way. The last thing she wanted to do was to be near another insane person. The truth was she was utterly petrified by them. She did believe that she had a severe mental episode and did worry that she perhaps suffered from a form of schizophrenia, but compared to the other patients in here she thought she was sane. She didn't know why she had been put in this particular hospital instead of a different one, but had figured they were all the same and the sanity levels of patients would be similar in all of them. But she wasn't one hundred percent sure of this fact and it nagged away at her.

During this particular session, someone did come and sit in the armchair next to her. It was a kind looking lady, who looked quite a lot younger than Jane. She may have even been in her twenties. Jane had watched her come through the doors to the left of where she was sat and look around nervously, listening to the mutterings, to the shouting, to the ticking clock that ceaselessly went about its business. She had wondered over towards another of the ladies who was sat on a couch on the other side of the room from Jane. As this new woman had approached her, the one sat down had begun screaming, shouting that she was trying to kill her and calling the nurses. She kept looking round wide eyed and asking the other people in the room if they could see this new woman, that she didn't know who she was and thought she was a murderer. The new woman had turned away sharply and scurried over to where Jane was sitting, not really looking where she was going and had tripped a couple of times over her own feet.

She flopped into the armchair next to Jane and was clearly panic stricken. Jane didn't normally talk to anyone during the hour, but she felt almost a motherly tie over this new girl, who looked even younger than Jane had previously thought up close. She didn't look like she could have been more than 19 or 20.

"Hello, are you okay?"

The girl looked at Jane with a deeply embedded fear in her eyes. Fear that had tormented her for an extraordinarily long time.

"Fine." She mumbled in a voice that was barely audible.

Jane went back to looking straight ahead, away from the girl. After a couple of minutes of silence, it was the girl who spoke again.

"I had no idea anyone could scream so loud at someone who just wanted to sit down."

Jane let her words hang in the air for a moment and continued to look straight ahead.

"I just wanted to sit down." The girl repeated.

Jane let out a long breath of air. "You're new here aren't you, I haven't seen you in here before?"

"I arrived a couple of days ago, they said I had to come in here for an hour today."

"Yes, it's compulsory, apparently it is good for us to spend time with other humans, helps to keep our heads from exploding." Jane tried to be funny to relax the girl but found that the humour came out forced and as a result sounded a little too serious. The girl probably thought she was insane.

"I hate it here." The girl said bluntly. "I want to leave."

"Don't we all? The best thing to do is try not to think about it. Try to forget that this is a mental hospital and take each day as it comes."

"That's impossible, you can't just forget where you are. You can't just close your eyes and pretend to be somewhere else the whole time, because you're always brought back around. The dream ends, you wake up and you're here. There's a nurse prodding you with this and telling you that you have to eat that. You can hear wailing and screaming and pain from all around you. You can't escape this place. I can't escape this place."

They sat in silence again for another couple of minutes.

"Maybe we can make it easier for each other, at least just for an hour or so a day. We can meet and sit here and just chat. We can pretend we are in a waiting room waiting for our dentist appointment, only there's a boy Billy who went in before us and needs some emergency care. So we're going to have to sit here for an hour together whilst he gets it done and just chat so the time goes quicker. What do you say?"

The girl considered it.

"My name is Jenny."

"Lovely to meet you Jenny, my name is Jane."

They shook hands and smiled at one another.

Chapter Fifteen

Jenny

For the next two years, Jenny and Jane spent an hour a day together. Generally, they didn't chat for the whole hour, they would speak for between 5 and 10 minutes and bitch about the nurses and how awfully they treated all of the patients. They had taken to calling the nurse who had force fed Jane the pills (and had subsequently force fed Jenny) Nurse Angry, plainly because she was always bad tempered, always just on the edge of snapping and forcing pills on you or shouting at you or spitting in your food or water.

Jane finally felt as if she had a friend again in the world, and talking and sitting with Jenny each day made her feel as if she was almost sane.

Jenny had done the rounds when it came to mental institutions in the past ten years or so. She had been brought up with her two brothers in Winchester and had been born into a wealthy family. Her father had been a director at one of the big banks in London and her mother had run her own fashion label.

Three days after her tenth birthday, her mother passed away in a car accident, along with two of her friends, one of which had been driving drunk. Her father had lost himself completely and had quit his job, spending his days alone in his study drinking. Her older brothers had been at boarding school and couldn't bear to be at home, which reminded them too much of their mother, and so Jenny and her father were the only two living in the large house.

She would often be woken in the middle of the night to the sound of cutlery and pots and pans being smashing and chucked around the kitchen as her father tried and failed to make a snack to curb his alcohol induced hunger. One particular night when Jenny was woken up, she had decided to be a nice daughter and go and help him make some food. When she went into the kitchen she was greeted by the sight of her father sprawled out, face down on the floor. This didn't come as a great shock to her, Jenny was used to going down to breakfast in the morning and find her father passed out on the floor in the kitchen from the previous night.

She knelt down by him and shook him gently in an attempt to wake him up, but her effort was in vain so she spoke softly to him, urging him to get up so that she could make him something to eat. Still he didn't stir, so Jenny picked up a pan and a large metal serving spoon and starting banging them together loudly by his ear. This time her father bolted upright, his eyes completely glazed over. He was blind drunk. Her father had panicked and assumed that he was being attacked and shoved his arms out towards the loud noise of the pan. Jenny had been caught completely unawares and fallen over backwards, the back of her head colliding heavily with the floating island they had at the centre of the kitchen. The blow knocked her unconscious, and her body had then lolled sideways and she had smashed the side of her head onto the hard stone floor.

If Jenny had been reached even an hour after this, she would have been fine, or at least very close to fine. However, her father had passed out again almost immediately, and Jenny had been unconscious on the floor for over six hours before anyone was alerted to come to her aid. She had been in a coma for over three weeks before she finally pulled through, though the Jenny that came out of the accident was very different from the Jenny that had gone down the stairs to make her father something to eat.

Her father had quit drinking straight away, appalled at what he had done to her. He vowed to give her the best treatment in the world and had spent thousands and thousands of pounds on giving her access to the best doctors and technology. Eventually, the money had run out and Jenny was only marginally better. With his final penny spent, her father had killed himself, leaving a letter to Jenny that simply said:

"I couldn't live with the guilt. I'm sorry, my sweet."

After the passing of her father, Jenny had relapsed and any progress made following her accident was reversed. Her condition worsened and she became a danger to society, which led to her first hospitalisation. Since then she had been in and out of mental hospitals her entire life.

Jenny had told Jane her story once and only once. She preferred not to talk about her past or her present condition but said that as they were going to be best friends, Jane should have some understanding about her past and how she came to be here. Jane had thanked her for trusting in her and had told Jenny her story in return. Jenny had been transfixed with Jane's family life and had asked her hundreds of questions about her boys and having a husband. Jane had found it oddly relaxing to delve into her past and tell Jenny stories about the life she used to live. The more time that they had spent together; the more they liked one another. They seemed to compliment each other well and in the hour a day they spent together, they could have been anywhere in the entire world.

*

Jane was staring at a frail looking woman who was sat knitting whilst opening and closing her mouth and grinding her teeth together. There was drool hanging off her chin which must had fallen out of her mouth during one of the many times that it had been hung open. Her hair was white and very thin on her head. There were chunks of it missing; presumably the old lady had pulled it out from these patches when she was stressed.

Jenny suddenly hit her on the arm.

"Ouch! What are you doing?!" Jane said shocked, rubbing her arm better.

"You had a fly on you!" Jenny laughed, "Don't worry though, I got it for you."

"Oh! Thanks!" Jane laughed, "For a minute there I thought you were crazy!" She winked at

Jenny and they both laughed together. They had recently taken to making light of their sanity, it was their life after all, and they may as well be able to laugh about it.

They returned to both watching the room, waiting for something to happen.

"I bet you that Angry is going to walk through those doors within the next five minutes and put a pill down someone's neck." Jenny blurted out.

"How much?"

"How about if I win, you have to swap chairs with me for a week, I think you always sit in that one because it is the more comfortable of the two!"

Jane laughed, "What about if I win?"

"Hmm." Jenny considered for a moment. "If you win then I promise to pull Nurse Angry's pants down at the first opportunity I get."

Jane looked at her astonished. "You really are mad."

"What's the worst that could happen? We're already in this place after all. She's already shoved pills down my throat, which as you know is something second only to rape! Literally, what else can they do to me?"

Jane thought about it, there were probably numerous things that Nurse Angry could and would be willing to do to make Jenny's life even more miserable, but Jane couldn't think quite what those things might be.

"Besides, it's not like I'm going to lose anyway. If she doesn't come in the next five minutes then I'll cause a scene and make her force the pills down my throat." Jenny giggled.

Sure enough, almost precisely a minute later in came Angry with a handful of pills. She stood in the doorway for a second, her beady eyes scanning the room for a victim. Angry locked on to a target and then moved in for the kill. She stalked up to the woman that had shouted Jenny down when she had first arrived at the hospital and asked her to take one of the pills she was holding. The woman refused and hence ensued the wrath of Angry.

Jenny watched the whole exchange beaming from ear to ear. She slowly turned her head towards Jane, still beaming her smile, but also raising her eyebrows up and down suggestively.

"Looks like the chair's mine!"

"Starting tomorrow!"

*

Jane beat Jenny to the common room the next day and honoured the agreement she had made with her friend and sat in the chair next to her usual spot.

She waited for Jenny to turn up and start gloating, but as the clock ticked away in the background and the seconds turned to minutes, Jane realised that she wasn't coming and felt a deep hole of sadness open up inside her. She wondered if Jenny had gotten ill, it wasn't uncommon in the hospital as the meals tended to be on the dodgy side of right. Another possibility was that Jenny was out cold on pills. If she had an episode earlier in the day the nurses would have just drugged her up and knocked her out. It was the third option that scared Jane the most, though. Jenny was, after all, just a frail girl who she suspected put on a strong face for the hour a day that they spent together. Deep down she assumed she would be struggling pretty hard. She still had no idea what mental illness Jenny actually suffered from, but to be in a place like this she must have done something bad or be suffering with something bad. The third option was that Jenny might have committed suicide. It wasn't uncommon at all, and Jane actually believed the nurses preferred it if you did kill yourself, especially Angry. Three women had died this month at least. Jane had seen the bodies of the three being transported out. There was only one way out of the hospital and that was death. She had almost felt envious of the three for their suffering was at an end, whilst the women they left behind had to endure. Had to go on facing the dark of the day and the darker of the nights.

*

The next day Jane again sat in the seat next to her usual, continuing to honour her and Jenny's deal and waited with baited breath to see if she would arrive or not.

    She listened to the tick of the clock and counted with it to sixty as the first minute past, and then the second. After the fourth minute went by without a trace of Jenny, Jane gave up and sunk deep into the chair. One day could be down her being put out with pills, but a second day meant suicide.

On this day, however, Jenny wasn't another of the suicide victims. After seven minutes had passed, the doors to the common room opened and she walked in looking slightly worse for wear. She wandered over and took the seat that she had won next to Jane.

"Hey!" Jenny said in a voice brighter than she looked.

"Hey! What happened to you? Where were you yesterday?"

"Oh it was nothing really, I had a little episode - you know how it is. Show a little bit of crazy and they come at you with all sorts of pills and tranquilisers! I'm fine now though, slept for about 18 hours I think, new record!"

Relief washed over Jane and it showed on her face.

"Missed me that much, huh? Don't blame you really, I am pretty great!" Jenny teased.

"Yeah, yeah. I was just nervous for you that you would miss out on your chance to have the good seat. How does it feel?"

Jenny had almost forgotten about the seat, but upon being reminded she fell back into it dramatically and moved her body around, soaking up the comfort.

"Oh it's even better than I thought!" She cawed and Jane laughed.

"They're exactly the same!"

"They're not, this one is more comfortable with the mere principle that it's not mine! Oh hang on!" Jenny reached over and slapped Jane's shoulder.

"Ouch!"

"Fly!" Jenny shrugged her shoulders.

"They are very attracted to me at the moment, must be because I'm so sexy."

"I heard that flies are attracted to bad smells."

Jane hit Jenny back playfully. "I smell fine thank you, especially compared to the rest of the people here."

"Yeah you're not wrong there. I can't believe they don't have a daily shower requirement. Oh!" Jenny slapped Jane on her right arm this time. "Must have missed it the first time!"

"You know, I'd rather you just left them, you hit too hard!"

"Sorry, when I see a bug I just have to kill it, I can't stand to see them crawling over people, it really creeps me out. I'll try to rein it in in the future though!"

"Thanks." Jane smiled.

*

The months continued to drift by, every couple of weeks another patient would take their life and a new one would arrive in their place. Every three or four nights, the giggling would find Jane in her cell and torment her. Jenny remained the only anchor in Jane's life.

For the first time since Jenny had been at the hospital, she beat Jane to the common room and decided to sit down in Jane's seat, victorious. The lady who had shouted at her on her very first time in the common room was in the middle of a rant, screaming at anyone and anything within the near vicinity that she could see a man in the corner who she knew wanted to kill her. Jenny and Jane had taken to calling her Lady Shout purely because they didn't believe she had the ability to talk in a voice other than a deafening roar.

"HE'S JUST STANDING THERE WITH HIS HAND IN HIS COAT! HE'S GOT A GUN! SOMEONE PLEASE TACKLE HIM HE'S GOT A FUCKING GUN! SOMEONE PLEASE TAKE HIM OUT, PLEASE GOD HELP ME HE'S GOING TO KILL *US ALL!*"

It was the first time Jenny had heard Lady Shout show any concern for other peoples safety. Normally she just claimed that whoever she saw was just trying to kill her, everyone else was going to be fine. Jenny followed Lady Shout's eyes to where the man was supposedly meant to be and saw nothing but an empty space by the wall. No one was in any danger from a gunman in here.

Jane walked in on the dot of eleven and was taken aback when she saw Jenny sat smugly in her chair.

"How on earth did you get here before me?"

"I bribed the nurse with sex." Jenny said with a deadpan expression on her face.

"Who would want to have sex with you?"

"Apparently everyone in here." Jenny said and whipped her hair to the side as if she was starring in a shampoo commercial. "That, and I think the nurse who came to get me had a broken watch."

"Ah, now that would explain it!"

Jenny brushed the comment aside and told her about the revelation of Lady Shout and how she had become more empathetic towards other people.

"I just think that she's gotten clever. She realises that no one pays any attention to her and may have put it down to the fact that she never involves anyone else in her shouting, apart from asking them to save her. Maybe by claiming others are in danger they will be more inclined to offer her some help."

"Well I am certainly no more inclined to help her!"

"No, I don't think anyone – OUCH!" Jenny had slapped Jane on the thigh.

"Shit! Sorry! It was the biggest fly I've ever seen, I just couldn't help it!"

Jane rubbed her thigh, which was throbbing. "You know, I think you just like hitting me, I couldn't even hear a fly!"

"They don't always make noise, I found out they can turn their buzz on and off so when they are hunting they turn it off so they make no sound and can sneak up on their prey!"

"Where on earth did you hear that? From a three-year-old?"

"No, it was on some sort of documentary I saw one time I think."

"Sounds like a load of crap if you ask me."

"Well I didn't ask you!"

They continued to sit in silence for the next ten minutes or so, watching the other people sit and shout and scream around them, and listening to the clock that kept ticking along as it always did.

"Shit, Jane do not move a muscle."

"What? What is it?"

"Just don't move. The fly is on your face."

"What?! I can't feel it, where is it?"

"It's on your forehead just above your right eyebrow. Don't move!"

"No, it's okay I can get it." Jane began to lift her hand up towards the bug.

"NO!! Jane don't move."

Jane froze; the shrill with which Jenny had shouted the word 'no' had scared her.

Jenny lifted herself up off the chair slowly and positioned herself in front of Jane.

"Careful." Jane whispered, trying not to move her head too much.

"Don't worry." Jenny said, her face a picture of complete concentration as she continued to fix her eyes on the bug just above Jane's right eyebrow. She lifted her right hand and took aim, before ripping it through the air and into Jane's forehead. It hit her which such a force that there was a loud crack and Jane was pushed back into her chair.

"Bloody hell Jenny!" Jane cried out as she rubbed her head, but Jenny wasn't listening to her, her eyes were now fixed firmly on the bug on Jane's cheek. Jenny whipped her hand back and slapped her in the face.

"Shit! Jenny stop!"

But the bug was still there, it must have gotten in between her fingers as she'd hit Jane in the face. Jenny pulled her hand back and hit Jane again. The other patients had begun to shout and coo and caw at the scene that was unfolding, a nurse on the other side of the room began running towards them calling for help.

The bug was still on Jane's face, and this time Jenny didn't try to slap it dead, instead she reached towards Jane's face with her hand in a claw like pose, and she began scratching at Jane's face. Jenny's nails dug deep into her skin, blood trickled down her face as Jenny continued to scratch desperately. Jane screamed out in agony and begged Jenny to stop, but the bug was still there, and it was still alive. Jane squired underneath Jenny, but Jenny was too heavy for Jane, who had become extremely weak during her time in the hospital. Jenny continued to claw, the pain was unbearable.

Then Jenny wasn't on top of Jane anymore. She was rugby tackled to the ground by the nurse. Through the doors, Nurse Angry burst in wielding a large needle filled with tranquiliser. Never had Jane been happy to see her before. She rushed over to the spot where Jenny and the nurse were struggling on the floor, the nurse on top trying to get a hold of Jenny's arms to pin them back behind her whilst Jenny thrashed beneath her, trying to break free so that she could save Jane from the bug on her face.

Nurse Angry put a knee down on Jenny's right arm to stop its movement and then thrust the needle into her body, squirting the clear liquid into her arm. Jenny continued to thrash beneath the two nurses as a third and fourth ran into the room, one carrying pills and the other more tranquilisers. Jenny's thrashing became slower and slower as the drugs took effect and eventually she found that she was no longer able to struggle before finally being knocked out cold.

Chapter Sixteen

Friendless

Jane didn't see Jenny again after that. Jane was taken straight to the hospital where she was treated mainly for shock; she couldn't believe what had happened. They had been best friends, they spoke every day and laughed and joked like they weren't in a mental hospital for years. But the problem was, they had been in a mental hospital.

When Jane had asked her doctors why Jenny had attacked her like that, they told her that she suffered from severe hallucinations. She had been brought into the hospital after she had killed one of her brothers with a carving knife. She had slit his throat after beating him heavily with her hands, which had been bloodied and bruised, when she had been found next to the body that evening by her other brother who had come for dinner. She had claimed that there were bugs all over her brother and she had just been trying to kill them all to get them off him. She had just been trying to save her brother from the bugs.

Her episodes were infrequent and generally only lasted a few seconds, as with the cases where she had hit Jane before and then not done it again, the bugs having disappeared off her. The nurses she had spoken to had asked her how close she had been with Jenny at the time of the attack, and Jane had conceded that she was her best friend. The nurses nodded and said that the closer that Jenny seemed to get to people, the worse the hallucinations surrounding them seemed to become for her, until they became overwhelming.

Despite the attack that Jane had suffered at Jenny's hands, she wasn't mad or angry with her, she was just sad. She knew straight away that it would be unlikely that she would ever see Jenny again, and she wasn't sure how she was going to cope without her. Speaking with her every day had made her feel almost sane. Jenny was the only person Jane spoke more than two words to in the place. Everyone else in the hospital seemed to be on a different sanity level to them, or at least they had until the attack.

Jane spent three days in the hospital ward in silence following the initial conversation with the nurses in regards to the attack that she had suffered. Her mind began to drift back towards her family, something that she had become very good at avoiding since she had met first Jenny and answered her early questions about them. She realised that without her friend, without her rock, she would begin to torment herself again. She would be drawn back into her dark past and be forced to relive her horrific night over and over until it became all she knew, and it petrified her.

*

When Jane returned to her room in the mental hospital, she found it darker and even more uninviting than it had previously been. In fact, walking through the mental hospital it had all seemed darker and gloomier, she thought that they may have decided to turn the lights on later than usual as the days were getting longer, but more likely she realised that the darkness was coming from within her.

*

Tick-tick-tick.

"JAKA, JAKA, JAKA, BLOW."

Tick-tick-tick.

"Come on Rosie, squirm with all your might."

Tick-tick-tick.

"HELP US! HELP US ALL! HE'S THERE! OVER BY THE WALL! SOMEONE COME AND SAVE US! NURSE! NURSE! SAVE US ALL!"

Tick-tick-tick.

"Dear old Rosie didn't mean to give you fright."

Tick-tick-tick.

"Ding-a-ling the bells, ding-a-ling the bells, ding-a-ling-a ding-a-ling-a BOOOOO!"

Tick-tick-tick.

"Drip, drip, Rosie what's that on the floor?"

Tick-tick-tick.

"They're all plotting against us, against us all. I watch them buzzing around like busy little bees, going from one to the next giving their little message of death. They think we don't know what's going on around here, but I do. I know what is happening."

Tick-tick-tick.

"Drip, drip, Rosie why were you a whore?"
Tick-tick-tick.
"HAHAHAHAHAHAHAHAHAHAH."
Tock.

*

Months turned into years, and the memory of Jenny began to fade. She became just a distant dream in Jane's life. No one sat next to Jane in the common room; no new faces walked through the doors and were scared over to her by Lady Shout.

Jane was plagued by nightmares and no longer slept for more than a few hours each night, spending the rest of the time sitting up and staring at the door, waiting for the time to pass until morning was signalled by the arrival of a breakfast that she would only pick at.

Jane was extremely skinny and ghostly white. She spent each waking hour now in mourning for her family. She was no longer strong enough to block out thoughts of them. Her grief and despair was deep and dark. Every time she closed her eyes she was greeted with her family's battered bodies, with their eyes wide open and pleading for mercy. But Jane couldn't help them, she tried and tried but she couldn't help them.

"I didn't mean to." She would mutter over and over to herself. "I didn't mean to. I didn't mean to. I didn't mean to."

*

Tick-tick-tick.

"Do I smell weird to you? I think I can smell blood on me. Oh god, I think it's happened again! I'm sorry mummy I didn't mean to be a naughty girl. I smell of blood mummy, help me wash it off. Please mummy, get up I need you to help me wash it off."

Tick-tick-tick.

"Sad old Rosie lying on the ground."

Tick-tick-tick.

"Mummy? Mummy? Wake up mummy I smell of blood. Please mummy get up I need you to help me wash it all off."

Tick-tick-tick.

"All because of the messages I found."

Tick-tick-tick.

"Please help me, I can't see anything. Someone has taken my eyes out. Please help me find my eyes. They've gotten away again and I can't see anything. Please someone."

Tick-tick-tick.

"Drip, drip, Rosie what's that on the floor?"

Tick-tick-tick.

"HAHAHAHAHAHAHAHAHAHAHA HA!"

Tick-tick-tick.

"Drip, drip, Rosie why were you a whore?"

Tick-tick-tick.

"I didn't mean to. I didn't mean to. I didn't mean to."

Tock.

*

"I need you to take this pill for me, Jane."

Jane sat in her bedroom staring straight ahead, ignoring Nurse Angry who was stood holding out a pill towards Jane.

"It's going to help you with your nightmares, I promise you."

Jane pursed her mouth shut and shook her head.

"Jane, come on look at me Jane. I'm trying to help you get some sleep. Don't you want that? Don't you want a good night's sleep again?"

Jane didn't respond, she just kept her mouth tightly closed shut.

"Jane, you know you have to take this pill one way or another, why don't we do this the easy way for once? It'll make you feel so much better I promise you. I'm just trying to help you."

Nurse Angry gave Jane a few seconds to respond, knowing that she wouldn't, before getting closer to Jane and forcing her mouth open and pushing the pill to the back of her throat like she had done on hundreds of occasions now. Jane tried to cough it back up, but Nurse Angry clamped her mouth shut and just waited. The pill took 2 minutes to dissolve if it wasn't swallowed straight away, so there was no escape for Jane. One way or another the pill was going into her system in the next 120 seconds.

Jane chose not to swallow as she always did, and felt as the pill turned to foam on her tongue.

Nurse Nancy left a couple of minutes later, just as the effects of the pill began to take their hold on Jane's body and she drifted off to sleep.

*

Jane found that the pills didn't help with her nightmares; they just made it impossible for her to wake up from them. Now she got seven hours of sleep a night thanks to the pills, but six of those hours were filled with the most horrific dreams involving her and her family. Of Jane killing her family. Of Jane being attacked by her family. Of Jane and her family being attacked by the green eyed creature. They were endless. Each night felt like a year, and Jane thought that she would suffer in the hell of her mind for eternity.

Thankfully, that was never the case. And as the year of the night eventually passed, she would wake up in her room and wait for breakfast to arrive.

*

That day, as Jane was walked to the common room for the hour of social interaction, she saw a stretcher with a white sheet over it being pushed through the doors at the end of the corridor ahead of her.

As Jane assumed her usual seat in the armchair overlooking the whole room, she looked around to try and discover whom it was that would never be returning. The entire usual crowd appeared to be in the room. An old lady sat on a rocking chair and mumbled a poem about some girl called Rosie; she was currently reciting something that made it sound as if she had a penis which Jane thought was rather odd. Jane had assumed Rosie was her daughter and the poem was from the perspective of her boyfriend or husband or father. She didn't know and didn't want to ask. There was a woman in her fifties with thinning grey hair flecked with black that believed she was a child who had lost her mummy. From what Jane had picked up she had determined that the lady had killed her mother when she was a young child and had probably been locked up in here ever since. There were nine others in the room who were much less vocal and were more like Jane. They would come in, sit in their regular seat, and then just sit in silence. One would sit and constantly scratch her arm with her thumb Jane had gotten a closer look at where she scratched on one occasion and had seen it was blistered and red with clear puss shining on the surface.

It struck Jane that it was a lot quieter than it usually was in the room, and it dawned on her as to why. Lady Shout wasn't in her usual spot begging for someone to help her, to stop the people that only she saw from killing them all. Jane felt a twang of sadness that she was surprised at feeling. Lady Shout had been with her in this room every single day since she had been in the asylum. She had gotten used to her screeching, frightened voice and it had become almost a comfort to her, a part of her daily routine.

She sat for the rest of the hour close to tears with only the ticking of the clock finding its way into her ears. Just before the hour was up, the image of her family burst into her mind and she whispered to no one in particular six words.

"I didn't mean to do it."

Chapter Seventeen

Teddy

Jane stared dumbfounded at the man in front of her.

"You are winding me up, aren't you? This is some sort of sick joke that you are playing on me to try and make my life even harder than it already is!"

The man in front of her sat with his arms folded in his lap. "This is no joke Jane; you are free to go. The police found a murder weapon with prints of a known killer on it. They matched the blood on the weapon to both your children and your husband. You have been framed Jane, and I could not be sorrier for what you have had to suffer through. The Prime Minister himself has written you a letter expressing his deepest regret for the manner in which you have been treated and the traumas that you have had to face in the years that you have been locked away in the asylum. He has also pledged to provide you with an enormous compensation. You will never want for anything again, Jane."

*

Jane had just finished vacuuming her house from top to bottom when she realised how late it was. She must have been vacuuming for close to three hours! Oh how the time did fly when one was having fun. She checked the floor in the last room she had done, the spare bedroom, which was small and made to feel cramped by a queen-sized bed that was positioned under the window. There was very little free carpet space, but the area where there was looked spotless to Jane's eye and she was satisfied that it was a job well done.

She reattached the nozzle to the hoover, which she had taken out in order to do the skirting boards, unplugged the hoover from the wall, and then pressed the automatic recoil button and watched the cord as it zoomed back into place with a whooshing noise.

Jane picked up the hoover by its handle and carried it back downstairs, through her kitchen and into her little lean-to. She tried the door but found that she must have locked it without realising, fetched the key, and then let herself out into the garden. She opened the shed door, which had a lock on it but the door itself was broken and was thus always open, the lock was just there to act as a deterrent, and put the hoover inside.

When she went back into the house, the air had changed. It felt almost sinister. Jane thought this a little odd, her vacuuming hadn't been that bad after all, heck she'd just checked herself and the spare bedroom at least was spotless! She got a cup out of the cupboard and poured herself a glass of milk, before gulping it down quickly. She poured a little water into the bottom of the cup so that it would be easier to clean in the morning and then put it on the side, before heading upstairs to get ready for bed.

As she was brushing her teeth there was a loud crashing noise downstairs. She jumped and immediately stopped brushing, spat into the sink, decided not to run the tap in case it was an intruder, not wanting to give her position away, and quickly wiped her face on the towel that was hanging on the radiator. Jane carefully slipped out of the bathroom and tiptoed her way into her bedroom. She knelt down by the bed and felt around for the cricket bat she kept underneath it. She grabbed the handle and pulled it out, then gripped the bat with both hands and moved out into the landing.

Jane peered her head out over the bannister to see if she could see anyone moving below, but couldn't see or hear anything.

She followed the bannister to the stairs, being careful to avoid any patches she knew would creek beneath her feet, and then started going down them gently.

She thought the noise had come from the kitchen, and then realised she had probably forgotten to lock the lean-to door when she had come back in after putting the hoover away.

The door to the living room was directly on the left at the bottom of the stairs, and Jane had decided on her way down that she would check in there first, just so that she couldn't be snuck up on unawares. She took a deep breath, steadied herself, and then burst into the room wielding the cricket bat, looking this way and that to make sure that no one was in there.

The room was empty, and Jane felt a little relieved. But she hadn't really expected anyone to be in there, one glance into it would have revealed to an intruder that there was nothing worth taking. It was a bare room occupied by a small, old TV, a couch and a couple of chairs, and a bookshelf with nothing of any great note on it. Jane wasn't a collector and so none of her books were worth more than a few pounds at best.

Jane had managed to run three quarters of the way into the room when she entered, pumped with adrenaline, and now turned ready to walk out and inspect the rest of the downstairs. She decided the best bet was to check out her little snug and conservatory first, again as a prevention to anyone sneaking up behind her, before finishing in the kitchen which was attached to the only place the intruders would be able to exit, as the front door was bolt locked and Jane always had that key on her or in her room.

The door to the snug and conservatory was directly opposite the living room door, and so Jane would be able to quickly jump across the hallway and into the snug without being out in the open for very long.

Again, Jane steadied herself and took a deep breath. The adrenaline was pumping hard again and was making her head ring. She could almost feel her brain pulsing on her skull, trying desperately to break free from her body.

Jane peaked her head around the living room door and saw that the door to the snug was wide open. She took a little run up and then leapt across the entrance hall, surprised at how far she was able to jump as she landed deep inside the snug. She lifted the cricket bat again and looked around wildly, making sure first that the snug was empty, before moving into the conservatory, which was also clear. She let a big sigh of relief go. Only the kitchen left to check now. She hadn't actually heard any noises since coming down with her cricket bat in hand, and guessed that whoever had broken in had run off when they had made the loud crashing noise, spooked that they may have been heard. Jane hoped that was the case as she turned and walked toward the snug door.

For the third time in a matter of minutes, Jane had to pluck up the courage to be brave and enter a room that she had no idea who was in. It was odd that the rooms in her house, which had always been so familiar, felt so alien to her tonight. That is what fear does to people, she thought.

Jane lifted the bat up again and slid out into the hallway, making sure to strain her ears in every direction in order to be able to hear any noise that was made in her house that night. The kitchen door was also open, and she put her back to the wall, bat drawn up across her body ready to be swung at a moment's notice. Jane turned the corner into the kitchen and surveyed the room quickly, trying to spot an intruder, the bat shaking in her hand as she anticipated having to bring it round in a large arc to take out anyone who tried to come at her. After what could only have been a couple of seconds, she lowered the bat. She was alone in the house. As she moved further into the kitchen, she saw what had made the crashing sound. On the floor under the sink was a shattered glass in a pool of very lightly coloured, milky water.

Jane felt relief wash through her body and the adrenaline drained out of her. She must have put the glass too near the edge of the sideboard, and the vibrations from her walking around upstairs must have knocked it off, or maybe she had slammed the door to the bathroom and the vibration through the house had caused the glass to shuffle towards the edge.

Though, despite Jane attempting to find some sort of logical justification to the glass falling on it's own, she couldn't help but feel uneasy. She was pretty sure she had put the glass very far from the edge; it wasn't like there was anything else on the sideboard waiting to be washed up in the morning. Why wouldn't she have put it as far away as possible from the edge to make sure it wouldn't have fallen off? She had never put it near the edge before.

Jane, still feeling unsure, went to check the door that separated the lean-to from outside, and found that she had remembered to lock it. She must have just left the glass close to the edge without realising. She was feeling very tired after all of her hovering, after all.

She climbed back upstairs, deciding to wait until morning to clear up the mess in the kitchen. She had sweated quite heavily as she scouted her house out and went back into the bathroom to wash her face. She locked the door behind her, as she also needed to spend a penny. After flushing the toilet, she washed her hands with soap and then splashed cold water all over her face. She then ran the tap over her wrists, a trick her dad had told her about for cooling her body down quicker. She was thankful for the tip now, as she immediately felt a lot cooler and also more relaxed. The stress of fearing an intruder's entry was leaving her, and that coupled with the loss of adrenaline made her exhausted.

As she unlocked the bathroom door by sliding the bolt lock to the left, she could hear an alarm going off on the other side of it. A faint, *duh-duh-duh-duh duh-duh-duh-duh,* classic alarm sound. She must have accidently set hers for the wrong time. As she opened the door in towards her, the alarm became deafening and was all around her head. It felt like it was penetrating her from inside her head.

DUH-DUH-DUH-DUH

It chimed all around her, and there was a great whoosh of air, so forceful that it pushed her back into the bathroom. Her back collided with the doors to the shower and she was being lifted into the air by some invisible force.

DUH-DUH-DUH-DUH

The alarm cried all around her. Jane screamed and writhed as she tried to fight against the air. She was shaking her head from side to side, trying to get the sound of the alarm out of her system and away from her body. But it was screaming at her.

DUH-DUH-DUH-DUH

Jane began to scream in time with the alarm, it became a part of her body. Still she continued to struggle against the wind. Her back was in a lot of pain now, she had been forced onto the handle of the shower door, which was no more than a rusted metal rod sticking out and jagging into her back.

DUH-DUH-DUH-DUH
DUH-DUH-DUH-DUH
DUH-DUH
DUH-
DUH

Jane screamed furiously, frantically. She struggled and struggled against the wind, but was so exhausted. The alarm was surrounding her body, engulfing her

DUH-DUH-DUH-DUH

Jane screamed and fainted.

*

Birds chirped in the trees at the bottom of Jane's garden as she sat in her conservatory with the doors open looking out with an open book in her lap. She had been sat in there for as long as she could remember, and felt the breeze of the wind on her face and listened to the trees rustle under its pressure. She stretched back out onto her conservatory couch and burrowed herself into its pillows in a state of total bliss and closed her eyes.

She opened them again as she felt the sun burning her face, she must have fallen asleep as it had moved a long way across the sky. She blinked the fairies in her vision away and was surprised to see that the trees at the bottom of her garden had vanished and had instead been replaced with a very large field that looked as though it had been recently ploughed, with very short thin stumps that Jane assumed must have been the base of some sort of crop not long ago.

Jane got up from her chair and walked out through her garden to inspect the new field that was now attached to it. She stepped over the low mesh metal fence that separated the field and her garden from one another and walked out towards the middle of the field. It really was very vast and it took her a great deal of time to get anywhere near the centre. She turned around to find that her house was just a small speck in the distance. Jane did a three-hundred-and-sixty-degree turn to see what else joined onto the field. She couldn't see anything else in all the other directions except more fields, and decided to head back.

As she moved closer, she stepped onto one of the crop bases and found that it made a very satisfying crunching noise under her foot. She decided to see if she could get all the way back to her house stepping only on the crop bases and making as much noise as she could with only her feet. After a couple of minutes, she found that she was very tired from the effort of crunching down the bases and decided to walk normally. She looked up toward the house and saw that it was still a little way off.

There was something climbing over the fence and into the field from her house. It was very small and she wouldn't have spotted it she had been much further away, but it was unmistakeable. Something small was scaling the fence. Jane thought it was probably a bird, though the outline of the shape that she could see didn't look very bird-like

Whatever it was, it eventually reached the top of the fence and launched itself off it, landing just short of where the crop bases began. Jane squinted her eyes at it, and still couldn't make out exactly what it was. Its head was only a couple of inches above the crop bases and started bobbing up and down as it moved towards her. Jane continued to walk towards it, curious about what it could be. As she got closer she began to make out some of the details. It was a light golden colour that almost glowed in the light of the sun, with two semi-circular ears that were the same colour as the rest of it jutting out of its head. The closer Jane got, the more familiar the creature looked to her, until she realised that it looked exactly like the old vintage teddy bear that used to sit in the middle of her mum and dads bed when she had been a young child. She could now clearly see the very dark brown eyes and black nose with an upturned mouth, that made it look almost sad, bobbing up and down, moving in and out of sight behind the larger crop bases, before becoming very visible again as it moved behind shorter ones.

The teddy was moving directly towards Jane, who was smiling happily at it. When the teddy was right in front of Jane, she bent down to pick it up and give it a cuddle, but as she did so the teddy's eyes changed colour. Jane scrambled backwards and fell onto her bum. Its eyes had gone bright green in colour, and its upturned mouth had begun to twist into a devilish smile.

Jane pushed herself off the floor, half turning as she did so. Once she was on her feet she began to run across the field. This time not caring where her feet were landing, not hearing the crunch they made as she stepped on crop bases. She sprinted as fast as she could away from the teddy until her feet would no longer carry her, and she was left bent over with her hands resting on her knees, panting hard, trying to suppress the vomit that had built up from too much anaerobic exercise. She turned around to see if she had managed to outrun the teddy, and believed she had when she didn't immediately spot it. But then its head bobbed up from behind a crop base. Up and down and up and down, unrelenting. Jane was completely exhausted, but there was no way that she could stand to be close to those big, bright green eyes again. She turned and tried to run again, this time only managing to run for about a hundred metres or so before her legs completely gave up on her and she dropped to her knees and vomited on the ground.

She was struggling to breathe and the heat of the sun was weighing heavy on her back. She managed to pull herself onto her feet and looked behind her. The teddy was only about a hundred metres away now. Jane couldn't outrun it. She looked around to try and find some sort of weapon that she could use to whack the bears head right off, but there was nothing around her except the crop bases. Thinking that it was better to have something rather than nothing, she pulled one of the bases out of the ground, roots and all, and turned to face the teddy that was closing the gap quickly.

She pulled the base back behind her head and got ready to swing it. Once the teddy got to within reaching distance, she began her swing and connected hard. The teddy flew into the air and was carried a few metres away by the momentum of the swing. Jane followed the teddy's flight with her eyes and chased after it. She stomped her foot down on top of the bear, chucked the crop base aside, and bent down. She grabbed each ear in separate hands and pulled as hard as she could. The head came straight off, much more easily than Jane had anticipated it would, and she fell back, letting go of the bears left ear with her right hand before using it to steady her fall. With her balance regained, Jane lifted up the teddy's head to inspect it. The green eyes had been replaced with the black ones she remembered the bear having when it sat on her parents bed, there was yellowish stuffing hanging out of it's neck and it was blowing slightly in the breeze.

She went over to the body, which lay motionless, as a teddy's should, and kicked it away. She had always hated the teddy that had guarded her parent's bed, and it felt good to finally be able to destroy it.

Jane dug a small hole in the ground that she intended to use as a grave, and then dropped the head into it. The lifeless black eyes looked up at Jane pleadingly, as if being buried was the last thing that this teddy wanted. Then they turned bright green again.

*

Jane stood in the middle of her bedroom in the pitch black. She wasn't entirely sure how she had gotten to be in her bedroom or why she was stood in the dark. Or how long she had been stood there, for that matter. She was just stood, staring at her wall. She tried to move but found that her legs wouldn't carry her. Jane looked down at her feet to try and see what the problem was, but found that she couldn't bend her head down far enough, she could only move it to the extent that she could see the bottom of the wall. She couldn't get it to move any further; she couldn't even see the floor that she was stood on.

Fear bubbled beneath her skin. She was stuck here. She couldn't move. She could never escape. She stared at the wall, and noticed that there was something on it. Something was drawn on the wall. She strained her eyes trying to make out what it was in the dark. It didn't appear to be writing of any sort; in fact it looked more like the outline of some sort of blurred object. She strained her eyes even further but to no avail.

She quickly jolted her head down, trying to catch out the spell that was holding her in place, but it was too clever for her, again she could only see to the bottom of the wall in front of her.

Jane tried to cry out in frustration but found that she couldn't feel her mouth, let alone open it to let anything out. She shook her head violently from side to side, trying to break free. She couldn't escape, not ever.

She realised that she could only turn her head far enough so that she could see the end of the sides of the wall. She tried to look down again whilst looking at the far right side of the wall, but found that she couldn't even go as far as the bottom right corner. Instead, Jane changed tack and looked up towards the top right corner. Again her neck wouldn't allow her to see this far up. Jane tried to scream again but had no voice.

She wanted to cry, but her face was numb. It was like she had just had her wisdom tooth removed again, except this time the doctor had numbed her entire face and not just her jaw.

Suddenly, she could feel her mouth again, she felt her bottom lip droop with the numbness and knew that drool was spilling out all over the floor around her, but she still couldn't look down to see her feet, which were now covered in her saliva. She could feel the drool almost pumping out of her body, more liquid than she could believe her slight frame could hold.

Her legs were soaked, drool was still teaming out of her mouth and she looked towards the bottom of the wall directly in front of her. She couldn't see it, but this time it wasn't because her neck wouldn't let her; it was because the floor was covered in a slightly foamy, watery liquid.

Her drool.

Her drool was taking up the whole floor, and it continued to pour out of her. Jane's eyes widened with shock, the water level was rising faster and faster. It was at her shin, then her knee and up towards her waist. Now up and over her belly. Over her boobs. Towards her neck.

It was no longer pouring out of her mouth but into her mouth. Jane, who was still rooted to the spot, was being drowned by her own drool. It filled her up and still the level was rising, she tried to close her eyes but found that she couldn't do that either.

It rose and rose, and then her eyes stung as the level reached her bottom eyelid and the liquid found its way in, stinging sharply.

Jane gurgled through the water in pain as the drool washed into her eyes freely, and was then up and over them. She couldn't breathe; she was drowning in her own drool.

The last thing Jane saw was an object drifting through the liquid toward her. It looked like a teddy bear. There was no escape.

*

The old clock chimed somewhere deep below Jane, who was sprawled out on the guest bed in her parents' house. It was a small room that had just enough space for a single bed and a chest of drawers, that were currently holding 3 days worth of clothes that Jane had brought with her to the house.

The clock chimed three times to signify that it was 3am, and Jane still hadn't fallen asleep. She just lay looking up at the ceiling, thinking about nothing at all in particular.

She heard a creak in the corridor outside her bedroom door. She had always gone on to her parents about how she believed that the house was haunted, and that she always heard noises in the middle of the night. Footsteps and creaking floors, and once or twice she could have sworn she had heard an old man grunt, followed by quick footsteps and a lot of creaking. Her parents had always brushed her aside and explained that very old houses did often make noises of their own accord, simply because they were so very old. It was just the house settling down for the night, its creaking boards tossing and turning to find a comfortable resting spot.

Jane turned over to face the wall and tried to close her eyes, but she was so wide awake that she couldn't keep them closed for more than a fraction of a second before they shot open of their own accord. She heard another creak outside her door, this time the sound came from further away as if the boards near her door had found their comfortable spot, and the ones further away had gotten jealous and were now trying to find their own perfect spot for the night.

Jane was just beginning to drift off when she heard something very soft brush against the door. It was so soft that at first she thought it must have just been a part of a very light dream she had fallen into. Then she heard it again. The faintest, gentlest of brushes, as if someone had spotted a little too much dust and was trying to remove it with a feather on the other side. Jane rolled over back the other way so that she was facing the door, and listened out. It was possible that she had made the same mistake twice and that her brain was just playing tricks on her, it wouldn't be the first time. After a few minutes of staring at the door, trying not to move or make too loud a noise breathing so that she could hear exactly whether or not anything was touching her door, she was satisfied that there was nothing out there. She turned back over to face the wall, which was her favourite position for getting to sleep, lying on her left hand side, and closed her eyes again to the world.

BANG-BANG-BANG

If the brushings against the door had been quiet, this noise was the complete opposite. Jane's eyes had bolted open and her head had whipped towards her door.

"Who is it?" She called out.

There was no response.

She lay there for half a second and then began to second-guess herself. Had there really been a loud banging noise or was it all just in her head? It might have been part of a dream that she had instantly forgotten when she woke up to the noise.

BANG-BANG-BANG

NOPE! That was her door. Someone was banging on her door.

"WHO IS IT?" She shouted much louder this time, figuring they hadn't heard her call out the first time. Again there was no answer from the other side.

"Come in! I'm awake!" She tried again, but the door did not open. Her dad must have forgotten to put his hearing aid in. Jane reluctantly pulled herself out of bed and put her naked feet down on the carpet. She went over to the door, twisted the handle, and opened it, expecting to see her dad.

Instead, she saw nothing.

She opened the door wider and glanced into the corridor, but there was no one about. Jane wondered out into the corridor and checked that no one had gone into the bathroom. The light wasn't on and the door to the bathroom was wide open, so there certainly wasn't anyone in there. Jane felt uneasy, though wondered whether her dad had given up and gone back to join her mum without her hearing. They never actually closed their door fully so she wouldn't have heard it shut, though it did seem unlikely that he would have made it back to his room without creaking any of the floorboards. Jane gave up and assumed he must have known every crack on the floor and avoided them, and went back to bed, shutting her door behind her.

She snuggled down under the covers, and pulled a pillow close to her so that she could snuggle it as she slept.

Something tickled her feet.

She immediately pulled them up. This house attracted large spiders and that was the last thing she wanted to have crawling all over her as she slept. She jumped out of bed and ran over to turn the light on, turning her head away from the bed for only a split second to locate the switch.

The light flickered as she turned around to try and find the spider, but instead, sat in the middle of her bed looking back at her were two big green eyes, attached to a small brown body.

The teddy launched itself at Jane, who lifted her hands up and caught it mid air. The teddy squirmed in her grip, and she turned to find her parents. She swung open the door, ran across the corridor and flung open her parents bedroom shouting for help, but her parents weren't in there.

Jane ran down the stairs shouting out for help, hoping that someone, anyone, would hear her calls. When she reached the bottom of the stairs she saw that the living room door was shut, but there was a soft golden light seeping through the crack at the bottom of the door. Jane burst into the living room to see her parents sat on the sofa watching TV.

"Oh hello love." Her dad smiled at her.

"Hello dear!" Her mum echoed cheerfully.

"HELP ME!" Jane screamed at them, thrusting her hands, which were now both gripping the teddy, towards them. "It's your teddy! It's trying to kill me!"

"What on earth are you on about Janey? And what is wrong with your hands, they look all twisted?"

Jane gave her father a perplexed look. "The teddy! With the green eyes! It's trying to kill me"

"What teddy, dear? What are you on about?"

They couldn't see it. Her parents couldn't see the teddy that she was holding.

Jane screamed and ran out of the room and into the kitchen. The teddy had managed to get one of its arms free and was using it to try and leaver its way out of Jane's grip. She let go of its legs with her right hand and pulled open the cutlery drawer, before pulling out the sharpest knife she could see.

She hacked at it, cutting it in half at the waist, the head end still clutched tightly in her left hand. Its eyes still shone bright green. Jane screamed and continued to flash the blade wildly at the teddy's top half. Yellow innards flew all over the kitchen and covered Jane's clothes. She hacked and hacked and hacked until eventually the light in the teddy's eyes began to go dark brown again.

When they were fully brown, she dropped the carcass onto the floor and went back to the drawers, searching frantically until she found what it was she was looking for, a blowtorch that her mum had bought a few years back so that she could crisp the top of her crème brûlée's.

Jane turned the safety switch off and held down the button. There was a brief clicking noise, and then the top of the blowtorch ignited with a blue flame. She bent over and put the flame into the teddy's carcass. The yellow innards caught immediately, and the flame engulfed the teddy in a matter of seconds.

Jane stood over it triumphantly, but then the flame caught the tablecloth that had been overhanging the kitchen table. The table was soon covered in hot yellow flames, which then began to spread to the chairs surrounding the table. Jane screamed as the flames grew around her until she was surrounded with no escape.

Everything was on fire, even the floor and the ceiling above her. It was coming in closer and closer, soon she would catch, her clothes would be first, and then it would burn the whole house down with her parents too. The flames licked at her feet, white hot, and then Jane was flying through the air. Away. Far, far away. She was up above the clouds. She could see her house on fire below her but it was no longer of any concern to her. She was flying. She was a bird. She was free, floating and soaring away in the clouds without a care in the word.

Then her wings began to fail her, and she was falling. Tumbling down towards the earth with no parachute and nothing to slow her down. The earth grew bigger and bigger beneath her, she saw cars and people hustling and bustling about below her. She would join them soon; she would escape from the fire and the teddy. She would be free at last, and she wasn't scared, she wasn't frightened of the impact. It wouldn't kill her; it would save her. Jane smashed headfirst into the pavement.

*

Jane was wandering through town, looking to pick up some bits and bobs for her new flat. There was a market in town every third Saturday, and Jane realised this must be one of those Saturdays as she wandered though the high street, greeted by the sounds of fruit and veg salesmen shouting at passers-by about all the great deals they had on that day.

"Buy a pack of strawberries and get a pack of blackberries absolutely free! Absolutely free, ladies and gentleman. £3 for 800 grams of strawberries *and* 400 grams of blackberries! Can't get that value anywhere else! Buy strawberries, get blackberries…"

The fruit seller tailed off as an elderly woman bought a pack of strawberries off him and he handed her some blackberries also. Once the exchange was complete, he continued trying to persuade people to take up his deal.

Jane walked on past the fruit seller in search of some fudge. She could see a sweet stand up ahead that appeared to be selling just what she was after and headed towards it.

The gentleman stood behind the table was serving a bald man who had the same slightly reddened scalp that Anthony would have had on a sunny summers day like this.

As she got closer to the stand, the bald man took the sweets he had just bought off the gentleman, and turned about 90 degrees to the right before walking off in the direction of more stalls. Jane stopped instantaneously, her jaw dropping. It was Anthony.

Jane tried to call out to him, but she had lost her voice in her excitement. She tried again but realised it was helpless; she was too in shock to speak. She snapped herself from her stillness, and started to run towards Anthony.

She pumped her legs, but found that she wasn't moving fast enough, Anthony seemed to be getting farther and farther away. Jane tried to pump her legs even harder but to no avail. If anything, Anthony was getting further away even faster.

Jane was sweating all over, trying desperately to reach her husband. Tears were streaming down her face with the effort she was exerting. She looked down at her feet, dismayed at how slowly they were carrying her forward. As she looked down she saw that she was running on a treadmill, which was fighting against her. She tried to cry out but again found that she didn't have a voice to cry out with. She jumped to the left and landed heavily bending her knees as she touched the ground. She then propelled herself to her feet and ran off in the direction that Anthony had gone.

In the time it had taken her to jump off the treadmill, however, a hoard of people had come out to enjoy the sunshine and see what the stalls had to offer. Jane frantically pushed and weaved her way around and through the faceless crowd. Craning her neck to see where Anthony was going. She had lost sight of him and began to panic that he was lost to her again, before she spotted his shiny, bald, slightly red head about 30 metres up ahead. Seeing him made her all the more determined to reach him, she moved faster, continuing to weave and dodge around all of the people blocking her way, using her hands and elbows as levers to fight through. Anthony was only 15 metres ahead of her now. She couldn't believe it; she was actually going to see him again after all of this time.

Ten metres to go, Jane tried to shout at him again, but again there was no voice, nothing, breaking free from her body. She was breathing extremely hard and sweating profusely, but she barely noticed. All that she could feel in her mind and heart now was a great yearning to be with Anthony again. Her rock. Her love.

Five metres to go, she could almost smell his aftershave in her nostrils. She wanted so desperately to be wrapped up in his arms, surrounded by that musky smell for the rest of her days.

Two metres, she practically jumped towards him, but suddenly there was a wall of people in her way appearing practically out of thin air, three or four deep. She tried to shout at the wall, but again there was no sound coming out of her. She opened her mouth and let out a silent cry, before throwing her hands, bunched into fists into the wall. Hitting the people who were preventing her from seeing her husband as hard as she could, battering them with her fury. People fell all around her, but more and more seemed to take their place. She could see Anthony getting further and further away up ahead. 10 metres, 20…

Jane was desperate, frantic. She scratched and bit and pulled her way forward, trying desperately, so, so desperately to break through the final line. There was just a single row now of people blocking her from her beloved Anthony.

She picked one of the fallen women's bags off the floor and swung it up into the faces of the human wall closest to her, knocking them aside and out of the way. She was so close; behind them was nothing but clear space, all the way up to Anthony. He was approaching a housing estate beyond the market. She knew she had to catch him before he got there. She knew if he got there she wouldn't be able to find him.

With one last humungous effort, Jane swung the bag around, knocking three people over and most importantly creating a way for her to break through the line. She took her opportunity and sprinted through the gap. She didn't look back, her eyes focused on Anthony and where he was heading.

Anthony moved into the housing estate, Jane was closing in fast. He turned to the right, and a couple of seconds later Jane followed him, skidding on the floor as she had been moving so fast and turning to see him.

But Anthony was gone. Jane screamed, sound finally returning to her. She looked around manically and shouted, "ANTHONY, ANTHONY, PLEASE IT'S ME. IT'S JANE. ANTHONY PLEASE!"

She couldn't see him.

She turned her head away in grief, and there he was. Walking away from her ten metres ahead.

Jane sprinted toward him, grabbed his shoulder, and turned him around and embraced him. "Anthony, I can't believe it, it's really you!" She squeezed him as tightly as she could, and then released her grip slightly so that she could kiss him.

As she did so, she recoiled.

It wasn't Anthony. It wasn't anyone. There was no face on his face. It was just a blank oval space. No nose, or mouth, or eyes, or eyebrows.

She fell away from the nothing creature that had been her Anthony.

*

Jane was back in her kitchen, cooking a Sunday roast. She was stood over the stove when behind her she could feel the gaze of the teddy coming at her. She turned and grabbed it, one hand around its neck and holding its arms tight against its body, the other holding its feet together.

The teddy squirmed around in her grip, before going completely still. Jane looked around to try and find something that she could secure it down with, but couldn't spot anything obvious.

The teddy suddenly became motional once more, it's mouth opened wide revealing a set of small sharp teeth. It stretched its jaw as far as it would go and bit down on Jane's hand. Jane let out a terrific scream and threw the teddy at the hobs. It was a gas cooker and so there were naked flames shooting out around the pans of boiling water ready for the veg and gravy. The teddy fell into an unlit hob and got trapped between the metal pan stand that went over the top of the hob, and the hob.

Jane went over to try and set it on fire, but the teddy turned to her with big sad eyes and pleaded with her not to light it up. Jane tried her hardest to ignore the teddy, but it was so little and so cute. The teddy began to try and dance for her. "Look, I promise to be a good teddy, we can dance and play and have the best of times together." The teddy pleaded and pleaded as it tried moving its little limbs. "We could have the best fun."

Jane began to dance with the teddy, music boomed into the kitchen where she was cooking and they danced and danced around. She rescued the teddy from the hob and held it by its arms, swinging the teddy around and around to the music. They were transported into a large ballroom, and were surrounded by hundreds of people, all dressed up. The ladies in long flowing dresses, the men in tuxedos linking arms around them as they swirled and swirled together. It was bright and joyous, and everyone began to laugh and shout.

But then the laughter turned dark, and so did the room. The chandeliers up above that had been sparkling with diamonds and other brightly colour jewels turned dull and grey. Jane stopped spinning and the crowd around her and the teddy moved in. The teddy's eyes turned bright green, and it grinned again, barring its small sharp teeth. It twisted its neck slightly to the right, and blood began to drip off its teeth. She strained her head away from the teddy, and saw that green-eyed creatures, all moving in at her as one, surrounded her. She screamed as the teddy bit her hands. She let it go and fell to the floor. The teddy jumped up onto her belly and walked towards her face, still baring its teeth.

It stopped when it got to the top of her right boob and stood over her, its green eyes penetrating Jane's.

The teddy flared its nose and then sprung at her neck, digging its teeth in and ripping and tearing. Blood spurted everywhere, and the teddy continued to bite and tear and rip. Jane screamed and wailed until she was shaken awake. Her eyes shot open and then immediately closed again as the harsh white light of the room burned them. There was a dark figure standing over her, still shaking her body, not realising that she was yet awake, as Jane didn't realise that she was still screaming. She stopped, and Nurse Angry let go of her.

Chapter Eighteen

Psychiatrist

For the first time in nine years, Jane had an appointment with a psychiatrist, which she assumed was to alleviate the nightmares that she had been having. The pills that the nurses had given her had not worked, and Jane suspected that it was the pills themselves that were causing her dreams to be quite so horrific.

Nothing remained of the woman that she used to be. The mental hospital had taken everything that she was, lifted it up out of her body, and then systematically smashed it to pieces with endless pills. In the first couple of years, patients went to a psychiatrist on the off chance that they might improve. After this period, only pills were left. The fact that they used pills rather than an actual psychiatrist to try and solve what were deeply held problems had astonished Jane when she had first been told she would no longer see the hospital psychiatrist, but she had come to realise that this wasn't a place of healing. This was a place for pushing the problems under the rug. No one wanted to save mentally deranged women who had committed all sorts of heinous crimes. The people that came here could not be saved, they were too far gone.

But, for some reason, on this occasion Nurse Angry had told her the night before that she was to see a man about her dreams, someone who believed they could help and was willing to spend time with Jane to make sure that she got better. Jane assumed it was part of a study he was conducting, and she would be interviewed rather than helped. Maybe he'd film her and she'd be put on a documentary on TV. 'The crazy woman who killed her whole family.' She could see it now airing on prime time television. Millions would tune in to see what sort of monster she was.

Jane was led down a long, bright white corridor, that had a blue streak down the middle that split the floor into two lanes, by Nurse Angry, past the common room where she had spent an hour a day for as long as she could remember. Jane's white, baggy dress billowed around her weak frame as she followed barefooted. She was led into a small room where a man was sat waiting for her. He wore a black suit with a red tie and looked very much like a businessman; nothing like any other psychiatrist that Jane had seen in her life. He smiled brightly at Jane, as if he were reuniting with a long lost family member who he hadn't seen in years and had spent months trying to get in contact with.

"Jane!" He said warmly, "It is so lovely to finally be able to meet with you. You wouldn't believe the strings I had to pull to be able to get in this place. But no matter, no matter, here you are and here we are!"

Jane looked at him with tired, untrusting eyes. His cheerfulness immediately set her on edge.

"Sit down, sit down! Mary, could you grab us a couple of coffees? Would that be okay? I'd love a couple of sugars in mine, no milk. And what will it be for you, Jane?"

Jane shook her head, she couldn't remember how she had her coffee, or even if she liked coffee for that matter. She was also shocked that Nurse Angry could be referred to as Mary. This man must have no idea who the woman really was; she wasn't normal or nice enough to be called Mary.

"Just the two sugared one for me then please, that would be very kind of you, Mary." The stranger beamed at Nurse Angry and she gave a weak smile back, Nurse Angry wasn't used to being around jolly people and it made her uneasy, and she scampered out of the room to fetch a coffee.

The man looked away from Nurse Angry and back to Jane, his smile still stretching almost all the way across his face from one ear to the other.

"Jane, Jane, Jane. Where do we begin?"

Jane continued to just watch him, totally perplexed as to what was happening.

"Introductions!" The man's face became an expression of complete shock. "My word, you must have no idea who I am! And here I am already on a first name basis with you Jane, ever so sorry, ever so sorry! My name is Joshua and I work for an organisation that has become very interested in your case, Jane, very interested indeed."

Jane tensed up at the mention of her case. It had been years since anyone had mentioned it to her. It was obvious now that he wasn't a psychiatrist here to try and help her; he worked for a TV company and wanted to produce a documentary. She had been right.

236

"You see Jane, the reason we are so interested in your case, is because it is almost identical to my case." Joshua said, still smiling cheerfully.

"Yes Jane, well, no let me correct myself, not my case, that would be bonkers, no, my son's case." The smile began to drop from his face.

"You are most probably wondering what I am doing here, and why I pulled so many strings to get a chance to talk to you? The answer is really very simple. I want to help you. I believe you, Jane. I believe that you shouldn't have ever been put in this institution, that you are a victim of something far, far greater than you or I.

"Jane, I know that you are hurting still. I know you will hurt from this day until your last and each day you wake up into a world that your family aren't a part of will eat you up and rip your soul, every single day. I know it. The rawness of the sights you saw fades and numbs, but the pain of your loss will never subside.

"There is nothing you can do to bring your family back, I understand that too and I know how much it will have destroyed you. I know the pain you feel because I feel it too. I feel it every second of every day. I felt it when the authorities failed to come up with a single suspect for the murder of my son. I felt it for every painstaking hour I spent in a holding cell, being asked the same questions over and over again and giving the same answers over and over again. I felt it when two years after his murder, when there were no other new leads or avenues left to pursue, the case was ignored and thrown into filing, never to be opened again. And I still feel it now, more than fifteen years on. The injustice still cuts me open from the inside out, ripping through who I am to my very core. The anger at the authorities, at the police, at the establishment, for not discovering and prosecuting the person who killed my son in cold blood wells up inside me each and every day. I was lost, though in a better state than you are now because I didn't have the misfortune of arriving at the murder scene soon after my boy's death.

"My wife and I separated following it, we couldn't bear to look at each other anymore, it just reminded us too much of our boy who was taken too soon, far too soon from us. She killed herself three weeks after, overdosing in the house on the spot where our son had been found. In my darkest, most desperate hour I too tried to kill myself. I had lost everything and couldn't imagine spending another second on this planet. I couldn't cope with this world anymore. I tied a noose in some rope and tied the rope around the bannister on my stairs. But I hadn't done a good enough job. As I jumped over the bannister, the rope snapped under my weight and I fell to the floor, still very much alive.

"It was fate. I had survived for a reason, there had to be a purpose. Why wouldn't God let me rejoin my son and wife in heaven?

"I had assumed all along that my son's death had been a one off. Some bastard had just walked into the house through the front door, spotted an opportunity, and destroyed him. The scene that greeted me when I climbed those stairs will live with me forever. I will never be able to un-see the mess that my son was in. But what I failed to think of was this: what if this wasn't an isolated incident? What if it had happened before to someone else? Maybe the reason why we hadn't found the murderer was because the murderer had already been caught for another crime.

"So I started searching for murderers that had been jailed. I analysed the way they had killed, the state of their victims when they were found, where they were found. I learned the motivations behind the kills, why they killed in the way they did. I learned about their psychology, what drove them to kill. And do you know what I found? Nothing. Nothing came close to the state that my boy was in. Not even remotely close. The killers I profiled were disgusting. They were cruel, calculating, ruthless animals. But despite this, they weren't cruel enough. They weren't clever enough to conduct a murder and not get caught for it. They weren't ruthless enough. There was always a trail left behind, a join the dot puzzle that eventually a good detective would crack. But I wasn't dealing with that. There was nothing in the house. There were no fingerprints, no hairs, not even any skin flakes. Literally nothing. The forensics came in, swabbed every damn surface in the place and came out with nothing. It was the perfect murder. Nothing rivalled it. Nothing came close. The murderers that had been caught were sheep compared to the lion that killed my son. And that got me thinking, what about other unsolved murders? This surely wasn't the only unsolved murder in the area, perhaps there were more. Perhaps there would be a pattern, and so I began to dig deeper.

"There were no other unresolved murders in the nearby area, which didn't surprise me. Andover was a grotty town, full of horrible people, but it wasn't a murder capital. They were few and far between. My son's was the first murder there in over 30 years, and the other murder in the town had previously been solved. A signed, sealed and delivered case in actual fact, the husband was sat in his armchair, in the living room, still holding the knife coated in blood when the police arrived following a neighbours' noise complaint. That certainly wasn't the type of killer I was looking for.

"I broadened my search to the South of England. That did bring back a lot of results, and I realised I wouldn't be able to sift through the details of every case. I needed to narrow down my results dramatically. So I simply cast out anything that was solved, and anything that lacked gore. And still there were too many, and so I continued to refine and refine and refine. Until there were only two recorded murders left. One was my son's, the other one was from ten years before, and I was worried that it would have been too long ago and couldn't possibly be related to my son's murder.

"There wasn't a photograph of the body that I could find online, but I knew instantly from the description that this was the same. The pool of blood, the slashing's all over the body, on the neck and the legs, a deep one right across the belly. The victim's eyes, wide open and staring almost petrified, as if the killer they had seen last had been truly monstrous. It didn't surprise me in the slightest that the human that had committed such atrocities should be anything other than revolting, most probably physically deformed.

"It was the last little detail of the description that I had thought nothing about at the initial reading; it was almost entered in the description as an afterthought by the coroner. On the right hand, at the tip of the index finger and on the tip of the middle finder were holes that were about half a centimetre in diameter. At first I couldn't see why this was important. I felt like it was deep inside me but couldn't think why. But then I realised that my son had

the exact same markings. It seemed odd that the murderer would bother taking the care to put the holes into the fingers when he had spent no care whatsoever slashing up the rest of the body. I thought that maybe it was like a signature, like the one that an artist might leave on their latest masterpiece. I asked my son's pathologist about what he had thought about the holes, and he had replied that they had perplexed him. They went straight through the bone. He suspected they had been drilled in, perhaps as a form of torture. They were immaculately round and went down to roughly the knuckle in both fingers.

"Naturally, I remained very much unsatisfied. I became curious as the why there had been such a long time between the two murders. If a murderer believed themselves to be an artist, then why was their work so few and far between? I thought that perhaps this artist didn't just produce within England; maybe they had lived elsewhere during the years between the England murders. So I looked at America and murders there. That is when I decided to quit my job and pursue the killer full time. What I found was that during the ten-year period, there had been four unsolved murders with exactly the same criteria, down to the holes in the fingers, as the ones in England. I also found that I wasn't the first person to spot the pattern in the murders There were forums, and I began chatting to others and finding out their thoughts on them.

"There were theories from people from all over the world on these murders. But, the general overriding consensus was that there had been multiple murderers, people who had been inspired by the ways that the killings had been done and had tried to copy them. I found that there were 6 people who had been arrested and charged with very similar murders, and as it turned out, there were hundreds of cases of murders of this type that had been solved all across the world, where people had copied the brutal nature of the original killer right down to his signature. I began to become disheartened and believed that my son had just become very unlucky, caught up in an insane person's fetish for killing like the original.

"I had given up hope on solving my sons murder, and had resumed my work when I was approached by an organisation called Heirdonus, and they told me that they knew who had killed my son."

*

Nurse Angry had returned with the coffee for Joshua, who had thanked her kindly and asked for her to wait outside so that Jane and he could finish their chat in private.

For the first time in as long as Jane could remember, she was being talked to by someone who apparently did not think that she was crazy, and it made her feel uncomfortable. This man knew nothing about her, how could he know she hadn't killed her family when she didn't even know. She believed that she had, but she didn't know.

"It is my understanding that you were lost in the forest in the period before your husband's death, during which time you heard voices in the forest. When you woke up, you said that you saw green eyes off in the distance near the forest that you and your family had entered the clearing through, is this right?"

"How do you know this?" Jane spoke out loud for the first time in she couldn't remember how long and had to stop and clear her throat after attempting the first word. Her voice had become weak and grainy and she thought she sounded like a frail old woman who was lying on her deathbed trying to say her final farewells.

"During my investigation into my son's murder, I spent a lot of time with a number of psychiatrists, one in particular you met just after the murder of your family, Dr. Henrey. For professional reasons he wasn't allowed to tell me the specifics of your case, however he owed me a big favour and left me with his office key one night. He left your file on his desk and in it was exactly what I had been looking for – another unsolved case like my son's. I knew straight away that you hadn't killed your family and I believe the reason you have a large blackout period is down to the creature that murdered your family.

"Now I don't imagine you will believe me for a second, but I implore to you that what I have to say is the truth. The organisation that approached me has been tracking the creature that killed your family for decades. I can also tell you that what killed your family is exactly that - a creature. I imagine this creature will be extremely familiar to you, though all you will know of it are the whisperings passed down from generation to generation. Myth and legend sprawled and twisted through the warp of time. No one knows exactly when the creature came into being, people have only guessed and speculated. It is estimated to be hundreds of years old, and although it takes a human like form, it is far from it. The organisation I belong to believe it crashed to earth up to a thousand years ago, and has walked the planet ever since living mainly off animals and insects. However, once in a blue moon it seeks other food sources. The creature has been known by many names during its time on earth, but the one most familiar to me and I am sure to you will be its most recent, Dracula."

Anne looked at the man incredulously, and found her voice that had been lost for so long in this bleak place.

"You mean to tell me that my son was killed by a vampire? You're telling me an actual vampire exists and walks the earth and slashed my family to pieces, presumably drank their blood, and then morphed into a bat and flew away leaving no trace?" Anger coursed through Jane, an emotion she had forgotten existed within her, surfacing on a day that kept springing new surprises.

"How dare you make fun of me? Either you are madder than I am or this is some cruel joke that you have been allowed to pull because of your so-called 'connections'. What is it, a rich man's stag do? You think you can just come in here and have your fun with a crazy person? Go back to your lads afterwards and hit a bar up and talk and laugh all about it? I killed them. I killed them all. I have to live with that forever. I don't need people to come in and make fun and remind me of what I did!"

Joshua shook his head painfully at her and looked genuinely upset by Jane's outburst at him.

"Do not be fooled by the fiction you have read. This isn't Bram Stoker's Dracula, though his character was loosely based on the creature Heirdonus continues to pursue and fight today. Stoker himself was a member of our organisation. The creature, as far as we are aware does not possess the ability to turn into a bat. It does not speak in a Transylvanian accent like those you may have heard in films. It doesn't have familiars that it controls with its mind. We believe it is a member of an alien species and was separated a long time ago from them whilst on some sort of space mission, crashing down to the earth in a ship that has since disintegrated.

"The creature is nigh on impossible to find, and hunts only at night. It is the eyes that give it away. There are thousands of accounts from farmers who hear their animals crying out in agony during the night and run to their aid, only to arrive to a devastating scene of slaughter. Away in the distance they see these two balls of green light, the same green that you saw in the forest. It is a creature of blood, not of this world. One that survives off animals, but lives off humans.

"I am here to tell you that you are not insane Jane, you were right all along. You did not kill your family, you are innocent and have been framed by the creature as an act of its self-preservation."

Jane found herself believing the man, more out of hope than anything else. The hope that she hadn't killed her family, and that was enough for her. "How do you know all of this?"

"Heirdonus has been fighting this creature for over three hundred years. They have an entire library devoted to it. We work hard every day to try and track it down and stop it and we have made so many breakthroughs in the last few years alone. We want you to help us capture it at last. You possess the skills that we believe will be the final piece in the jigsaw."

"I can't help you. They aren't ever going to let me out of here, I am a crazed murderer to them, and they're certainly not going to let me go because of the word of a man who claims that Dracula exists. They're more likely to lock you up with me."

"Don't worry about that. Heirdonus is extremely powerful, how do you think I was able to get a one-on-one interview with you? We have been watching you for a long time, Jane, and it is time for you to come with us and join the fight."

Part Four

Heirdonus

Chapter Nineteen

Release

Two weeks after her first meeting with Joshua, Jane stepped onto pavement that wasn't surrounded by a high brick fence topped with barbed wire. She had hoped there would be a bright blue sky with not a cloud in sight so that she could feel the warmth of the day on her face, but it felt more real when she looked up and could see only grey cloud across it. Although she had only just left the mental hospital behind, she felt as if she was home already. She was back in England. The hospital had felt foreign, as if she was in a completely different land that was independent of the country that it was located in. It could have been anywhere in the world and it would have been and felt exactly the same on the inside.

But she was free of it now, and already the memory of it began to become hazy in her mind, like a dream you had during the night that as soon as you wake up begins to disappear from your memory.

Joshua stood beside her and watched as Jane took a moment to breathe in the fresh air and listen to the sound of the world for a few moments. The road was lined with trees and Jane had never seen anything so vivid as their bright green leaves, never seen anything as sharply as the patterns the bark made. She listened to the bird's chirp happily to one another about their daily business. One flew down from a tree just off to the left and landed on a patch of grass in front of where Jane and Joshua were standing. It was a robin with a breast that was shining bright red despite the dullness of the clouds in the sky. It shifted its head quickly left and right, up and down and then called out to one of its friends and flew off almost as quickly as it had landed. Joshua cleared his throat, and Jane looked around at him startled and embarrassed. She motioned that she was ready to move on and he put his left arm onto the curve of her back and gestured with his right hand in the direction of where the car was parked.

They slowly made their way towards the car, Jane looking around her with her mouth hung open, appreciating everything she saw as if she was seeing it for the first time. And she thought to herself that she almost was seeing everything again for the first time. She was a new person, completely different to the one that had gone to that campsite with her family all those years ago. Her oaky brown hair was now grey. Her eyes had sunken into her face and were surrounded by two large dark rings. There were deep wrinkles dug into her forehead and protruding from her eyes out towards her ears from excessive frowning and pain. Jane looked as if she was well into her seventies, despite only being 43.

Joshua guided her to a long, black Mercedes. As they approached, a driver got out the car and opened the back door for her. Jane peered inside and was awestruck by the soft cream leather of the seats. She reached out and put a hand onto the material and found that it felt even better than it looked She slid her body into the car and melted back into the seat, relishing the deep smell of the new leather that filled her nostrils.

Joshua walked around to the other side of the car and got in. He told Jane to put her seatbelt on; she was so unused to cars that she had completely forgotten about this detail of travel. The driver put the car into gear and pulled out of the car park, taking Jane away from the place that had tormented her for the last decade of her life.

They drove in silence for about an hour. Jane stared out of the window and watched as the world flashed by outside. The uncountable number of hedges and trees and electricity pylons whizzing past in a great blur. The sun had broken through at one point and had shined golden on the wet road, causing Jane to squint, not wanting to look away, trying to take in everything she possibly could and enjoy every moment of her new life. She felt like she was back in one of her dreams, but for the first time in over ten years the dream she was having was not a nightmare. There was no teddy chasing her, driving in a large truck on the other side of the road waiting for Jane's car to be just in front of it before swerving and killing her. The car wasn't moving through quicksand, unable to ever reach its destination, always falling just too short, just not quite quick enough to escape the pull of the sand. This was a real car; travelling at a real speed in a direction she neither knew of nor cared about. Where the car eventually ended up didn't matter, what mattered was that she was free. She wasn't a killer; she hadn't betrayed her family and couldn't have done anything to save them. What she could do by helping Heirdonus would be to save other families by helping them to capture and destroy the monster that had haunted her life for so long. She would get her closure; she would get her redemption.

*

The car pulled into a great, narrow winding lane that was just about wide enough to squeeze through. On either side were thick bushes that blocked out the light, and despite the day still being relatively young, down the lane felt like it could have been late evening. The lane itself was more pothole than flat road, and the going was uncomfortable for Joshua and the driver. Jane on the other hand didn't mind it; she felt every bump and jolt of the car with joy, each one was an electric shock that was wakening her from her long absence. She was the monster and the road was her Doctor Frankenstein, breathing life back into her, allowing her to feel something physically rather than just mentally again.

After what felt like forever for Joshua and the driver, the road widened and the bushes surrounding it thinned before disappearing altogether and were replaced by a long row of the most beautiful trees than Jane had ever seen. They had thick trunks, which rose five metres into the air, before splitting into three or four smaller trunks that jutted off in their own directions. These smaller trunks then split again and reached out over the road and above the car creating a magnificent natural arch.

Attached to the tree branches was a flurry of light green leaves that were almost yellow. The trees were beginning to bloom with a white flower that became almost translucent in the areas where the sun broke through the now thinning clouds above. It was a scene identical to one out of a fairy tale that Jane had read as a young child, about a prince who galloped up to a castle high in the mountains to rescue a princess from an evil emperor. The castle had only one entrance that had been guarded by two rows of golden-branched trees that had bloomed the moment that the prince had come out of the castle carrying the princess in his arms after defeating the evil emperor. The building at the end of this road wasn't a castle, though it was the closest thing that Jane had seen in an extraordinarily long time.

Three great pillars stretched from the floor to three quarters of the way up the building, where they merged into a top story that was painted bright white. The building itself appeared to have three stories, with a balcony on the second floor that stretched the whole way across the front of the building. In between the three pillars on either side on each floor there were large windows. In between the central two pillars was a huge white door. The outside ground floor was painted a soft pink colour that was close to that of the flesh of a freshly caught salmon.

The driver had slowed the car down to a crawl as if he had felt the awe that Jane was exuding from the back seat. Jane lapped it all up, hungrily filling her eyes with the wondrous site before her, not wanting the drive to ever end.

When it did end and the car pulled up before the house, she found it to be even more monstrous in scale than it had originally appeared. The pillars were almost two metres in diameter each, and towered into the sky. Each floor looked to be around three times the height that Jane's room had been in the asylum.

Joshua couldn't help but laugh at the expression on Jane's face as he opened the car door to let her out.

"Welcome home." He smiled.

"Home?" Jane replied in complete awe.

"This is where you'll be staying whilst you recover your strength and detox from your ordeal. You will be given as much time as you need to get back into the real world, an awful lot has changed in the time that you have been away." As if to confirm this fact, Joshua reached into his pocket and pulled out a small device that looked like a tiny television. "This is your new phone, it's slightly more advanced than ones you may have previously had! This is one of the simplest phones that has ever been made in terms of its ease of use and so will be especially good for a first timer in this level of technology like yourself."

The doors of the house creaked open, and a tall, handsome man who looked to be in his early thirties walked out wearing a plain white shirt with its sleeves rolled halfway up, exposing deeply tanned arms. The shirt was tucked into blue chinos with a brown belt and matching brown shoes.

"Ah-ha! I thought I heard the car approaching!" He beamed at them both. "I'm Harvey Jones, and I'm going to be looking after you and teaching you about the new world during your time here. I'm here to try to catch you up as quickly as I possibly can! How was your journey?"

"It was incredible!" Jane said excitedly, whilst Joshua just shrugged his shoulders at Harvey as if to say 'it was the same old, same old really. Average traffic.'

"Brilliant! Brilliant! I am glad! Well do come on in and I'll show you up to your room. Grant will cook you up something nice. What do you fancy? He is really exceptional and will make you anything you want!"

Jane's mind went completely blank and she gave herself a second to think. She had been so used to the bland food at the mental hospital; the flavourless, colourless portions that were put in front of her that was just fuel that kept her alive, that she couldn't think of the names of any meals or snacks. She had loved cooking in her previous life and would spend hours in the kitchen each day preparing dishes and experimenting to find a new favourite combination. Maybe one day she would have that again.

Harvey waited patiently and after a minute or so Jane just sighed and shook her head deflated. "I'm sorry I just can't think; I haven't had a choice of food in so long."

Harvey smiled and said he'd ask Grant to prepare a few snacks for her to try and that he would be happy to prepare some sample menus of the sorts of things that she could have. Hopefully she could get some inspiration from that and start to come up with her own suggestions of what she might like. Jane smiled and nodded and said that sounded like the perfect plan as Harvey led her into the house.

*

The house was as breathtaking on the inside as it had been from the outside. Jane walked in to a truly ginormous reception area. The floor was white marble and made everything the eye could see shimmer. There was a double staircase that weaved its way up towards the second floor. In the middle of the double staircase, and hanging directly above it, was a large drooping chandelier that was rich with shining silver. The droplets of glass that dangled down away from the lights looked like the clearest water. There was an exceptionally polished circular wooden table, which was the deepest, warmest brown that Jane could recall seeing. The whole place oozed class.

Harvey led Jane up the stairs to the left of the door, and she ran her hand along the top of the bannister that appeared to be made of the same wood as the table. Jane did find that her hip ached a little as she climbed up the stairs, apparently just another side effect of a decade cooped up in the same couple of rooms. At the top of the stairs she was greeted by yet more feasts for her eyes.

The wall was decorated with elaborate artwork. Portraits of what she assumed were the previous owners of the house were separated by incredible paintings that reminded her of Van Gogh's 'Starry Night', with elaborate stroke work. There were more modern looking pieces too, packed with bright, sharp, colours that provided a glorious contrast in comparison to the simple white wall that they hung on. One in particular caught her eye; of a lone figure in a bright red top holding up an umbrella, walking down a street that looked like it was made of water, with trees that changed from a deep red colour to yellow to green the further down the street they were. The sharpness of the colours was the closest Jane had been able to get to describing to others what it felt like when she had first left the mental hospital and seen the colours of the trees and world again.

Just as Jane thought it couldn't get any better, Harvey led her into her bedroom, which, like the reception room, was utterly gigantic. The floor was the same marble that was a feature throughout the house. Pillars separated a mini living room with a golden couch, complete with red pillows and two deep burgundy red armchairs sitting either side of the sofa, from the bed.

The bed was the largest Jane had ever seen, bigger than any king-size and far more luxurious. It was draped in red and gold and piled with soft looking, inviting pillows. The wall opposite the bed was dominated by one of the huge windows that was in the middle of two of the outside pillars. Jane moved towards it and looked out at the arch of trees that the car had driven up through. To the left and right of the rows was a huge lawn area of luscious green, perfectly trimmed. Over to the right stood a fountain with a multi-tiered statue at its centre, water shot from the top, through the head of a figure that Jane couldn't quite make out from her position in the bedroom, and she made a mental note to herself that she would explore it soon and memorise every detail. She wanted to fill her head with positive memories and dispel all of the ones that had haunted her for so long.

"I'll leave you to it and go and get Grant to prepare you with some snacks, he's been chomping at the bit waiting for you to arrive so that he can wow you with his talents!" Harvey laughed, and if truth were told Jane had completely forgotten he had still been in the room with her. She turned and smiled politely as him as he turned to leave. Once he had gone she brought her head back around to gaze out of the window and stood in a stunned silence at the beauty of the world that stood before her.

Chapter Twenty

One

Jane spent the next few weeks enjoying the house and learning about the new world that she found herself a part of. She had been given a light fitness regime to follow in order to slowly build her strength back up, and was receiving treatment for her hip.

Every morning, she would spend two or three hours with Harvey, mainly getting up to date with the latest technologies, especially those that she would need to use in the coming months and years in the fight against the creature. She learned how to use her phone very quickly, it turned out to be easier to use than her old Nokia. She had been completely blown away by how much the phone could do. The internet and speed of it were the first things that grabbed her attention, and the revelation that there was an app store with millions of games and useful tools as opposed to just the game of snake that she had on her old phone made her head hurt.

She spent her evenings watching movies in high definition on a screen flatter and bigger than she thought possible. She hungrily ate up the James Bond films, Inception and the Batman movies before crying her eyes out at Toy Story 3 and Les Misérables. Once she had watched all the films that Harvey had recommended as must see, she moved onto television series with Breaking Bad and Game of Thrones.

Jane had let Grant have complete freedom in the kitchen and encouraged him to be as inventive and creative as he possibly could be with his menus. His flavours always wowed her and made her wish that she could produce to the standard he was able to time after time.

In the period just after lunch, Jane would go for a swim in the Olympic sized indoor pool, as part of her daily exercise that her regime specified. With her hair still wet, she would go off to explore the gardens that accompanied the property. The first day that she had done this she had headed straight to the fountain with a book and sat for hours listening to the birds and the water of the fountain. She admired greatly the beautiful female angel that stood at its centre, surrounded on the lower levels by baby angels with small wings that Jane had assumed to be the woman's children. She had debated with herself at first regarding whether or not angels could give birth, before deciding that of course they could. In fact, they probably had relationships much like people on earth except that theirs would last for an eternity.

After three weeks of the luxury of the food and the house and grounds, Jane said that she was ready at last to meet with the members of Heirdonus and offer up her services. She was ready to begin her training and was now in a position to start to improve her physical condition. Her hip was better and she was able to move much more freely, mainly down to the time she had been spending in the pool. In all the time that she had been at the house, not once had the giggling that had tormented her for years plagued her. All seemed right in the world.

*

Two days later, a large black car with tinted windows turned up at the house, and three men and a woman got out. Harvey greeted them at the entrance, much like he had greeted Jane, and he showed them into the boardroom on the ground floor. Grant had entered shortly after to offer them beverages and asked if they would like anything to eat.

Jane had been upstairs in her room watching television when they arrived and Harvey came up to fetch her.

"Jane, the Heirdonus council members are here, they're in the boardroom waiting for you."

Jane looked up and paused her programme. "Okay great, I'll be down in a minute; I'm just going to powder my nose."

Jane turned off the TV and went into the bathroom. She was completely transformed from the frail woman that had been driven up to the house. A hairdresser had come in and dyed her hair back to a colour that was close to her natural oaky brown, and a stylist had come in and provided her with make-up and creams that had dramatically helped in reducing her wrinkles. The bags under her eyes and black rings had been significantly reduced mainly because Jane was sleeping much sounder. She had been provided with a full wardrobe filled with dresses and beautiful tops. She was wearing a white dress now that had subtle birds patterned into it that were slightly raised off the dress, so that if one ran their hand over the material they could feel the bumps and trace to outlines of the creatures.

She gave herself a once over in the mirror, before adding some powder to her nose and brushing her hair behind her ear. She picked a hair off the shoulder of her dress, and once she was satisfied with her appearance left to head downstairs and meet the people she would be spending the majority of the next few years of her life with.

Harvey had waited outside her door, and linked his arm with hers as he led her downstairs and across the reception hall towards the boardroom where they had spent their time together as he taught her about the new world.

A long table that had twenty-four chairs around it, ten down each side and two at both ends, dominated the boardroom.

The four people who had arrived by car were all sat at one end next to each other on one of the rows of ten. The woman had a hard face and was sat in the middle left, with a man who looked to be in his seventies to her left with a head of thinning, grey hair. Joshua was sat to her right, and a man who looked like he wanted to be somewhere else completed the quartet.

As Jane entered, they all stood up and wore warm smiles. The woman, who appeared to be in charge, motioned for Jane to sit in one of the seats opposite the four of them. Grant had come back in and asked Jane if she would like anything, but Jane was fine having some of the water from the large jug that had been put on the table. Grant and Harvey then retreated outside and left the five to talk.

"It's lovely to finally meet you Jane, I've heard an awful lot about you and the horrors that you have had to endure because of the creature through Joshua here. My name is Maggie, this is David." Maggie said gesturing towards the man who appeared to want to be somewhere else. "Obviously you know Joshua, and finally on the end is Michael. I must say, you are looking remarkable for a woman who has been through so much, what is your secret?"

Jane smiled, flattered. "Rest! You would be surprised how much better I felt after a single night of good sleep, how much more human I felt. In the hospital... The people in there are nothing more than animals. Mentally insane people are closer to animals than human; you live off pure instinct rather than using your brain to think everything through. You are completely unhinged from yourself, which makes you completely unhinged from the real world.

"Psychiatrists can only do so much, like a dog trainer. They can try and reward you for good behaviour and reinforce you with positivity, and for a while some people will appear to be getting much better. If you ask them how they are they will tell you they are good. If you ask them if they still like children, they will tell you no. If you ask if they still hear voices in their head, they will tell you no. If you ask them if they would go back if they could and change their actions, they will tell you yes.

"But if you dangle a picture of a naked child in front of them, their eyes will light up. If you leave them in a silent room on their own and put on a secret microphone, after an hour or so they will start talking to people that are not there. If you took them back to the moment they committed their actions and gave them the choice of stopping themselves from committing the crime, or being able to watch it all over again, they would watch. But I was different. I was made to believe that I had done something that I had not. They convinced me that I had killed my own family, and then they locked me away for good. These were seasoned professionals who had spent their life dealing with genuinely insane people, and yet they couldn't spot the difference between an insane person and a sane one. They had become so used to dealing with insane people, that when a sane person tried to prove to them that they were sane, they thought it a sign of ultimate insanity.

"They viewed me as not only insane but also clever enough to try and hide it. When you spend years and years of your life locked away trying to convince someone who is unwillingly to believe you when you explain who you truly are… That is what completed my insanity for them. I freely admit that I lost my mind. They broke me to the point that I felt… Jesus no I knew in my heart that I had killed my family. And it destroyed me. I hardly ate, I didn't sleep, and I stopped exercising. I ceased to be human, like everyone else in that place, and I transformed into an animal. Until the day that Joshua came and rescued me. Going back into my cell after our meeting, I felt human for the first time in years. I ate well that night; I even slept a little better. I was innocent, and not only that but I would be given a chance to take my revenge."

The four of them had listened intensely to what Jane had to say, leaning in and engaging with her. It was Joshua who now spoke.

"You are braver than all of us put together, Jane. The recovery you have shown from that frail, old, if you don't mind me saying, shell of a person that I met just over a month ago now is staggering, truly staggering. I couldn't be more over the moon for you. When I first caught sight of you as you walked into that small interview room, well I'll admit that I had serious doubts. Serious, serious doubts. It appeared as if you were too far gone to be rescued at first, heck you wouldn't even talk to me!" He laughed, and Jane smiled back at him. "I am so glad, ecstatic really at the woman I see before me now. You are no animal, Jane. You are certainly no animal."

Jane blushed red at the compliment and lowered her face slightly to hide her embarrassment.

Michael folded his fingers in front of him on the table and looked at Jane warmly. "So Jane, how has Harvey been? Has he been looking after you properly and teaching you well?"

"Yes, he's been lovely and extremely welcoming. I was a wiz on my new phone after just a couple of days thanks to him!"

"Good, I am glad. I only ask because he's my son and I remember him as a young boy, always off gallivanting and forgetting his responsibilities. It was a long time ago now of course, but I still like to keep an eye on him."

"No, honestly he's been wonderful to me. I wouldn't have believed myself how quickly my life could turn around and he has been the main factor in that."

Michael smiled and nodded to himself, clearly proud of the man that his son was becoming. "That is really good to hear, I assume he has been the utmost gentleman?"

"Enough about Harvey." Maggie interjected, "I'm afraid I'd like to get down to business as quickly as possible. I need to get back to headquarters before 3pm for a very important meeting regarding the current location of the creature and I don't want to spend the next hour watching you drool over what a great man your son is turning out to be. We can all agree that Harvey is great! Now Jane, are you sure that you are ready to join us?"

"Yes, I am ready. The couple of niggles that I had picked up from my time in the hospital seem to have passed. I'm caught up on all that I need to know according to Harvey, and I want to get started. I want to get fit again and be prepared for the fight to come."

Maggie nodded her content. "We shall get our doctors to give you a full assessment before you begin any intense exercise regime, but once you have been given the all clear from them then you will be able to commence training and get up to the fitness level required to be able to go up against the creature.

"The house you have been staying in is one of four Heirdonus safe houses in the country. We like to stick to large, private manor houses since they are very useful for holding meetings. People don't look twice at a large gathering at a manor house, and so we find that we are able to be discreet about our business.

"We try to avoid large meet ups as much as possible. Due to the high profile nature of some of our members, a gathering involving them would be likely to draw media attention. We have a website that is only accessible by members. The website itself can only be found online by typing in a very obscure combination of letters and numbers that was originally created by David literally mashing his keyboard. Although this makes it is a pain to access the site, it means that no one is able to stumble across it by accident. In the unlikely event that someone is able to come across the site, they would be greeted by what appears to be an old garden centre website. To access the Heirdonus site, one has to login in using a unique username and password combination that is scrutinised by David to make sure that it is as strong as possible. You won't be allowed access to the site until being ordained as a full member of the organisation, and that can only happen once you have completed our training and the council accepts you. Access to the site probably won't be necessary for you anyway since you will be around to attend most of the meetings we conduct. The site is more for members that work abroad and have too high a profile to attend meetings. For the time being you will be none of the above, which isn't a bad thing.

"We are taking you to the Heirdonus headquarters with us. It is a manor house not dissimilar to this one, though it is slightly bigger and more accessible. You will be given a room and your training will start immediately after the doctors deem you fit. You will have to pass a series of fitness and mental tests, which are as much to do with your reaction times as anything else. We anticipate it will take you roughly three months to reach the physical condition necessary, based on the fact you have spent the majority of your time doing very little over the past few years and so your muscle mass is much lower than would ordinarily be. The Heirdonus fitness coach, Marcus, will train you personally. Be careful with him, he is a flirt and will stop at nothing to get in your pants!" Jane smiled politely assuming this was a joke, but Maggie gave her a hard look. "I mean it Jane, be on guard. That is not something you want to pursue."

"It won't be a problem, my passions for love died with my husband."

Maggie gave Jane a rueful smile.

"You will be trained in hand to hand and knife combat. We believe the creature can be killed, but only with a stake. From what we have heard from reports of members in America, bullets do not do any damage. From our study of the history of the creature, this does seem to be in line with other papers on the matter. There is a diary entry from the American civil war that explains how a creature came from the night and attacked men as they slept. Three men were killed; all gruesome, bloody deaths. Two of the men killed had tried to shoot the creature whilst it attacked the other. It is thought that the creature only intended to kill the one man, but upon being attacked killed the other two. What is so fascinating about the diary entry, aside from the fact that the guns appeared to be useless against the creature, was that the other two men were not killed in the usual way. They did not exhibit bleeding from the fingers, and they did not have multiple slashing's across the body. They simply had their throats slit, and were dealt with quickly.

"Now, we are not sure of the validity of the diary entry. The main problem we have with it is that it is the only recorded time we had that the creature had killed more than one human at once. Due to the fact that the other two only had their throats slit and were not killed in the usual manor, we actually believe that the creature did not kill the other two. They were killed by an opportunist who found the mutilated body that the creature had left behind, and thought that they could kill off a couple of guys that they didn't like and frame it as being part of the darker murder. The only other recorded time of the creature killing more than one person at a time came recently, when your boys were found murdered in the forest.

"This led us to believe that the way that the creature generally kills its victims is important. It may be some sort of religious sacrifice to the creature's Gods to kill in such a way. It may also be that the creature feeds on the humans it kills in this way, and the meat may need special preparation; the best way to think about it is Halal meat. The fact that the bodies of the animals found do not exhibit the same marks on the body as the humans killed has lead us to believe that the human killings are more important to the creature. The animal deaths are probably just a way for it to survive. The animals that are found dead tend to be drained of most of their blood, whereas the humans have a lot of blood left behind.

"Now Jane I am going to be perfectly honest with you. The reason we didn't come for you sooner to join the fight against the creature was because of your children. The creature has never before killed three in the same, sacrificial way as seen in your family's murders. Nor has the creature ever buried any of its victims before, it has never needed to because it doesn't leave a trace of itself behind. It doesn't leave fingerprints; it doesn't leave hairs. There is never a murder weapon. So why would it bury your children in the forest? We believed that it hadn't, that yours was a case of a copycat murder, and not the doings of the real creature. Copycat murders are rare, but there are a number of notable ones that have occurred and it wasn't inconceivable that yours was an example of one and that you were the murderer."

"So what changed? Why did you decide that I wasn't a copycat killer?"

"We got a hold of Pete's phone. He received a call just before his death that was from an unknown number and lasted precisely thirteen seconds."

"What has that got to do with anything?"

"That call comes from the creature. It is the mark of death. We don't know what is said during those 13 seconds, but we do not believe that the warning is given in a human language. Every victim of the creature receives a warning message before they die. Part of the sacrificial process is that the one who is sacrificed should be offered a chance at saviour. The creature offers them a warning. In the days before telephones, the warnings were scratched into the ground in a place where the sacrifice would see them before their death. The markings are unlike anything from this planet. They are sharp and twisting and ancient in origin. They look like a scream on the earth. Of course, no one ever understood them fully. They thought there were kids vandalising property and the like. But Heirdonus knew. That 13-second phone call was the creature. It called your husband and warned him. We know you couldn't have made that call, because your phone was dead at the time. David our tech wiz assures us of that fact. That 13-second phone call marks the creature as the murderer and tells us that you were innocent.

"Jane, the reason your children were buried is simple, the creature wanted you because it could sense that you would be a great threat to it. You stumbled back out of the woods and found Anthony's body, but you also found something else. You saw the eyes of the creature that night, and it looked into your eyes in turn. You knew that the creature lived. It would have killed you then and there if it weren't for the arrival of the kayaker. You had survived, and because of this the creature had to go after your children. The creature itself was unable to track you down and we believe that the reason for this is linked to a prophecy made close to a thousand years ago.

"It had to frame you for the murders in order to save itself. Burying your children not only made you look guilty, but also distanced the creature from the murder of your husband and made it look as if you were a copycat killer. Not only would the authorities be fooled and tricked into thinking you were either guilty of the murders or mad, but we wouldn't try to recruit you as it led us to believe that you were a copycat killer. It was quite simply brilliant.

"Now, the family that moved into your house following all of this did a renovation to the property about 8 months ago. They knocked down a wall in order to build a new conservatory extension onto the side of the house, but to their surprise discovered that the wall they had knocked through wasn't the wall they thought it was. Hidden behind it was a secret staircase wedged between the wall that they had bashed through thinking it was the outside wall, and the true outside wall. At the bottom of it, in a small cellar, they found themselves surrounded by high tech equipment, plans, and drawings. Jason, who owned the property, is highly tech savvy and attempted to break into the computers with some of his friends from work, but they couldn't get through the firewalls that had been put in place. They realised that what was lurking beneath was of great importance, and eventually grew worried that it might have some link to terrorism. It was at that point that Jason decided to contact the government.

"Naturally, we have members that are involved in the government and they alerted us to the discovery. We thought little of it at the time and presumed it had just been the private workings of an architect or tech guru who had been scared that someone might try and steal their work. We weren't interested in those computers in that small basement until we heard what it was that had been worked on in there.

"The work was your husband, Anthony's. He had been developing a new type of recon device, one that was able to detect light of a frequency that was previously untapped. We believe the frequency that this machine works in is the frequency that the creature hides in when it is not hunting. Once finished, the machine will be able to do something that hasn't ever been possible before. It will be able to track the creature. We will be able to find it, Jane.

"Now, this is where the prophecy that I mentioned earlier comes in. The prophecy tells of a creature from an earth that is not our earth. A creature that roams alone, seeking no friends, claiming no lands, fighting no wars. For a thousand years the creature would roam, before men would stand against it. The men would fight and strive but would always fall short, until a coming. The one who comes would be unfounded and would stare into the eyes of the creature and see only grass. The one who sees grass would be found with the power to discover the creature and would be presented with the opportunity to avenge. Jane we believe that the prophecy is about you. You looked into the creature's eyes and saw a bright green light. The creature went for your family rather than you, making you unfounded. Your family perished at its hands, meaning you have the chance to avenge them Jane. And what finally convinced us was the discovery of Anthony's plans in that basement. You were found with the tools to defeat the creature, as you were lying next to Anthony when the kayaker found you."

Chapter Twenty-One

Marcus

"ONE, TWO, THREE, UP! ONE, TWO, THREE, UP! ONE, TWO, THREE, UP!"

Marcus' voice rang out loud and true in the gymnasium as Jane continued to do squats, holding each for three seconds before rising on Marcus' command.

"Good Jane, good! Well done! Top work, really top work today Jane, you're getting closer and closer!" Jane stood bending over her knees and breathing hard, trying to regain her breath. She had completed a 5 mile run and thought that was all she would have to do today, but Marcus had run her straight back to the gym and got her to do a full body workout.

"Great work Jane, really well done."

Jane continued to pant away, but even she let herself smile a little. She was making exceptional progress. It was only two months since she had arrived at the new manor house base, but already she was consistently running 5 miles every other day without too much bother. She had put on muscle weight and was looking and feeling much healthier and stronger. The woman she had been in the mental hospital was a mere echo of what she had become under Marcus' supervision.

Jane was highly motivated by her quest for revenge against the creature. There was nothing that could stop her now. She felt that it was her destiny, she was the one from the prophecy, and she could feel it in her bones. The work she was doing with Marcus was both mental and physical.

When she arrived, it had been mainly physical work, building up her strength slowly and not trying for too much too fast so as to avoid an injury which would have acted as a major setback to her recovery plans.

Now, she spent roughly half of her day doing mental exercises to increase her reaction times and make her sharper, and a quarter of the day exercising. The rest was left to her to eat and relax and recover. The chef at this manor wasn't as good as Grant had been, and practically every meal she would miss Grant's ingenuity with his flavour combinations. But she knew that the work she was doing here was important and that she couldn't dwell too much on her wonderful time at the pink manor.

Marcus handed Jane a bottle of water and she squeezed it gratefully into her wide-open mouth. He then took it back off her and handed her a second bottle that was filled with a cloudy liquid that looked like lemonade. It was as bitter as lemon, but contained none of the fruits juice. It was a combination of water and recovery vitamins, and was in use by the top sportspeople all over the world, or at least Marcus claimed as much. Whatever was in the drink, it always helped to refresh Jane and quenched her thirst.

In the first few days of being under Marcus' stewardship, he had tried briefly to seduce her like Maggie had said he would. After reproaching his advances several times, he got the hint and had since stopped trying to get into her pants. Their relationship had been a little strained in the days following her reproaches, but as time had worn on they had found that they enjoyed each other's company and Jane began to see him as a brother that she had never had. Albeit a brother who made her work harder than any normal sibling would.

"Okay Jane, that's all for today, you've done really well. I wasn't sure if you were quite ready to jump straight from a run into a full body workout but you showed great grit and determination and I am very proud of you ."

Jane smiled broadly at the compliment, she still hadn't gotten used to the positive and flattering messages that Marcus would finish every physical session they had together with. After spending so much time being put down by nurses and told by doctors and psychiatrists that she was mentally unstable and would lead a normal life again, she wasn't sure she would ever get used to being complimented and encouraged.

"Because we went so hard on the exercise front I'm going to give you the rest of the day off, and we can continue with the mental exercises tomorrow morning. I'll see you at 8am."

Jane was relieved at this, she felt far too exhausted to solve any mental problems and would probably sleep for most of the afternoon to let her body recover, maybe even try and sneak in a massage if Helen was about. Helen had given her some of the best massages of her life since she had been at the manor, but unfortunately she was very seldom around to give them as she had a young child at home that she wanted to spend time with. Jane didn't begrudge her this; God knows she would spend every waking second with her family if fate hadn't been so cruel to her. As Marcus left through the gym doors, Jane took another few glugs of water before sitting on one of the benches that lined the wall, finally giving her legs a rest from a hard day's work.

She had pushed her body to its absolute limit in the time she had been at the manor, running until she threw up, punching hanging bags in the gym until her knuckles cried out in agony for her to stop, squatted until her legs could no longer push her body back up. She had pushed herself to breaking point and when she reached a moment where she didn't believe she could push herself any further she would think of the creature that had robbed her of her life and family, and she would dig even deeper and give even more than she thought possible.

Due to her willingness to give so much, she was a long way ahead of schedule. The council believed that soon she would be strong enough to be allowed in any raiding groups on their missions to hunt for the creature. Thanks to the technology that they were now developing using the blueprints that Anthony had left behind, Heirdonus believed that they would finally be able to find the creature and bring an end to its monstrous crimes.

According to David, who was the chief technician for the whole of Heirdonus, the blueprints had been even more impressive than first thought. Anthony must have been mere days away from their completion at the time of his passing.

David had instructed a team of six of the best brains in Heirdonus to set to work on finishing Anthony's work. It had taken them about three weeks to work out exactly what was needed to build the machine, and the materials that they would require would not be easy to procure, but then they hadn't expected that so complex a device would be easily constructed. That was probably the main reason that it appeared that Anthony hadn't once attempted to begin to build even prototypes of the machine. Jane didn't really understand what it was that the machine was capable of doing, but from what she gathered it was a bit like a recon drone, only it could see a spectrum of light that no other device could see. The reason the creature could not be found by conventional recon methods was that it was able to hide itself in a different spectrum of light when it was not hunting.; like a chameleon that can change its skin. Heirdonus believed it to be the best defensive mechanism the world had ever fought against and probably would ever have to fight against. It was the reason why it had gone hundreds, if not thousands of years without detection from those who had sought it out. Anthony's work would be sufficient for Heirdonus to pinpoint its exact location. What Heirdonus was now currently working on was a way in which to draw the creature out once it was found. If the creature remained hidden in the other light spectrum, they couldn't be sure whether or not they could apprehend it if they did find it. They needed to find a way to lure it into its visible light state.

Jane had an epiphany. She jumped off the bench despite the complaints of her muscles, and ran out of the gym towards the manor house.

*

"A family!" She panted furiously at Michael, who she had nearly knocked over whilst sprinting into the house.

"What are you on about Jane?"

"A family! The way to lure out the creature. Offer it a sacrifice. Offer it a family!"

Michael looked over her with tired eyes. "It wouldn't work, Jane."

"Yes it would, if it thought it had easy pickings for a sacrifice of course it would! A family, out alone in the woods somewhere on a holiday, like my family had been. The creature would be drawn in, I know it."

"You know that the creature can sense a trap, and this would be the most obvious trap we could possibly come up with. How would we get to the family in time to save them? We don't have a cure for the creature's poison that infects the body. We don't have a location where we would be able to isolate the creature. Plus we would have to find a family that would be willing to sacrifice their own lives in order to bring the creature to justice."

Jane shook her head frustrated. "I am sure it would work, I know it would."

"Jane, do you not think we have discussed this possibility before? It is too dangerous, there is too much risk and there is no guarantee that the creature would even show. And, for arguments sake, let us suppose that the creature did turn up; how could we guarantee that we would save the family."

"What if we started today? What if we told only the parents of the family, the children wouldn't have to be involved? We could get them out and to safety before the creature arrived. The children would exhibit real fear. If the dad were to tell them a truly horrific story, I believe that their real fear would override the fake fear of the parents. Jesus, the parents would probably exhibit real fear too. You have just said yourself that you wouldn't be able to guarantee their safety, well that is precisely what we need. We need their safety not be guaranteed because that makes it real! Their children will be in grave danger, which makes it real! The fact that we cannot protect any of them and that they could actually die makes it real, Joshua! The creature will not sense a trap because the fear will be too real."

"What you're proposing is a suicide mission then? A test of our own abilities as to whether or not we will be able to save an innocent family from a terrible, terrible fate. The odds are stacked against us coming out on top. We have a zero-percent success rate when it comes to saving people. We simply cannot ask this of a family unless we can be one-hundred-percent certain that it is not a death sentence."

"What I suggest is a chance to rid the world of a monster! We get every member of Heirdonus to the location, armed heavily in order to bring the creature down. I am the one from the prophecy; you know that as well as anyone. It will work this time; it has to work this time. What is the point of believing in the prophecy if you are not willing to take some action or some risk in order to make it come true?

"The forest where my family was killed; that is the perfect location to trap the creature. Three sides of the clearing where we set up our camp are engulfed by trees, meaning that the creature is able to sneak up on the location. I imagine it chose that place and my family to attack in the first place because of this security. The fourth side backs onto a river. We could have members in boats on the other side of the river, maybe further upstream. Then teams located in the forests with camera feeds to the family so they know when to move in. We could surround the creature on all sides before it even knew what was happening!"

There was a light in Michael's eyes that hadn't been there moments before. She watched his eyes flicker as he scanned through in his head all the possibilities, as he attempted to calculate the risk levels to what she was proposing. Jane could see him visualising the setting, seeing the open canopy and the forest and the river. Desperately trying to find a way to make the plan work and make it all come together. After a few minutes, his eyes stopped their flickering and he was back in the room with Jane, beaming at her.

"I have to consult the others, I need more opinions on the matter. I need to speak to those who know the doctrines of Heirdonus, who know the history of the creature. We need to make sure we are armed correctly. Stakes are a must, but it may be worth taking other types of weaponry. For starters, if we are unable to kill the creature we will need to have some way of at least capturing it and holding it prisoner." Michael nodded furiously to himself, his eyes began to flicker again and Jane knew that he was back in the forest making plans. When he arrived back in the room again, he was even more confident. "It could work."

Jane was drawn in by Michael's enthusiasm; she had never seen this side of him before and had no idea that this side of him even existed up until now. If anyone had told her he was capable of such excitement she would have rubbished them away.

"The big issue we face is that I don't think there is a family capable of it. I have never met a mother who would risk her children's lives like this."

The light drained from Michael's face and he looked at Jane gravely.

"You may not have met such a family, and few have, but I do know of one. I shall call a meeting and we shall discuss in full all that you have put forward and if the council accepts it then you will be granted permission to join the organisation as a member. If it is passed then you will be introduced to the head of the organisation, and in doing so will meet the head of the family that will be vital to the success of this plan.

Chapter Twenty-Two

Member

Jane lay in her bed the night after the council had gathered to discuss her idea. She had waited impatiently in the gym, trying to take her mind off what was happening by having an intense workout with Marcus, but no matter how hard she attacked her exercises, her mind kept drifting to the meeting and whether or not the council would pass her idea and allow her to become a full member of the organisation.

Marcus knew she was distracted but didn't press the matter, instead taking Jane through her paces for three hours before saying enough was enough and that she would injure herself if she kept going any longer.

Jane slumped onto the bench where she had originally had her idea and stared at the doors to the gym, willing them to open and Joshua or David or Maggie or anyone for that matter involved in the council meeting to walk through and give her a nod to let her know that it had passed. She sat for close to half an hour before finally giving up and getting up to shower.

It wasn't until she was sat on her bed with wet hair, another thirty minutes later, that there was a knock on her door. She tripped on the dressing gown that she had been cloaked in during her rush to the door and then swung it quickly open, her eyes wide with expectation. At the door were the four council members who had originally visited her at the house; David, Maggie, Joshua and Michael. Maggie looked at her and smiled.

"Your idea was unanimously accepted. The head of the organisation, himself, presided over the meeting and he wishes to meet with you on the day of your acceptance as a member. The family have agreed to take part in the mission. The children will not be told but will be retreated from the area before darkness falls and the creature arrives, similar to how you took your children away from the campsite to get ready for bed. Preparations are going to begin at once with regards to the setting up of camera equipment and securing live feeds of the whole area so that we can capture the creature once it comes into the visible spectrum. We have drawn up plans for the construction of a vast cage in case we cannot kill the creature. Once Anthony's machine is finished and working we shall use the two to determine the optimal location. We need to be sure we can get the cage to the campsite you stayed at before confirming it as the location. We are going to use helicopters to airlift members into the chosen location when the creature arrives. This will prevent the risk of the creature coming into contact with anyone but the family and running away. It also gives us flexibility if there is a pursuit.

"We believe that by planning the trip 6 months in advance in the same area that you camped, there is a strong chance that the creature will show there again. Naturally this is not guaranteed and in general it is rare that the creature frequents the same place twice. If it is true that you are the one, however, we believe that the prophecy is going to come true and you are destined to stop the creature. It is fate that wherever we decide the location for our assault to be, the creature will be."

Jane was ecstatic. She thanked them all for accepting her as one of their own and for all of the help that they had provided her with, especially in getting her out of the mental hospital and allowing her to find a new lease of life.

"Your members ceremony will be conducted within the next week, at a time when the leader of Heirdonus will be available. Well done Jane, and thank you. We'll leave you to rest."

*

Jane was sound asleep when she was taken. She didn't hear her kidnappers enter the room, nor did she hear them cross the floor to her bed where she was sleeping. She did, however, feel numerous rough hands grab her and put a black bag over her head. Her eyes burst open into the blackness of the bag and she cried out in panic and thrashed under their grip, but it was no good. Moments later, a hand reached into the bag and thrust a cloth over her nose and mouth. Seconds later, Jane was unconscious again.

*

Jane's head lolled to the side and then back round to the front of her body as she slowly regained consciousness. The bag was still over her head, leaving her blind to the world, but she could feel that the world she found herself in was hot and sticky. She could hear flames in the air around her, which would explain the heat. She was tied to a chair with rope around her waist; her arms were wrapped tightly behind her. Her legs were also bound together tightly.

"DO YOU ACCEPT THIS WOMAN?" A booming voice called out and echoed back off the walls of the space that Jane was in. The room must have been large because the echo bounced six or seven times before eventually fading away into silence.

"Heirdonus accepts." Whispered a large number of voices.

"WILL YOU GUIDE THIS WOMAN IN HER WORK FOR THE ORGANISATION?"

"Heirdonus guides."

"WILL YOU PROTECT THIS WOMAN SHOULD DANGER COME HER WAY?"

"Heirdonus protects."

There was a shuffling behind Jane and then she felt the ropes loosen around her waist and then fall to the ground. She was lifted onto her feet and pushed forward, falling to her hands and knees.

"WOMAN!"

Jane felt the eyes of everyone in the room turn to face her.

"DO YOU WISH TO JOIN THE ORGANISATION HEIRDONUS?"

"Yes." Jane whispered in reply. A whip cracked behind her and Jane screamed in agony as it made contact with her back, causing a line of red-hot pain to shoot through her body.

"WOMAN, DO YOU WISH TO JOIN THE ORGANISATION HEIRDONUS?"

"Yes, goddammit, please I want to join!" She cried out this time. But the whip cracked again, it collided with her back just to the right of the original blow, and Jane screamed out. She begged for them to stop.

"WOMAN, DO YOU WISH TO JOIN THE ORGANISATION HEIRDONUS?"

Somehow, through the pain that Jane's body was subjected to, she realised what she had to say.

"Woman wishes!"

The whip cracked again behind her and cannoned into her back, harder than before. Jane didn't scream this time, the pain was too intense for her to be able to make a single sound, and it felt as if she was on fire from the inside out. She could feel her top sticking to her back where the whip had broken her skin and caused her to bleed. Her eyes were streaming under the black bag that was still covering her face. She had no idea what they wanted her to say and could no longer think through the pain. She was going to pass out at any moment. The big, booming voice did not give her any respite though.

"WOMAN, DO YOU WISH TO JOIN THE ORGANISATION HEIDONUS?"

Jane decided her best course of action would be not to reply; maybe that is what they wanted of her. In any case, if she didn't reply then they couldn't beat her because she hadn't uttered the wrong words.

The whip cracked behind her after 10 seconds of silence and collided with the mark that the first whip had made. The pain knocked Jane out cold.

*

Jane came to, not knowing how long she had been out for. The bag was still over her head, which was now resting on the floor in the position that she had fallen into when she passed out. She tried to lift her body up, but couldn't.

"WOMAN, DO YOU WISH TO JOIN THE ORGANISATION HEIRDONUS?"

From her position on the floor, Jane managed to mumble, "I wish." She closed her eyes and waited for the crack of the whip to smash into her back once more. But this time the whip did not come.

"WOMAN, WILL YOU GIVE ALL YOU CAN FOR THE ORGANISATION HEIRDONUS?"

"I give." Jane replied tentatively, clenching her teeth together firmly in anticipation of the crack of the whip. But she had sussed out the required formula.

"WOMAN, WILL YOU HIDE THE EXISTENCE OF THE ORGANISATION HEIRDONUS FOR AS LONG AS YOU LIVE?"

"I hide." This time Jane spoke the words confidently.

A chorus of whispers started up as footsteps moved towards Jane.

"Heirdonus accepts. Heirdonus accepts. Heirdonus accepts."

The bounds on her arms and legs were untied and Jane was lifted to her feet. As she rose she felt blood trickle down her back and absorb into her trousers. Once on her feet, the bag was lifted off her head, and Jane was thrust into a dark room lit only by candlelight and a fire, which was gently roaring behind her. It appeared to be some sort of cave, with a vast ceiling that the light from the flames did not reach up to. Jane was surrounded on all sides by hooded figures in black robes with white belts that all held their hands behind their backs. Directly in front of her was whom she assumed to be the leader of Heirdonus, the man who had called out the questions to her, in a white robe with a black belt. The man's hands were not behind him like the others, instead they were wrapped around an elaborate golden pole that reminded Jane of the ones that Bishops carry. Though, instead of a cross at the top of the pole, there was an orb surrounded by golden loops that met at the centre of the top of the orb. He approached Jane.

"Woman." He spoke in a much softer voice, "Swear after me: I swear to serve Heirdonus truly and faithfully for all of my time."

"I swear."

"I swear to hide nothing from Heirdonus, for they are my brothers and sisters, my mothers and daughters, my fathers and sons."

"I swear."

"I swear to use all of my skill and cunning to bring the creature that we fight to justice."

"I swear."

"Jane, welcome."

The cloaked figure turned away from her and went back to the edge of the circle. He leaned in and whispered something to the figure on his right who rushed toward Jane at his word, quickly followed by the figure to the leaders left. They took one of Jane's arms each and led her out of the cave, back towards civilisation, as a member of Heirdonus. As they were leaving, Jane glanced up above where the leader of Heirdonus had been stood. She squinted her eyes. It looked like the small green light of a camera in record mode.

*

That night a doctor visited Jane and saw to the wounds that the whip had inflicted upon her.

"Was the whip really necessary?"

"It is a tradition that has been going since the formation of Heirdonus. Only the strong willed are able to get through the initiation ceremony, and it is only the strong willed that are wanted by the organisation. If anyone were to reveal the workings of the organisation to outsiders there would be mass panic on the streets. An alien creature walking our world, killing our people and our animals, being able to live potentially indefinitely… It would drive people insane. It could bring governments to their knees. Now you are a full member you will learn who is a part of the organisation, the high profiles. If the list of the members alone got out there would be anarchy. It cannot be risked. That is why the whip is so important."

Jane shook her head slowly. "Well I think it sucks."

The doctor laughed. "You actually did remarkably well. Most people pass out at least twice during initiation. I passed out a grand total of four times. It took me fourteen whips to figure out how I was meant to answer the question, now that is unimaginable pain. You got off lightly!"

Jane smiled sympathetically at him, but didn't feel as if she had gotten off particularly lightly.

"Now, this is going to sting a lot. Put this in your mouth." The doctor pulled a thick piece of rubber out of his bag and handed it to Jane. "This will stop you from biting your tongue in two, which I assure you would be worse for you that a few scratches on your back! Put it in and bite down on it as hard as you possibly can."

Jane took the rubber off the doctor and did as she was told, clenching her jaws as tightly as she possibly could.

The doctor moved around behind her, and she heard as he undid a bottle and tipped it upside down. He patted at her back with a sponge that he had tipped some of the liquid onto, and for the second time that night fire shot through Jane's body. Her teeth dug deeper into the rubber, she closed her eyes and twisted her head down and to the right trying desperately to stifle the scream that welled up inside of her. The doctor continued to pat away at her back a few more times, and the fire continued to burn white hot.

The doctor paused for a moment and shuffled behind Jane. The fire calmed down into just a small flame on her back. She heard the bottle tip up again and no sooner had the pain begun to abate then it began to roar up again as he began dabbing her back once more.

After a few minutes the doctor stopped.

"Okay that's you all sterilised. All that's left is bandaging, then you can go back to bed and try and get some rest, I imagine you'll need it! I would try to avoid sleeping on your back if it is at all possible though."

Sleeping on her back was the last thing that Jane had been planning on doing that night.

"Lift your arms up, please."

Jane lifted her arms above her head and the doctor strapped one long bandage around her body until all of her wounds were completely covered.

"Right, that should just about do it. I'll help you back to your room."

"Thank you."

The doctor linked his arm with hers and walked her through the manor from his small private office on the ground floor over to the lift that would take them up to Jane's room.

As they were walking along the corridor to her room, Jane slowed her pace and looked at the doctor.

"Hey, on my way out of the initiation I thought I saw the light of a camera above where the leader was standing?"

"Ah yes, your initiation was live streamed to the other members of Heirdonus thanks to some handy work by David. It is a recent policy that all members watch the initiation of new recruits, even if they are unable to attend in person. We do, after all, have members all over the world."

Jane wasn't sure how she felt about her anguished cries being broadcast all over the world but at this point was too tired to continue the conversation, all she wanted to do was get into bed and forget her pain. They didn't speak the rest of the way to Jane's door.

Chapter Twenty-Three

Founded

It was two weeks before Jane was able to continue with her exercise programme, much to her frustration. In that two weeks she spent much of her time working on her mental reaction times and Marcus said that she was getting to the point where she was quicker than most of the members of Heirdonus. Once she was fit enough, she would be able to join the search parties.

Anthony's machine had been completed days before and was currently undergoing testing, but the initial signs were good and it would soon be taken to the air to search for the creature. The engineers had stripped out an army grade recon device that had been decommissioned from its use in Afghanistan and reconstructed it to Anthony's specifications. It was remote controlled from a mobile base that had to be within twenty miles of the device.

Jane had been involved in council meetings and had met with the leader of Heirdonus, a man called Pete who turned out to be much nicer than Jane had expected the head of an organisation to be. He was witty, sharp and extremely clever. What's more, he was a brilliant actor and apparently his wife was too. They had two children and were willing to put themselves at risk in order to bring the creature to justice. Jane was completely in awe of him; it was no surprise that he was the leader. He had this magnetic pull about him that made you want to hear every word he spoke, as if what he said was gospel.

David had managed to source a lot of cameras of all different types. He had small ones that the family would be able to have on their person and in their clothes in order for the other members of Heirdonus to see where they were at all times. He had also acquired hand held cameras that members could carry with them as they surrounded the creature. He had planned for one in six members to be camera people. If they weren't able to apprehend the creature then they could at least document how it behaved, how it attacked and defended, whether any of the weapons they used were indeed any use against it. They had ruled out guns entirely at this point. The records of the creature indicated that they wouldn't work anyway, moreover due to the fact they were surrounding the creature on all sides there would be too great a risk of friendly fire. Instead, they would use a variety of knives and nets combined with a large number of stakes, made from materials ranging from steel to wood, in their attempt to kill or capture the creature.

Joshua had designed a cage that was layered with different metals and materials that he believed would be able to hold the creature if they were able to capture it. Layers of plastic, iron, and steel, as well as glass and titanium were to be used in its construction. Jane had spent an evening listening to the reasoning from Joshua for each layer and what sorts of creature each material could realistically hold. Together, he was certain that some part of the cage would prevent the creature from escaping. The cage itself was currently under construction, though Jane wasn't allowed to view it. A number of radioactive and hazardous materials were being used to bind some of the layers of the cage together. It just wasn't worth the risk of someone who wasn't working on its construction being near.

Pete had planned the trip for six months time, as had been discussed. This set a strict time deadline on the members to get everything ready and source everything that was necessary. To begin with Jane thought that there wasn't enough time, however, she soon realised that the high profile members had friends in very high places and the sourcing turned out to be the easiest part. Construction was the difficult bit. The majority of the engineers had been working on building Anthony's machine, which meant that the cage was falling behind schedule. Each layer took a number of days to fix into place and secure properly, and there were an awful lot of layers.

Jane was still extremely busy training each day. It had been decided that she would be given a metal stake lined with silver as her weapon to face the creature with. The council had decided that it was fate that the one prophesised about would use a weapon often touted as the ultimate vampire killer. Vampire stories throughout the ages had been based on the creature, so there was as good a chance as any that a stake would work.

Jane spent hours a day training with Marcus and the stake, apparently there was more to it than just stabbing the creature with the pointy end. She had to be able to wield it much like a sword in case the creature attacked her back and she had to defend herself. They spent hours together doing drills where Jane was given a wooden stick and was only allowed to defend, no matter how angry she got, as Marcus continued to hit her with blow after blow. Slowly but surely Jane got better, and after about a month of training Marcus' stick no longer collided with her flesh.

Pete had broken off connection with Heirdonus about a week after Jane's initiation, once the plan had been finalised, so that the creature would not be able to sense the strong link between him and Heirdonus. He went back to his day job, and his wife Anne continued to look after the children and keep the house in order. Anne, who had a much weaker link to the organisation, was still able to attend the most important meetings, in case any of the details of the plan changed. She regularly met up with Helen as their children both attended the same school.

Meanwhile, transportation of the cage was being arranged, despite the cage still not being finished. Anthony's machine was ready after completing its testing stage and was now being flown over the country to scout the earth for any signs of the creature's movements. They flew the machine in the North of the country, as far from the forest as possible so the creature would think the location was safe As yet, the creature hadn't come up on the machine's radar but the organisation felt confident that it was because it was already in the forest scouting out the area and making sure nothing was out of place.

There had been several arguments about how the group would approach the area. They thought about ground troops in the forest, but the issue with that was that they could be detected by the creature, which would then flee the scene. They had eventually decided on airlifting the members in using helicopters. Once the creature was lured into the open space, provided the camp was set up near to the middle of the clearing, there would be plenty of room around it for helicopters to drop members down who could then quickly form a circle around the creature. The cage was more difficult, it was too large to be brought in by helicopter, and no other aircraft would be able to land in the area. It had to come by boat, which meant that it couldn't get near to the creature's location before it was encircled. It would therefore only be used as a last resort.

Jane was halfway through another session with Marcus when the doors to the gym were flung open and Maggie rushed in looking frenetic and excited.

"We've found it!" She called across the gym. "Heading south towards the forest. It was picked up by Anthony's machine, moving quickly. It doesn't appear to suspect a trap. It's fucking working. I don't believe it! Jane you beautiful thing!" She rushed up to Jane and surprisingly kissed her full on the mouth. "And Pete, I mean I knew he and Anne were superb actors but to fool the creature? It is unprecedented. You are the one Jane. Unbelievable. What a dream!"

Maggie turned and dashed out of the room, presumably to go and find other members to tell. Jane was stood blushing, no one had touched her lips since Anthony had passed and she didn't think that anyone would again. She started laughing, and then became hysterical.

"It's really happening!" She laughed at Marcus, who couldn't help but laugh along with her, infected by the sound of her joy.

Chapter Twenty-Four

Helen

Helen stood in the kitchen finishing up the spaghetti bolognaise that she had been preparing for her husband David's arrival home from work. She walked through the small archway that separated the kitchen from the dining room and checked the time on the old grandfather clock. It was 5.57pm; David's train would have gotten in about 10 minutes ago. He would be home soon. She watched the clock tick for a few seconds; Helen had inherited it from her granddad who had passed away a couple of years before. She had always loved to watch it tick whenever she had visited him in his home as a young girl, and because of her obsession with it he had actually taken to calling the clock Ticker. Helen had been devastated when he passed away suddenly following, what her and the family had thought was, a routine operation. She had greatly admired her granddad, he had looked after her grandma in the last years of her life as she had suffered with Alzheimer's, and in the end he had been so focused on her and making her last few years on earth as comfortable as possible that he had entirely ignored himself and what his body had needed.

In the end, the operation had led to additional complications that had needed additional operations. The strain on his body had been too great, and following the second of his additional operations, he had been left in a critical state. Thankfully, Helen had gotten the chance to say goodbye, he was just about conscious when she arrived at the hospital and had managed a weak smile and to whisper "Ticker," as she perched on the edge of his bed. Their conversation had been short and mainly one way, with her telling him that she loved him and that he would be able to look after nan again, lord knows she would give him a hard time for making her wait so long. Though, Helen was sure, she wouldn't have minded the wait, as his family down on earth had still very much needed him in their lives.

Helen heard David push his key into the door and twist it, before pushing the door open. She heard him wipe his feet on the welcome mat and chuck his keys into the bowl that sat on a small but tall round table in the entrance hall. David let out a huff as he sat himself down on the bottom step and undid his shoelaces, and Helen heard the thud as he plonked his shoes down under the stairs.

"I'm home, love." He called out, grunting again as he picked himself off the bottom stair. Helen took this as her cue and walked out of the dining room, through the kitchen and out into the hall.

"Hey Hun, how was your day?"

"Not bad, not bad, have you got everything out and ready?"

"Yes it's all downstairs, I've cooked spag-bol so we can eat it as soon as you get changed and then finish off. It doesn't normally take us much more than half an hour to get it all sorted does it?"

"No, half an hour should be more than enough time I'd imagine, plenty of time indeed. I'll just run up and get changed."

As David walked relatively quickly up the stairs (he wasn't as thin or spritely as he used to be), Helen wondered back into the kitchen, drained the water from the pasta in the sink, distributed it onto the plates she'd put out on the side earlier and then poured over the bolognaise sauce.

She grated some Parmesan over the top, putting extra on David's, as he liked it cheesy, and then put them on the table as David was trundling back down the stairs.

Once they had mopped up the extra sauce with some garlic bread, David got up and took his and Helen's plates and put them in the dishwasher.

"Right," he said, turning to Helen, "Time to get this show on the road I guess!"

Helen got up from the table and followed David back through the entrance hall and into the living room. They had two sets of windows, one facing directly into Culver Street with the other looking at their cars in the driveway and up the road. The windows both had white shutters on the inside that Helen and David began manually closing. Once they were closed, Helen and David each grabbed one end of their two seated sofa which had been pressed tight against the back wall, directly under one of the two sets of windows, and picked it up, moving it into the middle of their living room.

David went back to where the sofa had previously been placed, knelt down, and fiddled around with his fingers on the carpet until he found the spot he was looking for, a little bobble on the floor. He pinched it and then pulled. The carpet gave way and moved off the floor. Using his free hand, he grabbed more of the carpet and tugged it hard. Once he had pulled enough of the carpet up, he stepped over the uprooted carpet, pivoted and then knelt and rolled the carpet up to the sofa in the middle of the room. Helen, meanwhile, had gone into the garden shed and brought in a big, pristine garden gnome, complete with a large red hat, a jolly smile and rosy cheeks. She moved over to David, being careful to hold onto it tightly so as not to drop it, and then together they placed it in the middle of the rolled up carpet, which David continued to hold in place with his foot. David slowly moved his supporting foot off the carpet. It didn't unravel itself, but David waited a fraction longer, ready to slam his foot down if it did start to unravel. Satisfied that it wouldn't, David turned back around, knelt down and lifted up what appeared to be a front door knocker that had been inserted into the floor. He pulled, grunting as he did so, and eventually the floor rose up with him backpedalling away from the lifting door. When the trapdoor was at a 90-degree angle to the floor, David stopped backpedalling and Helen came over to help him lower the door gently onto the floor. It was on a 180-degree pivot, which saved them from having to lift the whole weight of the door between them.

With the door lying flat, David moved around to the entrance to the hole that was now in the middle of their living room. He bent low and stuck his hands out to rest them on either side of the hole. He then put the weight of his body onto his hands, grunting even more, and swung his body over the hole, before lowering himself slowly until his feet touched down on a step. He took his hands off the side of the hole, felt about on the wall to his right, eventually finding the light switch, and then flicked it.

Below him, there was the reluctant flicker of a bulb that was in dire need of being changed, before it eventually decided to give in to the electrical flow and lit the way below.

Helen had gone upstairs and came back carrying a load of electrical wiring which she handed to David. He took it and then began descending the stairs. Helen went back upstairs and grabbed more leads and wiring. When she returned to the living room, she plugged a couple of leads in to the wall and unravelled them as she approached the hole that David was now deep inside.

Helen lowered herself onto the steps rather more delicately than David had done. The stairs argued against her feet as she descended down them, they hated being disturbed and creaked out in protest, aching under Helen's weight. The second step from the bottom was missing. David had gone right through it last year and had ended up with a sprained ankle, his excuse to Doctor Richards being that he had gone over on it whilst out on a jog. He had even changed into running wear before heading off to Doctor Richards' practice.

Helen made sure that she carefully lowered herself onto the bottom step and then stepped onto the floor of their concealed basement.

The basement was large, spanning the same space as the whole of the ground floor of their house above, but without any walls to partition the space. Helen had entered a small living space that was occupied by a TV opposite a faded, green three-seated couch. A rug, patterned with orange and red stems and flowers, separated the TV unit and the couch. The rest of the space was filled to the brim with electrical equipment that David was now attending to, pushing buttons and looking at monitors. He got up from a red backed desk chair and systematically flicked about twenty switches that were all lined up on a long row across the wall opposite the bank of monitors he had been looking at. Hundreds upon hundreds of wires were fed into the roof above and criss-crossed their way to the top left hand corner of the room, where they disappeared out of the basement and up into the main house above.

David went back to his monitors and continued to press buttons and carry out what appeared to be a series of checks.

Meanwhile, Helen had switched the TV on and was tuning it to a HDMI channel.

"I'm just going to grab the laptop." She said in David's general direction, but David was oblivious to his wife and was completely engulfed in his monitors, which were now displaying streams and streams of white code over a blue background.

Helen went back up the stairs which continued to moan and groan at her and fetched the laptop from her and David's bedroom as well as a HDMI lead, and then went back down to the basement.

She placed the laptop on the floor near the TV and then plugged the HDMI lead into both. The TV display immediately changed from 'No signal' to the exact same display as the one on the laptop.

On the screen, the Internet shot up as Helen manipulated the mouse on the laptop. She searched the scramble of letters and numbers that brought up the Heirdonus site in a web browser, taking care not to make a single mistake. At the top of the page, she clicked the login button, which prompted her for her username and password. Helen entered them:

H4eL78enJa3m43eS7
YbV82KKkh31P

While she waited for the new page to load, she looked back at David who was now looking slightly less frantic as he seemed to be coming to the end of his checks. His monitor displays were no longer showing the code, and instead were showing a page that required a password to be entered. David entered a password, and was then prompted to present his fingerprint. He pulled out a drawer from above one of the monitors and placed his full hand on it. After a moment where his hand was scanned, the computer bleeped in approval, and asked for retina identification.

The page had fully loaded and Helen scrolled right to the bottom whilst David turned his head to look directly into a camera. At the bottom of the page there were a number of options, and Helen clicked the one that read 'LiveVid'. A pop-up box came up asking for the session passkey. Helen dug into her pocket and pulled out the small piece of white paper that Anne had given her at the Fete just a few days before, and entered the random key that she had neatly written on it into the pop-up box.

"Let me know when you're ready to try it." She called out to David, who was now working back at his monitors.

"Two ticks honey." He replied, and attacked his keyboard for a couple more minutes whilst Helen sat on the sofa patiently.

"That should do it." David said with finality and nodded at Helen to press enter on her pop-up box on the laptop. Helen did so, and after a few seconds buffering Anne and her two sons appeared on Helens laptop screen and the TV display, and on the screens of people tuning in all over the world.

*

Tom Hopkins loaded the Heirdonus page up onto his laptop and entered the passcode, which brought up a blue screen with the words "No signal" gliding across it from the bottom left to the top right of the page. He checked his watch; it was about 15 minutes until the stream began. Perfect timing, as per usual.

He reached over and grabbed a tissue from the box on the table in front of his armchair and blew his nose before shoving the used tissue into his pocket. Tom then got off the couch and went through a small archway into a tiny kitchen that seemed to have been built for half a person, rather than a full one. An oven, a sink and a small half-size fridge dominated the kitchen with little else being able to squeeze into the small room. Tom opened the fridge and pulled out a ready meal, piercing the lid several times with a fork that he had gotten out earlier and left on the side in preparation. He checked the packet before putting the meal in the microwave that was sat on top of the oven and set a 7-minute timer. He went back into the fridge and grabbed a cider. Tom used a bottle opener to remove the cap and then poured the liquid into a pint glass. He reached into the fridge and grabbed a couple more bottles in his left hand and then picked up the glass of cider and took them into the living room. He glugged down a third of the glass before setting it on a coaster and putting the other two bottles on the table. He went back into the kitchen and picked up the fork and a knife and stood leaning on the side waiting for the microwave to ding.

He watched as the seconds ticked away to the dull whirring noise it made, and eventually the ding went. He opened the door and was greeted with a face full of steam that clouded his glasses. After a moment, they began to clear and he pulled the lid off his meal, emptied it out onto a plate and carried it into the living room. Tom set the plate down on the table in front of him and opened the tub of Vaseline that was balancing on the arm of the chair. He gently rubbed his middle finger in a circular motion in the middle of the tub as he reached for the glass and downed half of the remaining cider. Tom belched, and then applied the Vaseline to his lips, which had been chapped for the past couple of days..

He checked his watch; there was less than 30 seconds until the stream would start. Tom dug into his ready meal and was just finishing swallowing his first bite when the screen changed from the no-signal blue to a live stream of a pretty woman and her two children.

*

"Send the children to bed." He whispered in a hushed but urgent tone to his wife.

"It's too early for them, you know that."

"They cannot be awake for this; you know that as well as I do. We have made sacred vows, to break them means death."

"I know, I know."

"You know and yet you do nothing! Come on Em, I don't care if you lock them in their rooms, I am not missing this for the world and neither are you."

Em nodded. She got up and went into the play area where her twin girls were sat playing with dolls. "Come on girls, it's time for bed."

"But mum our bedtime isn't for ages yet!"

"Don't argue with me Nat, you know to respect your elders. I need you to get up bright and early tomorrow which means you need to go to bed earlier today."

"But mum we don't want to get up earlier."

"Please girls just do as I say, you don't want your father to come in here, and you know what he's like when you misbehave." As if on cue, a voice boomed out down the hall. They couldn't make out what their father was shouting, but they knew it wouldn't be anything good. The girls glanced at each other sheepishly before slowly rising to their feet and carrying a doll each over to Em.

"Okay, mum." They both spoke simultaneously.

"Thanks girls." Em led them upstairs and helped them get changed into their pink matching pyjamas. She watched as they brushed their teeth, making sure they didn't cheat by swallowing a small amount of toothpaste in order to pass her breath check. Once done, they clambered into their beds and Em kissed them both on the forehead, then wished them a good night's sleep.

Em shut the door on them, and quietly twisted the lock shut so that they wouldn't go wandering and see something that they shouldn't. She went back downstairs, where John was already getting ready for the stream.

"All tucked up."

"It's about bloody time, Em. It starts in 2 minutes. If I'd missed the beginning I would have been extremely angry Em. Extremely angry. Now hurry up, fetch me a beer and get yourself something too. I want it in my hand before it all kicks off, do you understand? Well come on get a bloody move on Em, stop standing about like a statue, who the fuck do you think you are?"

Em lowered her eyes to the floor and rushed off to fetch his beer. She took it back to him.

"Just going to pop to the loo quick."

She ran back to the kitchen, opened a cupboard, and pulled out a box of Coco Pops. She opened the top and pulled out a 70cl bottle of Vodka. Em unscrewed the cap and took three huge mouthfuls, wincing as it burned its way down her throat. She took another swig and let out a deep breath. She returned the bottle into the cereal box and hurried back to her husband, wobbling slightly on her feet as she did so.

*

Mr Harson finished reading through his notes for the following day's Prime Minister's Questions and set them down in front of him. He had told his house staff to take the evening off as he was just going to finish up his reading and would be able to make himself a sandwich afterwards, he didn't need a chef in the house for that task after all.

It was the first night that Mr Harson would be spending in 10 Downing Street on his own since he moved in. His wife and children had gone to visit his wife's mother who was ill in hospital. Mr Harson had said he was extremely sorry that he wouldn't be able to make it that night and that he would endeavour to go and visit her before the end of the week. Tonight he was busy, far too busy.

He felt a twang of regret that he wasn't able to tell his wife everything about him, there were certain secrets that one had to take to the grave and tonight would be one of those. His position meant that he had to be very good at keeping face even when confronted by great challenges, and he was very apt at doing so.

He had kept face when half of his party had given him a vote of no confidence following the election loss 5 years ago. He had stayed strong and held onto the belief that he was still the best man for the job. He had repositioned cabinet members and made sweeping changes. He had scrapped and fought his way back from the brink in the chamber. He had made allegiances with old foes. He had done everything he possibly could to survive, and then the economy did everything it could to help him into power 5 years later. The pound crashed, unemployment was at an all-time high and there was rioting on the streets. Government was untenable, there would only be one winner at the next general election and so it transpired. He won a 60% majority; it had quite frankly been a landslide. He had faced and survived everything the country and indeed the world had thrown at him thus far, and tonight's secret would be no different. He would watch, he would enjoy every moment, and then he would keep the secret, like he kept every secret, to himself. He had sworn a vow to Heirdonus, and like every one of its members he would honour that vow. He was after all an Englishman, and an Englishman always backed up his words with his actions.

Chapter Twenty-Five

Creature

The plan was ready. They would approach the forest from all sides at precisely 11.16pm. The Runner family were set to arrive at the campsite at 8pm and would set up their tent in a similar location to the one that Jane and her family had used all those years ago. The family would drive down the same route as her family had done. They would park up as close as they could, right on the riverbed surrounded by forest on three sides and the river ahead. They would struggle through the forest with their tents and belongings, and would have to be careful not to trip over the tree roots that stuck above the ground. The children had been given cases that they could carry on their backs to make it easier for them through the forest. At 10.30pm, the children would go with Anne into the forest to go to the toilet. Once in there, they would go to the loo and then keep walking on to the designated safe area, finding their way there using the torches and Anne's impeccable sense of direction.

At 11.00pm, Pete would run into the forest in a panic looking for them. He would use his vast experience as an actor to give off the impression of being truly, deeply terrified that he had lost his children. Pete had been acting for over 30 years and felt like he had been preparing his entire life for this very occasion. At least that is what everyone hoped. They were as close to one hundred percent certain that the creature would show as they could be.

Unlike Anthony, when Pete returned to the fire where the creature would be waiting, he wouldn't be alone. The members of Heirdonus would join him. Helicopters stood by at four locations around the forest. Each helicopter had a live feed to the cameras that Pete and Anne were wearing on their persons so that the members knew exactly when to move into the site. They had decided not to wire up the children in the end so as to avoid any unnecessary suspicion on their part. Each person would be armed with a stake. Every third person in the circle that they were to form around the campsite was armed with a machete and had been told to prioritise its use over the stakes. Every second person also carried a variety of different weapons, including Joshua who had a special hand grenade that was only to be used if the situation became so dire that the risk was worth taking. If they were unable to kill the creature using all of this, one of the helicopters had a drop open door and would release a net onto the creature to capture it, at the same time the main cage would be coming by water on a boat.

As the clock ticked closer towards 8pm, the Runners were slightly behind schedule. They lost time between Leicester and Oxford due to some unexpected traffic. They couldn't travel down from anywhere closer than Leicester because they had to give the impression to the creature that they were genuinely weary from their drive. No detail had been overlooked; if this attempt went wrong it could be the last time in any of their lifetimes that the creature would present itself. The fact that they would arrive later than planned was also a good thing, as it may lead to some genuine panic as Pete would have to pitch the tents faster than anticipated.

They eventually reached the car drop off point at about 8.20pm. Pete unpacked the car and the boys collected their bags. Pete and Anne balanced their luggage on top of the two tents and then lifted them as one, and they began their journey through the forest to the clearing.

Pete constructed the tents as quickly as he could, starting off with the boys, which he managed to put up in record time. Not surprising as they had bought a new tent which required very little effort in assembly, just in case there had been traffic and they needed to cut time somewhere. He got started on his and Anne's tent and had nearly finished sorting out the components when Anne and the boys returned with the firewood.

The boys helped Anne construct a fire, using matches to get it to light. Once Anne was sure that the boys were capable of keeping it going, she went to help Pete finish off their tent. At this point it was close to 10pm and they still had plenty of time.

It turned out that Pete had almost finished the tent, and with Anne's help they had it up and ready in no time. They still had a lot of time to kill, and so Pete suggested that he tell them a story, hoping to scare the boys, which would help to draw the creature in. Pete told them the story of Jane and her family.

At exactly half ten, Anne took the boys into the forest to pee. And at 10.37pm, they made their way toward the safe zone where they would be transported away.

*

Jane watched them move into the forest on the screen in her helicopter. Maggie looked at her and then game her hand a squeeze. It was nearly time. Jane lifted her hand slightly and was shocked to see how much she was shaking. Jane wasn't nervous, she was excited. She was closer to getting revenge for her family's murders than she ever thought possible.

Meanwhile, Pete had begun his part of the mission and was pretending to be petrified, running into the forest like a mad man. At 11.10pm, Jane and the other members of Heirdonus' time had come. Jane made sure that she had everything she needed and whispered a quick prayer. Maggie spoke into her headset and the blades of the helicopter began rotating. As they were thrust into the air, they saw the other helicopters rising in the distance. Once they were all in the air, Maggie looked at the monitor again; Pete was near the break between the end of the forest and the opening where the tents were pitched. She gave the order, and the helicopters moved in.

Jane stared out the window and watched as the trees gave way below to the opening at the edge of the forest, and Jane saw the roaring fire below with Pete now stood about ten metres away from it. The helicopter came to a halt and hovered in the air. Maggie shouted out to the members as the side doors to the helicopter opened and rope was dropped down. Jane watched as three members began descending the rope before it was her turn. She grabbed hold, and jumped out into the night, down towards the creature below.

When she got to the ground, Jane ran off to the left, following Maggie who had gone before her and filled in a gap in the circle that the members were desperately trying to form around the campfire and around Pete as quickly as possible. Within no time, the circle was complete and the area was surrounded.

Jane took her eyes towards the fire but she couldn't see the creature. Her spirits dropped. It must have known. Of course it must have known, this was a creature that had survived for potentially thousands of years. It could tell real fear from fake fear. Jane was about to break down in tears and looked to her right to see if Maggie was equally disappointed, but she was staring straight ahead past Pete and into the flames.

Jane craned her neck, and sure enough, there, sat directly behind Pete from where Jane had been standing, facing the fire, was the creature that she had obsessed about for the best part of 11 years. Jane tightened her grip on her stake and inched closer, moving slightly away from the perfectly formed circle of members. She glanced across at Maggie, tasting blood in her mouth. She realised in her excitement of finally getting a chance to exhibit revenge she had bitten her tongue.

Maggie returned her glance, looking steely.

Jane wanted nothing more but to run up behind the creature and stab it through the heart, but she knew if she went at it alone she would surely die.

Maggie slowly raised her left arm, the arm not carrying her stake, signalling the advance. She quickly pulled it down, pointing directly at the creature, and the Heirdonus members moved in as one.

Jane felt the anger and hatred well up inside of her as she moved closer and closer to the creature; her hands were tingling in anticipation. She was clenching and then unclenching her jaw, going over the moment that she would plunge the stake through its body and be done, and have her revenge at long last.

Closer and closer they crept, until they were just a few metres behind Pete. She heard Pete begin to cough and raise his hand up to wipe the blood away from his nose. Jane began to panic; she really liked Pete and knew they had to kill the creature before it was too late for him. She looked at Maggie, who hadn't motioned for them to quicken their pace in order to make sure they got to the creature in time to save Pete. Jane couldn't understand what she was doing; Pete was dying right in front of them. As if on cue, Pete fell to his knees coughing and spluttering. Jane couldn't take it any more, she had to save him. She screamed incomprehensibly and bolted at the creature, not caring about if it hurt her or not, all she cared about was making sure that Pete would be okay, and that his children would grow up with a father. She sprinted past him, hoping the other members would be tight on her heels and brought up her stake ready to plunge through the creature, who was still sat motionless staring straight into the fire, like it had countless times before it had killed its victims, unafraid or unaware of what was coming up behind it.

Jane screamed out into the night and bared her teeth as she thrust her stake right through the creatures back, it slid into its body with so much ease that Jane's momentum carried her through with the stake, and she fell over the log it had been sitting on and fell upon the creature. She screamed again, wildly this time and withdrew the stake before stabbing the back of the creature again and again and again, trying desperately to rip it into a billion little pieces if she could.

The creature didn't move below her, it must be dead, she laughed crazily at the fire and then up into the night air. She looked back down at the creature and blinked in disbelief as she saw straw sticking out of the holes that she had made in it. She jumped back from the body, and looked around frantically, her eyes wide and full of panic.

"IT'S A TRAP! IT'S SET A TRAP! WE HAVE TO GO NOW!"

Jane got up and swivelled and began to run back the way she had come, but only managed two short steps before she realised she was surrounded by dozens of bright green eyes, staring at her from all angles.

Jane screamed again and turned to run back toward the fire, but approaching from the river were more bright green eyes, she turned again to see Pete break through the circle, which had overtaken him as it advanced. He was holding something in his hands.

"Pete... I don't... You're okay? Thank god! What have you got there?" Jane blubbered at Pete, who stopped a metre into the member's circle.

"My name is Pete Wicombs. Son of the founding father of Heirdonus, Jacob Wicombs."

Jane knew the name but couldn't for the life of her remember why, it was as if it was a name from a previous life and she knew only the echo of it.

"Sadly, my father is unable to be here today, though he would have absolutely loved the show we have put on. It has been a pleasure getting to know you Jane, though I am sure the pleasure we shall get from destroying you will be all the more delicious. Today, we shall complete our revenge upon your family."

Pete licked his lips, his eyes were madder than the words he was saying.

"I don't understand. Where is the creature?"

"Don't you get it? Stupid woman! The creature doesn't exist, at least not in the way you think it does. I mean really Jane? A demonic vampire child? The world we live in is crazy, but it's not mad." He cackled and raised the object he was holding up, before putting it on his face.

A new pair of bright green eyes was now staring back at her, and Jane screamed.

"Smile for the camera's Jane, you're live on Heirdonus TV all over the world!"

The creatures advanced on Jane.

Chapter Twenty-Six

Heirdonus

Jane was gagged quickly to stop her screaming and bound tight. Three of the masked members of Heirdonus dug a deep hole in the ground and put a large wooden pole into it, before filling it in around the edges to secure it in place. Whilst this was going on, the others went off to gather wood and increased the size of the fire, which began to roar and crackle behind the pole.

Jane's hands were untied and she was thrust toward the wooden pole. Her hands were then forced behind her and were retied behind the pole so that she could not get away.

Tears streamed down her face and snot fell freely from her nose, over her lips and into her mouth to be caught by the rag that was gagging her. Jane tried to comprehend what was going on, but couldn't. Heirdonus was meant to be fighting the creature that had killed her family, why had they bound and gagged her? And what was Pete going on about with Jacob Wicombs, she had heard the name before somewhere but she couldn't remember when or why.

It was the masks they were all wearing that scared her the most, the green eyes. It was as if they had delved into her deepest, darkest nightmares and pulled out the worst thing they could find and then replicated it over and over. The eyes came from bodies of all sizes, tall men and short men, she could see the long hair of women floating out behind some of the masks. But it was the little ones that scared her the most. There were children present. They were sat around the fire behind her out of sight, but she could hear them chatting and sniggering with one another.

One of the taller masked men was carrying a large recording device, and placed it down facing Jane. He then went off and she spotted the area over by the forest that all her family had broken through, jolly and excited about their holiday, all those years ago.

Another large masked man was struggling with an even larger camera. He shouted and she heard a couple of the children behind her get up and scurry over to help him carry it. This camera was placed slightly behind the other one, and Jane watched as it was set up onto some sort of wheeled cart. The man moved it from side to side looking down the lens whilst the children went back off to sit by the fire. It was if a whole studio was now being set up in the forest around her.

Eventually, the creatures buzzing around their equipment slowed as the final preparations were made, and the masked figures began to congregate into small groups before disappearing off behind Jane and out of her sight, presumably to be close to the fire whilst one of the shorter men went up to each camera and did a little check.

After what seemed like an eternity, a new circle began to form around Jane, slightly smaller than the one that had engulfed her earlier as several of the people who had made up that circle were now manning cameras.

The small man who had been checking the equipment stepped forward from the crowd and walked up to Jane.

"Heirdonus condemns." He spoke in a voice that soft and soothing. It was a voice she had heard a long time ago, in a beautiful room with oak furniture and a water feature that trickled away in the background. Henrey slapped her across the face and her head twisted to the side with her cheek burning red hot in pain.

Another approached her.

"Heirdonus condemns." It was Harvey; she knew his voice straight away. Jane tried to ask him why he was doing this to her, but the gag prevented any legible sound being heard. He must have been in one of the other helicopters. Jane braced her face, expecting another slap, but Harvey didn't hit her. Instead, he pinched each of Jane's nipples, and in a single motion squeezed them as tightly as he could and yanked them towards himself. The gag that was still in place dampened Jane's agonising scream.

A woman approached next. "Heirdonus condemns." She punched Jane in the stomach, knocking the wind out of her.

And then a child approached. Jane could tell it was a child despite it being relatively tall compared to some of the others as the masked face turned away from her and looked up to the man stood to the left of them. The man gave an encouraging nod towards Jane and gave him a gentle push towards her.

The child moved forward, glancing back once as if unsure about what to do and then stopped slightly further from Jane than the others had.

"Heirdonus… condemns." A slightly squeaky male voice said, before he reached out and pinched with both hands the skin on her neck. He then pulled his hands apart in a rapid movement and Jane had never felt anything like it. She thought that the skin on her neck was going to split in half and that would be the end of her. Her eyes continued to stream tears down her face. She thought he was never going to stop, that this pain was never going to end. Her neck was burning in fury; it was like someone had put a white-hot flame straight onto it and was pressing it up against her skin, unwilling to pull it off, enjoying the sight of Jane in pain far too much. And for some reason, this was the moment when the name Jacob Wicombs clicked in her head.

His name was a ghost from a past that she had almost forgotten. The copycat killer. He had been called this as he killed his victims in the same way described in the horror book 'Copy Cat' by Phillip Taylors. Jane's father had been the prosecutions lawyer and had sent him down for life imprisonment. The case had been all anyone had talked about for weeks, especially to Jane because they thought they could get some inside gossip on what was going on and whether or not she believed he would be convicted. Of course, Jane had always tried to change the subject, as she couldn't tell them anything even if she had wanted to. Besides, the details were far too gruesome.

One of her tears fell onto the boy's hand and he jerked away from her and let go of his grip, much to Jane's relief.

This ritual continued until everyone in the circle had come up and assaulted her.

Then, as one, they all began to chant, softly at first, but then it built and built until they were all screaming at her.

"Heirdonus condemns. Heirdonus condemns. Heirdonus condemns. Heirdonus condemns. Heirdonus condemns!"

Someone broke into the circle from directly in front of her, holding some sort of apparatus that looked like a cross between a gun, a power tool and a needle. It had two, thick, long metal screws on the end, coming out of quite a large main body that moulded round and down to a trigger. The figure walked halfway from the edge of the circle to Jane as the chanting went on, then turned to face the other creatures and raised the weapon high above his head. There was a hushed silence from the circle.

"Heirdonus condemns?" He called out.

"We condemn!" Came the thunderous reply.

The man turned to face one of the cameras and repeated his cry.

"Heirdonus condemns?"

Right across the world, in their basements and lofts, gathered around their laptops and TV screens, in number 10 Downing Street, the worldwide members of Heirdonus cried out in a bloodthirsty rage.

"WE CONDEMN."

The man wielding the weapon turned to face Jane and then crouched down to the earth, the members in the circle followed suit, crouching low. They started bouncing up and down slowly, and chanted in hushed tones.

"We condemn. We condemn. We condemn."

The man with the tool bounced with them, rising up, and then falling down further and further from the earth each time until he was stood on his feet, moving towards Jane. His green eyes flashing evil in her direction.

He went round behind her, and tied a new piece of rope, bounding her left hand only behind her back and to her body. He then cut the rope that was tying her arms together, and forcefully brought her now loose right arm around in front of her.

He turned toward the circle, and motioned at the boy who had attacked her neck earlier. The boy moved back towards her whilst the man grabbed her arm with his big right hand, and bent her fingers straight with his left.

"Do you condemn?" The man asked him.

"I condemn."

The boy picked up the weapon and balanced it by resting the end that didn't have the two metal holes against his shoulder. He flicked a switch on the side of the weapon, and Jane watched as a clear liquid oozed out of the end of both of the rods. The boy then pulled the trigger, and the two rods began to rotate faster and faster and yet were soundless apart from a very dull whir. Jane squirmed against the grip of the man holding her, but he tensed and she found that she couldn't move, he was far too strong for her. The boy aimed the weapon at her fingers, and slowly but surely moved closer. Jane frenetically squirmed, thrusting her head left and right, but it was no use. As the drill was about to penetrate her skin, she turned her head away and screamed into the gag.

*

Jane didn't feel the drill enter her hand. It was as if she was so frightened and so sick with fear that she was no longer able to feel. Her body seemed to have provided its own anaesthetic. When the boy pulled away with the drill, Jane thought that he'd either completely missed her fingers or didn't have the nerve to carry out the atrocity. Jane found that she couldn't feel her fingers and wasn't able to bend them as she tried to determine whether or not they had been drilled. She decided to brave a glance down towards them and lowered her eyes to get a look. Jane's heart thudded violently in her chest, trying to break out of her body as she saw blood draining from the end of her drooping hand. Though it was no longer tied down, she was unable to move it and it just hung limply by her side, letting the life drain out of her.

She tried to speak, to ask why she couldn't feel it, but her mouth was still gagged and it came out as a series of high pitched, muffled noises.

The man who had carried the power tool over to her smiled as if understanding what she wanted to know.

"Strange, isn't it. It doesn't feel like more than a pinprick, yet it goes so deep and bleeds so much. Rather beautiful when you consider it. Jacob spent the majority of his life as a chemist, and this was his greatest invention." The man gestured toward the end of the metal rods, which were now splattered in Jane's blood.

"He spent decades perfecting the poison, using a combination of different types of snake venom. His early experiments didn't work out, mixing the venom often caused the resulting product to counter react with itself and almost neutralise. He searched and searched for a way to combine them and eventually he found it. Honey. Would you believe it? Honey did the trick. As soon as it comes into contact with human skin, the poison completely numbs the surrounding area, which means that the drill can be used without one even knowing it. The second stage of the poison takes a little longer to kick in. It closes the airways and causes patients to cough violently as it feels to them as if they have something stuck in their throat. Finally, it attacks the blood. It thins it drastically in the veins, which is why often patients can suffer from intense nosebleeds. The final stage is when the expansion of the blood as it thins bursts the veins and arteries in the body, resulting in a large amount of internal bleeding that leads patients in most cases to throw up, if they are still alive at that point that is. I wonder, will you throw up for our audience, Jane? Will you be a good sport and put on a show for us?"

Jane's eyes were wide with fear, and were beginning to bloodshot as the poison inside her body caused her blood to thin and run faster. She could almost feel the pace increase around her body. The veins on her wrist began to throb and pulsate.

Pete slowly walked towards her, his green eyes shone more brightly than the rest.

"Isn't this a sight to behold?" He mused. "Here we are again, Jane. So poetic that we end in the same place that this all started. Except, it didn't really all start here, did it? It started in the courtroom with your father. I was devastated when I heard the news of his death. I wanted to be the one to watch the light leave his eyes. But no matter, no matter. You have proved to be much more entertaining than he would have been. Can you see his expression now, watching on from the beyond as his only child is torn from this world? ARE YOU WATCHING OLD MAN? CAN YOU SEE ME UP THERE?" Pete screamed up into the night air.

"I loved my father dearly; he was as good a man as any I knew. Yes his interests were slightly unusual and not in keeping with society, but then you've got to dig deeper. What you find is that his views and way of life was much more in keeping with society than people care to think. The human race loves murder and death and war, we have evolved through these things and thrive off them. My father should be celebrated for his invention of a new way of killing. Statues should be erected to him. What your father did was worse than murder, condemning a man to a life locked away in a cell."

Jane felt her throat beginning to tighten, making it even harder for her to breath and she now desperately tried to spit the gag out of her mouth, frantically manoeuvring her tongue to try and push it out. Sweat poured down her face. Her back and armpits were soaked. This wasn't how she wanted her life to end.

"I wanted to kill your entire family at once, but Anne stopped me. Anne has always been far more intelligent than I am. She told me to wait, to bide my time and plan a murder that fit your family's crime. I took over from my father as head of Heirdonus, and we planned a way to make you suffer deeply. You were imprisoned because of me. You were driven mad, because I willed it. Those giggling voices really were a touch of genius, don't you think? It cost a lot of money to get the sound just right and to set the speakers up all over the forest and in your cell. The noise would have driven anyone mad. Fuck, in the end, you even believed that you had killed your own family. The ultimate revenge, almost. It has all gone better than I could ever have imagined it!"

Jane could no longer hear the words that Pete was saying; she was succumbing quickly to the poison.

Pete realised this, and turned back towards the circle, disappointed that he didn't have any more time to gloat.

"Pity that we don't have any more time left together. I was really rather enjoying your company. Heirdonus condemns." He called out the last two words, and the chant began to ring out again. Members of Heirdonus began to break the circle up, and moved towards her with their stakes aloft.

The first member reached Jane, her long brown hair breaking free from the sides of her mask. She removed the mask from her face, and Jane stared dumbfounded at Jenny. She knelt down in front of Jane before bringing the stake right across her body, holding it away from herself with her right arm. Jenny then swung it hard and fast in an arc. The stake sliced right through Jane's shins as if they were made of butter, and Jane's blood spurted and caked Jenny.

Jenny moved out of the way quickly, and another took her place and did the same, swinging hard and fast just above where the previous wound had been made. The members green eyes dotted in the specks of blood that spurted from Jane's shins.

More members approached, each slicing higher and higher up her legs and towards her belly. Jane was shuddering violently, her head lolled to the right with eyes that were vacant and unseeing. Her mouth opened and blood dripped from its corners.

The last coherent thought Jane had was of Jack, Tom, and her Anthony. They were playing together in the river. She was leaving this world to find them in whatever lay beyond, and that thought gave her peace as she passed from the world.

Printed in Great Britain
by Amazon